Grave Web

Grave Web

Betty Sullivan La Pierre

2007

This novel is a work of fiction. The characters, names, incidents, dialogue, and plot are the products of the author's imagination or used fictitiously. Any resemblance to actual person, companies, or events is purely coincidental.

Grave Web

GRAVE WEB
'Hawkman Series' #10
Others in 'The Hawkman Series by
BETTY SULLIVAN LA PIERRE
http://www.bettysullivanlapierre.com

THE ENEMY STALKS
DOUBLE TROUBLE
THE SILENT SCREAM
DIRTY DIAMONDS
BLACKOUT
DIAMONDS aren't FOREVER
CAUSE FOR MURDER
ANGELS IN DISGUISE
IN FOR THE KILL

Also by Betty Sullivan La Pierre

MURDER.COM
THE DEADLY THORN

ACKNOWLEDGMENT

I want to thank
Matthew Alan Pierce
for naming this novel.
He's the author of the new epic horror novel
The Dark Curse of Whispers!
Available at:
Amazon.com
And most online bookstore
Visit him at:
http://www.myspace.com/emancipatedtales

GRAVE WEB
HAWKMAN SERIES #10
Cover Art by Author, Paul Musgrove

TO ALL MY FRIENDS AND FANS
WHO HAVE SUPPORTED
ME THROUGHOUT THE
YEARS.

CHAPTER ONE

Becky Simpson stood at the edge of the open grave. Long strands of soggy hair clung to her face as tears slid down her cheeks. Her lightweight jacket dripped water as the rain pelted against her slim body. Thunder rumbled in the distance while the coffin slowly descended into the gapping hole. Cory sidled up next to her and placed an arm around her waist.

"Come on, Sis. You're getting soaked. It's time to go. "

He gently led her toward the big black limousine, helped her into the seat, then scooted in beside her.

"What am I going to do without him?" She said, her voice quivering as she took the handkerchief he offered, and dabbed the water from her face.

"You'll be fine. Now you can do the things you always wanted to do."

"Do you realize without Dad, I'm all alone. You've at least got a wife and a child on the way. I've got no one."

He gave her a squeeze. "Hey, you're still young. You have plenty of time to find the right man."

She glanced at her brother. "You know what I'd really like to do?"

He shook his head. "No, what?"

"Find out what happened to our mother."

Cory straightened and removed his arm from around her shoulders. "Why do you want to go digging into the past trying to find the whereabouts of Mom? She left years ago and never made contact with either of us."

A slight smile curled the corners of Becky's lips. "I've dreamed of her many times. I can still see her cleaning the house and humming a cheerful tune. She always seemed so happy." Clasping her hands in her lap, Becky stared longingly out the rain streaked window. "There's bound to be a reason she left. I know she loved us. Why would she just disappear without a word?"

Cory bowed his head and dusted off his wet pants. "Have you ever thought she might be dead?"

Becky jerked her head around and glared at him. But before she could answer, the big car came to a stop in front of the church. Cory hopped out and ran around to open her door. He took her arm, and they hurried up the steps just as a bolt of lightening streaked across the sky, followed by another rumble of thunder. Dashing into the building, Susan, Cory's wife, met them inside the vestibule. She gave her husband a hug and took Becky's hand.

"I think you two need to get into dry clothes."

Becky nodded. "You're right. I'm getting chilled."

"We'll go by and pick up something to eat," Cory said. "See you in about thirty minutes."

"Okay. Meet you at the house."

As Becky drove home, many thoughts crowded her mind. She wondered why there were so few people at her father's service. Surely he had more friends. Of course, the weather may have played a role and kept many away. Not good for older people to drive in cold and stormy conditions. Maybe she should have offered to have a wake with food and drink. "Sorry, Dad," she muttered aloud. "I was just too upset."

When she reached the house, she ran upstairs and changed clothes, then brought in a big log from the covered back porch. Placing it on the paper she'd stacked on the grill, she set it afire. By the time Cory and Susan arrived with the food, the house felt cozy and warm.

After they finished the meal, eight months pregnant Susan groaned as she rose from the table. "It's been a tiring day and we have a long drive tomorrow. I think I'll go to bed." She turned to her husband. "Honey, could you help your sis clean up?"

Becky waved a hand. "You two go ahead, it won't take me a minute to get everything put away."

"Are you sure?" Cory said, picking up a couple of the plates.

"Yes." She gestured for him to leave the dirty dishes. "You go take care of Susan."

⮞

The next morning, Becky walked her brother and wife to their car. "Susan, are you okay?"

"Yes." She laughed. "Just big and fat. Believe you me, I'm ready to have this baby."

"Be sure and let me know as soon as the big event happens."

"Don't worry. You'll probably be the first we call."

Becky bent down and gave her a hug. "I pray everything goes well." She stepped back as her brother closed the car door.

He put his arms around Becky and gave her a squeeze. "Sis, stay in touch." Glancing up at the sky, he dashed around the front of the car. "We'd better get on the road. Hopefully, we can beat this next storm."

"Call me when you get home. Drive carefully." They waved as she watched the car turn the corner and disappear. Climbing the steps to the front porch, she rubbed the sides of her arms as the goose bumps rose from the chilly breeze.

The minute she moved inside, silence engulfed her. She leaned against the door and stared into quiet room space. Normally, Dad would have the news blaring on the television, regardless of the hour. She already missed his voice, calling for her to come and watch the latest storm alert or to tell her about an incident at the grocery store.

She wiped a hand across her face. It surprised her when she discovered her cheeks wet and warm with tears. Suddenly, a clap of thunder jolted her out of the intense thoughts. Running fingers through her long brown hair, she pushed the loose strands behind her ears and moved toward the hallway.

Becky hesitated outside the closed door of her father's office, bit her lower lip, then turned the handle. She moved cautiously across the room to the large oak desk in front of the window. Tracing her fingers across the worn smooth wood, she felt a guilty sensation flow through her, as though she'd intruded into an area where she didn't belong. She took a deep breath and slid into his desk chair. So many questions left unanswered. Her eyes welled with tears again as she thought about all the wonderful times she'd had with her dad. Now, all the kin she had left in the world was her younger brother.

Only two years separated their ages, but Cory had married soon after he finished college, moved to another town, and now had a baby on the way. Five years ago, due to the woeful pleading of her father, Becky had returned home. He said the big house seemed so empty and lonely after his children had gone off for school. Maybe all the chatter of a growing family might not be present, but if she'd come back he knew it would lift his spirits. He promised not to put a damper on her life, and she could stay as long as she wished. No love had entered Becky's life, so the decision hadn't been hard to make. Once she'd settled in, she had no desire to find a place of her own.

She'd found a good paying job in town at a mall, where she became the buyer of women's clothing at one of the well known department stores. This kept her wardrobe in the latest style and occasional travel kept her from boredom. Many people told her she had exquisite taste, and wearing the fashions she'd purchased, lured many people into the women's area.

She remembered how her dad teased her about one of the slinky outfits she wore home. He told her a beautiful woman prancing around in that outfit would cause nothing but trouble to the married men in her office. His laughter rang through the house when he told her she'd leave them panting and the wives ready to kill.

Becky wiped the tears from her eyes, and blew her nose. Having the full responsibility of being executrix of her father's will, she'd taken off a couple of weeks to get things in order. Cory would return to sign the final papers in the next few days.

He had no problem with her keeping the house, as he had no interest in it. The estate would be divided so that he'd be covered for his half.

She pondered again how she'd approach him on the idea of finding their mother. Cory was only eight when she took off. No trace of her had ever been found. But Becky remembered her twinkling blue eyes, big smiles and wonderful hugs.

Dropping her pen on the desk top, she strolled to the window and peered out through the sheer curtains. The rain had quit and she smiled at the squirrel guarding his nest in the crook of the oak tree. He kept chattering and scolding a blue jay perched on a limb a few feet away. The bird flew at the sound of the gate as it rattled open and Henry Harris, the gardener, entered. He'd taken care of their yard for as long as she remembered. Becky had never liked him as a little girl. When she told her dad the man scared her, he just laughed, telling her Henry wouldn't hurt a fly and he needed the job. Strange, she didn't recall seeing him at the funeral, but it didn't mean he wasn't there. In her state of mind, she probably didn't see anyone who wasn't right in her face. He tended to be very shy and could very well have been in the background. Becky crossed the room and went down the stairs to the main floor.

Slipping on a jacket hanging on the hook near the back door, she went outside. "Good morning, Henry."

"Mornin'," he said, ducking his head as he reached down to pick up the rake. "Sorry about your pappy. Very sad to have him gone. I thought I'd run over and see what I could do between the storms."

Before Becky could respond, he'd turned abruptly and headed around the corner of the house. She decided not to pursue him this morning. Her questions could wait until a less strained time.

CHAPTER TWO

Becky went back inside and made another pot of coffee. She straightened up the kitchen from the hurried breakfast with Cory and Susan. With that done, she poured herself a cup of the fresh brew, and gazed out the window where she could see Henry had rolled the wheelbarrow to the edge of the flower garden and proceeded to fill it with wet debris from the rain. He tenderly raked around the roses and pulled a few weeds. Scruffy, her dad's old dog, lay under the oak tree and watched the gardener with doleful eyes. Becky wondered how long the animal would live with her dad gone. They were inseparable pals.

She glanced in the direction her brother and wife had headed. Threatening black clouds covered the sky. The couple lived about an hour and a half away, so she said a silent prayer they'd reach home before the next storm let loose with a vengeance.

Reluctantly, she climbed the stairs to her father's study. One of the hardest jobs she'd ever encountered was cleaning out his belongings. Each suit, shirt, belt, or shoe she'd taken from the closet had wrenched her heart as she placed them in a bag for charity. Now, the job of cleaning out his personal papers made her balk. She didn't look forward to the undertaking, but knew it had to be done.

Removing the small vacuum with its hose and attachments from the hall closet, she carried it into the room and placed it beside the desk, then slid into the office chair. She wanted to take over this large oak desk as her own, and didn't know quite where to start cleaning. Opening the long drawer in front, she sorted out things she'd use. She placed the good pens and erasers in a pile, and tossed the others into the trash can, then fiddled with several staplers to see which one worked best.

A couple of hours later, she had everything of value stacked on the top of the desk, along with the bills. One of her future jobs would be to notify all the companies to transfer statements into her name. She stood, arched her back to relieve the kinks, then let out a long sigh. Glancing at the large safe standing next to the desk, she felt another strange sensation sweep through her. Her father had never revealed the contents, but had told her where he kept the combination in case anything happened to him.

Pushing the weird feeling aside, she vacuumed all the drawers and stacked the bills in the order they needed to be paid. Once she had the surface cleared, she gave the whole piece of furniture a heavy wax job, then stood back and smiled at how beautiful it turned out.

When the door bell rang, she wondered who it could be and hurried down the steps to the entry. Through the frosted front glass she could see a silhouette, and it appeared the person was holding some sort of object.

"Hello, Mrs. Bradley, what a pleasant surprise. Won't you come in?"

"Hello, dear. No, I only have a few minutes. I'm already late for my board meeting at the church. But I wanted to drop this potato salad off. I didn't know if your brother and his wife were still here, so hope I didn't make too much. It will keep real well in the refrigerator."

Becky took the large bowl from the woman. "Thank you so much."

She patted Becky's arm, her expression solemn. "I'm so sorry about your father's sudden passing. I'm sure he died of a broken heart." She turned and hurried down the porch steps.

"I'll return the dish as soon as it's finished," Becky called.

Mrs. Bradley gave a wave as she climbed into her car and drove off.

Knowing this woman had the reputation of being one of the best cooks in Medford, she lifted the lid and the heavenly scent of mustard and onions swirled around her nose, making her stomach grumble. "Oh, this smells and looks so good. I'll have some with my lunch," she said aloud, as she moved to the kitchen.

While eating, Becky thought of the woman's comment about her dad dying of a broken heart. Why would she say such a thing. It had been years since Mom disappeared. She shrugged her shoulders, picked up the soiled plate and took it to the kitchen sink. Nowadays time for older people tended to move fast; what seemed like years to some, felt like only a few months to others.

She glanced out the window and wondered why Henry was still here. He normally finished his work in a couple of hours. But he was still puttering around the rose garden. Suddenly, he took off his hat and held it over his heart. Becky watched as he crossed himself, then plopped the cap back on his head, gathered up the garden tools and disappeared around the corner of the house. Now what brought that on? she wondered.

Shaking her head, she grabbed a soft drink from the refrigerator, a can of almonds out of the cabinet, and headed back upstairs, hoping to finish cleaning out her dad's office this evening. She placed her snacks on top of the short stubby vault, and retrieved the combination from the desk drawer. When she heard Mr. Harris' truck start up, she glanced out the window as he pulled away from the curb. She knelt down beside the safe, holding the instruction sheet with one hand, twisted the dial with her other, and set the first number. Feeling the tumblers under her fingers, she moved to the next digit and soon, the door swung open. She couldn't believe her eyes. Stacks of files and envelopes packed the interior.

"Oh, my God," she gasped, "this is going to take forever to clear out."

She placed the code back into the desk drawer, then went to the corner of the room where she'd tossed some boxes for storing things, and picked out a couple of medium sized ones. Dropping them next to the vault, she pulled her hair back, twisted it into a bun, and plopped down on the floor. She shook her head as she scrutinized the packed safe. "Dad, were all these so important they had to go in here?" she questioned aloud. She exhaled nosily. "We'll soon find out."

Knowing each item would have to be examined, she pulled out a bundle of envelopes and placed them on the floor between her legs. After an hour, all she'd found worth saving were a couple of receipts for work done on the house before her father died. Groaning, she stood and rubbed her aching back. Taking a sip of the soda, she popped open the can of nuts and munched a handful. She walked around the room to stretch her tight muscles before moseying back to the vault. Her gaze caught the hint of a faded pink ribbon sticking out from a pack on the bottom. She bent down and wiggled the bundle forward until it came loose, and the articles on top flopped down with a swish. Sitting down at the desk, she gently placed the stack of what appeared to be old letters, on the surface. She squinted at the blurred return address and her heart gave a sudden thump. Carole Patterson, her mother's maiden name.

Becky studied the faded postmark of the envelope, and could barely make out the date, which turned out to be the year before she was born. Her eyes stung and filled with tears blurring her vision. Trembling fingers gently untied the bow. The letters spilled across the oak top. She quickly thumbed through them and noted all were from her mother, addressed to her dad, Al Simpson. Sorting them in order, Becky picked up the oldest. She held it to her heart and whispered. "At last, Mother, I have something of you."

CHAPTER THREE

Becky fondled the letter for several minutes. She stared into space remembering when her mother hadn't returned in a month, how her father had cleaned out every possession she owned, and either sold or threw it in the trash, not leaving even a trinket for her or Cory. Whenever she asked her dad about her mother, he'd cut her off.

"I have no idea where she is. Don't you worry your pretty little head, I'll take care of you and Cory." Becky had no problem recalling these exact words, because he said the same thing each time she asked. Finally, she gave up, and came to the conclusion it was useless to even inquire. But in her heart, she knew her mother wouldn't leave them and never come back without a very good reason.

She glanced at the letter in her hand. Would these hold any kind of a clue?

Slowly, she removed the first letter from the envelope. The paper crackled with age as she spread it open. The faint scent of roses swirled around her nose. "My Dearest Al," the letter began, "how I've missed you. I'm counting the days when you return to take me with you." Becky read through the stack of love letters and soon returned them to their holders. Securing the pink ribbon around the stack, she held them tenderly.

"You loved Dad so much, Mother, why did you go away, and not return?" she whispered.

Scooting the bundle to the corner of the desk, she glanced out the window. The sun had already dropped behind the trees. How long had she read? She looked at her wristwatch; it showed six o'clock. No wonder her stomach growled. She gazed longingly at the still three-fourth's full vault, and realized she hadn't made any headway in cleaning it out. Soon, Cory would drive down to sign all the papers and she wanted to share anything she found of her dad's that he might want. Tomorrow, she vowed to finish this job.

Slipping on a jacket, Becky decided to stroll around the yard before fixing a bite to eat. When she stepped outside, she zipped up the front of her wrap. The cool evening air felt invigorating, but chilled her to the bone. She stepped quickly around the yard and paused at the rose garden. Her mother loved the aroma of these beautiful flowers. Becky looked forward to having them in full bloom. Henry had cut the bushes back and they looked pathetic. That's probably why he'd stayed so long today. But she knew they'd be lovely in a couple of months. She noticed a spider web under the small table and looked for a stick to knock it down. Unfortunately, Henry had done such a good job of cleaning up, she couldn't find one. She'd bring a broom out tomorrow and sweep it away.

Scruffy meandered up to her side with his head down, and ears drooping. He finally looked up at her with mournful eyes. Becky reached down and rubbed his head. "Oh, honey, I know you miss him terribly. Come on, I'll get you some food and you can sleep on the back porch. At least you'll stay warm."

The dog followed her and they both went inside. After filling his water and food bowls, she placed an old piece of carpet on the floor. Her dad had spoiled his pet by letting him come in when the nights were nippy. Scruffy took a couple bites of the dry dog grub, a few laps of water, then plopped down on the rug. Becky felt sorry for him, as she knew he was grieving for his master. She knelt beside him and put her arms around his neck. "You're going to be fine, ole boy. We'll get through this together."

The next morning, Becky decided to finish clearing out the vault. She squatted in front of the steel box and pulled out a handful of documents. Some of the loose pieces scattered across the floor. She gathered them up and sat at the desk. Again she sorted, tossing old receipts into the trash box, and questionable papers into the save box, which she'd go through later. When she reached inside the safe to remove another pile, her fingers struck something hard in the corner. She bent down, placed the stack in her hand on the floor and pushed the remaining papers aside. Lifting out a small velvet jewelry box, she opened the lid and her mouth dropped open.

"Oh, my," she gasped.

Shoving her hair behind her ears, she stood, but her legs had turned to jelly. She fumbled for the desk chair and practically fell into it. Placing the container on the shiny oak surface, she removed the wedding ring set and stared at it for several moments. Then she took out the diamond tennis bracelet and placed it alongside the rings.

"Mother never went anywhere without these. Why would they be here?" Her voiced choked. "Unless she's dead."

Becky's hands folded over the jewels and she stared out the window. *Something's not right.* She knew in her heart, she'd have to find out if her mother was still alive. But how would she go about it? She didn't have the vaguest idea.

The rain pelted the pane and the wind came in gusts. Small branches of the big oak tree swished against the side of the house. When the phone rang, Becky punched on the speaker phone, figuring Cory was calling to tell her he wouldn't be down today.

"Hello."

"Hi, Sis. I'm sure you realize I won't be coming down in this storm. It wouldn't be safe to drive."

"I understand. There's no hurry. Just wait until these squalls move out of here. But before you go, I need to talk to you about something preying on my mind."

"Sure. What is it?"

Becky explained what she'd found in the safe and how she wanted to find out if their mother still existed. A silence fell between the two siblings.

"Sis, what you've told me is very mysterious. But the hunt

may cause you more grief than you're experiencing right now. Have you found anything else in the vault that might shed some light on her disappearance?"

"I haven't finished going through it yet. Do you have any idea of how I should go about finding her?"

"I'd imagine you'll have to hire a private investigator."

"I don't know any."

"Rumor has it there's a Tom Casey in the Medford area who's supposed to be one of the best in the county. He used to be a spy for the Agency from what I hear. You might check him out in the phone book and see if he does searches for missing persons. I might warn you, he wears an eye-patch and looks like a big cowboy."

Becky laughed. "Sounds like my kind of guy. Once I finish going through the vault, I'll get in touch with him. How's Susan?"

"Very grumpy and uncomfortable. She's definitely ready to have this baby."

"Give her my love. I'll give you a call if I run across any more suspicious items."

"Okay. Take care and best of luck on your endeavor."

After Becky hung up, she jotted down Tom Casey's name and then pulled out the phone book from the lower drawer. She thumbed through the yellow pages until she came to Private Investigators. Finding his name listed, she read the ad which stated he did searches for missing persons. She wrote down the number, and put the directory away. First things first, she thought as she scooted the chair around to the front of the vault. She unloaded another batch of items and placed them on the desk. Her shoulders and back felt chilled, so she went to her bedroom and removed a vest from the closet. "Might as well be comfortable," she mumbled, slipping it on, as she moved back to the study.

She continued sorting for two hours and finally removed the last items stuffed in the cubbyhole of the vaults interior. A small envelope with the word 'Al' on the front caught her attention. When she opened it, she immediately recognized the feminine handwriting. Her eyes misted as she read.

> Dear Al,
> I can't go on like this. Since your affair, things
> will never be the same. My heart won't let me
> believe you still love me. If you did, it would
> never have happened. I'm leaving, and I have
> no way of supporting Becky and Cory, so you'll
> have to take care of them. You've broken my
> heart and ruined my life. I hope you're satisfied.
> Tell the children I will always love them.
> Carole
> P.S. I've left my rings and bracelet, I have no
> more use for them.

Becky folded the paper and slipped it back into the envelope. Her insides felt like life had been squeezed from them. All these years she'd thought she knew her dad, but obviously not. Who in the world was his lover? She racked her brain and couldn't remember anyone coming around after her mother's disappearance, except neighbors. Slumping back in the chair, she fought back the clawing emotions wanting to surface. Of course, she must remember how very young she was when her mother took off, and lacking the wisdom of life, probably missed any loving glances passing between her father and someone else.

She gnawed her lower lip, and wondered how much information Mr. Casey would need before he could take the case. Surely, he'd need names to start a search. She let out an audible sigh. Looks like any private investigator will have quite a job on his hands with this cold case.

CHAPTER FOUR

Becky glanced at the throw away box, and decided she'd better not discard anything yet. No telling what hidden clues might be on those scraps of paper.

She gazed out the window. The storm had made the day dreary, and spooky dark. The rain fell in sheets and the wind kicked it around, making the drops hit the windows with force. Thunder rumbled and lightening lit up the skies like a horror movie. She hoped the power stayed on. Maybe she should go check on Scruffy. He didn't like storms. She'd let him in earlier, and made sure he'd settled on the rug in the enclosed porch before she came upstairs. Jogging down to the main floor, she went out to the back room. Scruffy looked up at her and let out a whine.

"You need to go outside?" she asked.

He slowly rose from the floor and strolled reluctantly to the door.

"I'll wait for you. Go do your job."

The dog hurried into the back yard, and returned within minutes, his brown coat dripping wet. Becky grabbed a towel off the washer and wrapped it around him before he gave himself a good shake.

She laughed, as she rubbed him down. "I caught you just in time, ole boy. You'd have splattered me good." Feeling his shivering body, she gave him a hug. "Come on, Scruffy. Let's go inside the house where it's warm."

The temperature had dropped a good ten degrees, so Becky flipped on the furnace and Scruffy followed her up the steps.

But when she turned into her dad's office, the dog stopped at the door.

"It's okay, you can come in."

He moved meekly toward her, his ears down and his big brown eyes solemn.

"I know, you miss him as much as I do. I'm sure you can still smell his scent. It'll be a long time before it's gone." She rubbed the dog's head, then pulled a small throw rug from in front of the door and placed it beside her chair. "Here, we'll call this your rug. We'll keep each other company."

The dog gave her arm a warm lick and settled on the piece of carpet. Becky returned to the last pile of items on the desk and began to sort through them. She found a small book tucked inside an envelope and flipped through the brittle pages. It appeared to be a record of payments. Her interest piqued as she noticed the dates started a year or so before her mother disappeared, and continued until her dad's death. Becky thought it odd; each entry appeared in a personal code. She wondered if her dad had been blackmailed.

She let out a sigh, and glanced down at the canine who had one ear lifted in her direction. "Sure wish you could talk. Bet you could answer a lot of my questions." She stood, and stacked the items in a neat pile. "Scruffy, let's go have some dinner. Tomorrow's going to be a busy day."

Hawkman stepped out of his 4X4 and the aroma of freshly baked goodies looped around his nose. "I should have eaten breakfast," he mumbled, as he pushed open the bakery door.

The bells jingled and the baker hurried from the back of the shop. "Hello, Mr. Casey. You're at work early this Monday morning."

"Yep, have a court date, but I shouldn't have left home without eating breakfast. The smell of these delicious pastries weaken my resolve to cut back."

Clyde chuckled. "They're good for you. Give you lots of energy."

Hawkman laughed. "Right, as they add on the pounds. So give me two of those bear claws."

Both men erupted in laughter, as the baker wrapped the delicacies and placed them in a white sack with ample napkins. "You have a good day."

Hawkman waved as he left and headed up the stairs to his office. The small room smelled like a confectioner's kitchen, so he left the steel door slightly ajar and cracked open the window. The stiff, cool breeze would air it out in no time. He glanced at the overcast sky and wondered if it would rain again today. They'd had a cold and wet winter this year, and he was ready for the Spring sunshine.

He'd no more settled in his chair than the phone rang. "Hello, Tom Casey, Private Investigator."

"Hello, Mr. Casey. My name is Becky Simpson and I'm calling to inquire if you do searches for missing persons?"

"I sure do."

"Even ones who haven't been seen nor heard from for close to fifteen years?"

"Whoa, that's a long time. But yes, I can sure give it a try, however, can't guarantee I'll find them."

"I understand. I'd like to meet with you as soon as possible and iron out what needs to be done to get started."

"Okay, let me check my appointments. Today might be tight, as I have a court date at ten thirty and I never know how long it could last. If you don't mind three thirty or four o'clock, we could make it this afternoon."

"That's ideal for me. Could you give me directions to your office."

"Are you in Medford?"

"Yes."

"I'm easy to find." He quickly gave her instructions.

"Do I need to bring anything to help you get started?"

"It would be nice to have the name, birth date and recent address of the person in question." He felt a smile form on his lips. "Also, your checkbook, as I require a retainer to start a case."

"No problem. I'll bring what information I can."

"See you then."

After hanging up, Hawkman wondered what he might have gotten himself into. He'd never had a case with a person missing over seven years. This should be interesting. The name Becky Simpson didn't ring any bells, so he looked forward to the afternoon appointment.

He gobbled down the pastries and chased them with a cup of coffee. Going into the small bathroom, he glanced in the mirror as he strung a tie, which matched his slacks and sports coat, around his neck, then smoothed down his shirt collar. This was the one thing he didn't like about going to the court house; he had to dress up. Jennifer said it was good for him. Little did she know how uncomfortable a tie felt, and after being out of the Agency for all these years, dressing casually had become his way of life. He vowed not to give up his cowboy hat or boots, and no one seemed to mind. They'd become his trademark, along with his nickname and eye-patch. Making sure he had no crumbs scattered down his front, he locked up and headed to his SUV.

He didn't get out of court until almost three thirty. Walking down the steps, he loosened the tourniquet around his neck and hurried to his vehicle. He reached his office, raced up the stairs, removed the tie and raked his fingers through his hair, then plopped his hat back on his head. After putting on a fresh pot of coffee, he had all of five minutes to spare, when a faint knock sounded.

"Come in."

A young woman with long brown hair and big eyes matching her tresses, peeked around the edge of the door. "Mr. Casey?"

"Yes. Becky Simpson, I presume."

"That's me."

"Have a seat and let's get acquainted."

She appeared a bit strained, but smiled. "Thank you for squeezing me in today. I really appreciate it."

"No problem. Glad I could do it. Before we get started, could I get you a cup of coffee?"

"Sounds wonderful."

Hawkman placed a couple of steaming mugs on the desk, then pulled out a yellow legal pad. He explained to her about the retainer fee he required if he took the case and how he'd give her a record of his monthly expenses. She listened and nodded.

"Now with the preliminaries out of the way, tell me about this person you want to find."

"My mother."

Hawkman shot her a look. "Your mother?"

CHAPTER FIVE

Hawkman leaned back and stared at Becky. "And how long did you say your mother had been gone?"

She twisted the strap on her purse. "Almost fifteen years."

"And she's never tried to contact you?"

Becky shook her head.

"Has anyone tried to find her?"

"No," she whispered.

He came forward in his seat. "Ms. Simpson, I think you better start from the beginning and tell me about your mother."

Becky revealed what she could remember and by the time she'd finished, tears flowed down her cheeks. She placed the small box with her mother's wedding rings and tennis bracelet on the desk, along with the note she'd found. "This is all I have of hers so far. And now that my father's dead, I wanted to see if I could locate her. There are so many unanswered questions."

Hawkman examined the jewelry and read the note. "To your knowledge, did your father ever try to hunt her down?"

"Not that I know of. However, I was very young and I'm sure he withheld a lot of information from my brother and me. We weren't old enough to understand what had happened. And whenever I asked him questions, he gave me the same answer and told me not to worry about anything; he'd take care of us." She sighed. "I finally quit inquiring."

"What's your brother's name?"

"Cory Edward Simpson."

"And what does he think about you trying to find your mother?"

She shrugged. "At first I suppose he thought me crazy, but when I told him what I'd found, he left it up to me. He and his wife are expecting their first child any day, and I don't feel like he wants to be involved in my pursuit. So I'm pretty much doing this on my own."

"Is this note and jewelry the only things you've found that indicated your mother and father were having problems?"

"I haven't gone through every item yet."

"Have you contacted your mother's family?"

"Both her parents passed away shortly after she and dad were married. And Mom was an only child. I know nothing about any other relatives."

"I'm going to need every clue you can find. I want you to make a list starting with your mother's maiden name, your dad's full name, then the people who knew your parents. Especially, friends of your mother. Even ones who might not be alive today. Get as much information as you can: addresses, phone numbers, and any other pertinent facts. I will be contacting these people and see what they can tell me about your folks. So the more I know beforehand, the better my approach."

She looked at him, puzzled. "How in the world could the deceased help?"

Hawkman chuckled. "You'd be surprised how the dead talk."

Becky removed her checkbook from her purse. "It sounds like you'll take my case."

"Yes, it intrigues me. I'll work on it until I see no hope, then I'll let you know. For now, I want you to spend the next few days going through the things you found in the safe and read every scrap of paper. Don't throw anything away until you've okayed it with me."

She wrote a check for a thousand dollars and handed it to him. "Will this do as a starter?"

"It'll be ample. At the end of each month, I'll give you a running account of my expenses." He scooted the box of jewelry toward her. "Keep these in a safe place. It might even be wise to get a safe-deposit box at the bank. I'll make a copy of this note and you put the original with the rings." He crossed the room to his scanner and made a duplicate, which he tucked into a file. "How soon do you think you can get back to me with the list of names and any other items you might find?"

"Give me a couple of days."

"That'll be fine."

Becky placed the small box and letter into her handbag and stood. She held out her hand. "Thank you so much, Mr. Casey. I truly appreciate your taking this on."

They shook hands and Hawkman walked her to the door. "I'll be looking forward to hearing from you."

᠍᠍ৡয়

As Becky drove home, she thought about Mr. Casey and how comfortable she'd felt talking with him. She made up her mind to trust him, and show him the strange little ledger she'd found. Maybe he'd know how to decipher it. And it might have something to do with her mother's disappearance.

She pulled into the garage, and hopped out of the car. The sky had darkened once again, and looked very threatening. Shaking her head, she went into the house by way of the small door leading into the kitchen.

Crossing the room to the back porch, she let the dog out, and decided one of her future projects would be a doggy door. After letting him back in, she headed for the kitchen, then glanced back at Scruffy. "You want to come inside and keep me company?"

He thumped his tail and trotted to her side. "If I didn't know better, I'd think you understood English." She laughed as he bounced around in the kitchen and almost slipped on the linoleum. "You're definitely acting like the old Scruffy again. I was worried about you, boy." She took some doggie treats out of the cabinet and made him run through his bag of tricks as she doled them out one by one.

He followed her upstairs to the office, but this time didn't hesitate about going into the room and headed immediately to his rug. "You learn fast," Becky said, giving him a pat.

She sat down at the desk, but stared at the canine a few minutes. Memories flooded her mind as she remembered the night, several months after her mother left. Dad carried in this dirty bundle of fur someone had discarded on the road. He brought him home, thinking Cory and she would like a pet.

The little thing was dirty, skinny and ugly. She recalled how she didn't even want to touch the mutt and Cory showed little interest. More than likely, even in their young minds, they knew he was just trying to fill the void of their lost mother. But Dad took control of the little beast, called him a scruffy little hound, and bathed the animal. After a few weeks of a good diet, the dog developed into a fat, adorable puppy. The name Scruffy stuck. With all the attention her dad gave the dog, the animal only had eyes for him.

A few months later, Becky remembered feeling guilty for not showing any interest in the new pet, as he turned out to be quite cute. Dad trained him to walk on a leash, shake hands, sit and lie down on command. The little runt turned out to be a well-disciplined animal.

She turned her attention to the stack of envelopes piled on the desk, then stared at the two boxes of stuff she'd pulled from the safe. Letting out a sigh, she knew she had to read every piece of paper. Putting her mind to the project, she set to work.

After a couple of hours, she stood and stretched. Scruffy raised his head and thumped his tail. "You hungry, big boy? Let's take a break and go eat." She pulled back the curtain and glanced out the window. It had started raining, but not a gusty storm like yesterday. She thought about Cory and Susan. They must be getting excited with the birth of the baby just around the corner. She hoped these storms would stop soon, so Cory could run down and sign the trust papers before the little one arrived.

Dropping the drape, she stepped over the box she'd placed on the floor for trash, and headed for the kitchen with Scruffy at her heels. After they both had a bite to eat, she locked up. The idea of having the dog inside, gave her a feeling of security.

Once back at the desk, she searched through each envelope. To her surprise, one of them contained a strange looking key.

She furrowed her brow as she examined the odd shaped piece of metal and came to the conclusion: it belonged to a safe deposit box. On the outside of the envelope, in printed block letters, she read aloud, "First National". Placing it on top of the envelope with the ledger, she made a note to check with the bank tomorrow.

CHAPTER SIX

After Becky Simpson left the office, Hawkman stepped to the window and watched her get into a metallic blue Toyota Camry and drive out of the lot. He poured himself another cup of coffee and sat down at his desk. A feeling in his gut told him this would be an odd case. How could a mother disappear for fifteen years and no one searched for her?

He glanced at the check and recognized the area where Becky lived, then jotted the address and phone number on the folder. She'd filled out a form he needed with her mother's name, social security number, but left blank the question about a missing person's report. But she'd have been too young to know if her father filed such a document. Those are not things you discuss with small children. So he'd first search the Social Security Death Index to see if the woman still lived. If he found no record of her death, then he'd go into the police files.

Checking his watch, he figured he'd wait until he got home to pursue the job on the computer, as it sometimes took a while. He placed the file and check into his briefcase, rinsed out his mug, turned off the coffee maker and headed out the door.

Becky continued working through the stack of stuff until almost midnight. She finally slumped back in the chair and stretched her arms above her head. Her gaze fell on the envelope with the safe deposit key. Would she be able to get into the box? She'd take the death certificate and the will, just in case they questioned her authority. Rubbing her eyes, she turned her attention toward the big brown fluff of fur sleeping on the rug. "I think it's time to hit the sack, Scruffy."

The dog lifted his head and cocked his ears.

"I'd like your company tonight, so you can sleep in my room."

Scruffy waited, his tail wagging as she gathered the debris from her snacks and carried them downstairs. When she opened the door for the dog to go out, she glanced at the sky. The rain had stopped and she could actually see some stars twinkling between the leftover clouds. She stepped outside and watched Scruffy take a run around the yard with his nose to the ground. "What in the world are you finding so interesting?"

He picked up a stick and tossed it in the air. Becky laughed. "You're acting like a pup again. Good. Glad to see you behaving more like yourself."

She let him play for a few minutes, figuring he needed the exercise, then called him in, as the chill of the night soaked into her bones.

The next morning, the sun's bright light coming through the window woke Becky. She got up, showered and hummed as she fixed herself a light breakfast of oats and toast. Scruffy could stay outside while she ran to the bank. She also doubted Henry would show up until the ground dried.

Tucking the will, death certificate and key into her purse, she drove to the First National Bank. When she approached the teller about getting into the box, it not only surprised her, but relieved her mind to find out she and Cory were listed as co-owners. Once the woman lifted the drawer to the table, she left, leaving Becky in privacy. When she opened the lid, she discovered it full of envelopes and legal looking documents.

She couldn't imagine what all these items involved. Fortunately, at the last minute, she'd grabbed a small plastic grocery sack as she left the house and had shoved it into her purse. She removed the contents, stuffed them into the bag and left the bank. Curious to examine the papers, she by-passed the grocery store. The bread and milk could wait.

Once home, not wanting to mix these items with the stuff from the safe, she dumped the bag on the kitchen table. She then plopped her purse on the chair, sat down without removing her jacket and opened the first legal looking document.

It appeared to be a deed to a house. Her eyebrows rose as she saw the address and recognized it as Henry's home. Yet the title showed not only her Dad's name, but also her and Cory as co-owners. She put that one aside and opened the next one. It also contained a deed in their names, but she didn't recognize the address. The next four were deeds of different homes, and again she and Cory were stated as the co-owners. She rubbed her hands over her face in disbelief and stacked them in a pile.

The next few envelopes contained bank statements in her name, along with her dad's. When her gaze focused on the total, she gasped. "Fifty Thousand dollars!" She flopped back in the chair. "Where the hell did all this money come from?"

The second batch contained statements with her dad's and Cory's names. It also had fifty thousand dollars stated as the closing total. "Oh, my word! Wait until Cory sees these. He's not going to believe what I've uncovered."

She checked the date of the last entry and it had been entered two weeks before her father suffered the massive heart attack that killed him. Then she noticed the entries on one of the forms had three different sums, but were duplicated a month apart. The same with Cory's. It appeared they were rental payments. Why had her father never mentioned owning such properties? It all seemed very mysterious.

The next few letters were from an agency that took care of rentals for people. They explained their procedure and what they did for their monthly fee. It indicated if they could take care of all six rentals, they'd give a good discount. There were several from different groups, but it looked like her dad had settled on the 'Rental Ease Company'.

She read through their contract and he'd obviously set up the First National Bank to receive the payments and put them into the two accounts, along with a third account in her father's name also with her and Cory's, which had the word 'maintenance' after their names. It also had a nice hefty sum.

She leaned back in the chair and stared at all the documents in front of her. Everything seemed so precise and planned. Yet her father never gave a hint he had any property other than the home she lived in right now. Surely, he knew she'd eventually find out, so why would he keep such a secret? This all stumped her.

The next stack of envelopes were bound together with a rubber band and sealed. She took the letter opener from a container on the table and slit them each open.

These were rental agreements. Nothing seemed out of place; they were dated and signed by the tenants.

When Becky gave a second look at the date, she sucked in her breath. Frantically, she opened each of the agreements again and noticed they were all dated the month after her mother disappeared. She grabbed the deeds and checked the dates. They were all dated the same. This seemed mighty fishy. Maybe she should tell Mr. Casey. As much as it hurt her heart, something told her Al Simpson had been up to no good.

CHAPTER SEVEN

Becky leaned back in the chair, pushed loose strands of hair behind her ears and let out a sigh. For sure she wouldn't let a scrap of paper slip by her without scrutinizing its content. Glancing around the kitchen, she tried to recall where she'd last seen her dad's briefcase. She needed it to put all the items she wanted to show Mr. Casey. Carrying it in a paper sack into his office just didn't seem quite kosher.

She hurried up to her father's office, searched the room, shelves, around the furniture and finally went to the small closet, which she hadn't touched since his death. Rummaging through shelves loaded with books and miscellaneous knickknacks, she finally found the valise on the floor behind some boxes. It struck her as an odd place to keep it.

Setting the case on the desktop, she struggled to get it open. "Oh, great," she said aloud. "It's locked. Now where the hell is the key?"

Snapping her fingers, she quickly opened the desk drawer, remembering she'd spotted a stray one while cleaning and decided not to toss it. Quickly locating it in a cubby hole, she pushed the small piece of metal into the latch, twisted and the case popped open. Exhaling in relief, she glanced into the interior, and couldn't believe her eyes. "Oh my word, more papers," she gasped. Rubbing a hand across her face, she grabbed an empty box from the corner, and dumped the contents, then carried the briefcase downstairs to the kitchen. "I've got to get organized," she mumbled. "This is getting a bit overwhelming."

She placed all the things she'd brought home from the safe deposit box into the case, closed the lid and scooted it to the end of the table. Just as she headed to the back porch to check on Scruffy, the phone rang.

"Hello."

"Hi, Sis, how's it going?"

"A bit weird."

She explained how she'd met with Mr. Casey, then about the deeds and account statements she'd found at the bank.

"What! Fifty thousand dollars in each one? Holy mackerel! Where'd dad get that kind of money?"

"I'm not sure, Cory. But I don't have a good feeling about this whole thing. I'd like for you to see it all before I take this load into the private investigator. Is there a possibility you could come tomorrow?"

"I'll see what I can do."

"How's Susan?"

"She's doing fine. The doctor told her she still had at least two or three more weeks to go. Needless to say, it didn't make her too happy. She'd like to have that baby tonight. My little, fat wife is pretty miserable."

Becky chuckled. "I'm sure, but tell her it's better for the baby to go full term."

"I think she knows that," he laughed, "but I'll pass on your advice. I'll see if I can get away from work early tomorrow and come down. Are you going to be home all day?"

"Yes, I just found another bunch of papers in Dad's briefcase and want to sort through them. I definitely won't be going anywhere. I plan on seeing Mr. Casey on Wednesday. He'd like to get started on the case as soon as possible, but he needs a lot of information first. And maybe you can help me supply some names."

"Okay, I'll think about it. I'll try to give you a call before I leave, otherwise, I'll call on my cell on the way."

"Sounds great. Thanks, Cory. Give Susan my love."

"Will do. Bye."

Becky continued her trek to the back porch and Scruffy gave a pleading bark from outside. She opened the door and he jumped up with a stick in his mouth, his tail wagging. "Oh, you silly pup. Looks like you're in a playful mood. Okay, I'll toss it for you a few times, but then I've got to get back to work."

After fifteen minutes of playing with the dog, Becky stopped and caught her breath. "Okay, boy, enough of this game; you've worn me out." She let him inside where he headed for his water bowl and lapped up a great deal. Leaving the door open leading to the porch, she went into the kitchen and poured herself a glass of soda. Scruffy came to the edge of the threshold, water dripping from his jowls, and waited for her to give him permission to enter.

"You can come in," she said, waving her hand. "It's going to be boring, but I imagine you're ready for a nap." Giving him a rub between the ears, she picked up the briefcase from the table and headed upstairs with Scruffy bouncing along at her side.

When they reached the office, the dog flopped down on his rug and she slid into the seat at the desk, placing the valise at her feet. She picked up the small ledger, thumbed through it, and wondered what type of secret it held, then placed it in the briefcase along with other papers. Not sure where to start, she decided to check the box of stuff she'd dumped out of the case and pulled it toward her. She gathered up several number ten envelopes and stacked them on the surface of the desk. Picking up the top one, she opened it and pulled out the sheets of paper. On the top, a letter from a lawyer stated Carole Ann Simpson had transferred the title of this property, and it gave the parcel number, to her husband, Clayton Al Simpson. Enclosed they'd find a statement they needed to sign and return to Mr. Simpson, stating all rental payments would be sent in his name to the First National Bank.

Becky wrinkled her forehead as she read, and then it slammed into her like a fist in the gut. The papers were signed one month after her mother's disappearance. She quickly opened the other envelopes and found six identical letters and contracts for each of the properties. What struck her as odd; her mother's signature appeared on each of the conveyances.

"How could this have happened," she said, loudly.

Scruffy got to his feet, walked over, cocked his head toward her, and gave a little whine.

She reached over and patted his head. "It's okay. You didn't do anything wrong, but I think your old master did."

The dog meandered back to his spot and stretched out, but watched Becky with worried eyes.

Reaching into the desk drawer, she pulled out the love letters her mother had written to her dad. She tried comparing the signatures, and they resembled each other quite a bit. Not being a handwriting expert, she had no idea if they were really her mother's writing on the deeds or excellent replicas.

Becky leaned back, stared into space and blew out a puff of breath rippling her bangs. "I hope Mr. Casey can help me unravel this whole thing; it's getting very bizarre." She shoved the latest findings into the valise and plopped the box of remaining items she'd brought out from the safe onto the desk. She groaned when she realized she still had to go through every scrap of paper in the throw away pile.

CHAPTER EIGHT

Becky worked continuously for several hours, until the print blurred. She rubbed her eyes and stood. Strolling over to the dog, she reached down and stroked his back. "Scruffy, I don't know what I should keep or throw away. I think I'll just bundle it all up and take it to Mr. Casey."

He let out a bark as if answering.

She laughed. "So you think it's a good idea, too."

The next morning, Becky decided not to work in her father's office. Cory could just look over the papers she'd already discovered. She decided instead, to make a trip to the market and stock the pantry, as next week she'd have to go back to work. The days off would have been much more pleasant under different circumstances.

By the time she returned from town and put the groceries away, Henry had completed the yard work. He waited patiently as she wrote out his paycheck. Before handing it to him, she gazed into his weather worn face.

"Henry, you've been serving this house for many years."

"Yes, ma'am."

"Tell me about my Mother."

He looked startled by her request and stepped back. "What do you mean?"

"What kind of a woman was she?"

"Very nice," he said, ducking his head.

"Did she and Dad have many friends?"

Shrugging, he glanced away. "As many as most, I guess."

"Did you know any of them?"

"I recognized a few who came by while I worked in the yard. Mostly neighbors, many have moved away, some died."

"Can you tell me the names of those still around?"

"Frank and Elma Bradley."

"Yes, I know about them. What about my mother's friends?"

He shifted from one foot to another. "I don't rightly recall."

"Would you think about it and if you come up with any, let me know?"

Frowning, he asked. "Why are you so interested in your Ma? She's been gone for years. Once she slammed that door and left, she never returned or showed any interest in you kids."

Becky sighed. "I know, Henry. Dad never told us anything about her, but I'd just like to know the reasons behind Mother's leaving."

He turned to go out the door. "Miss Becky, forget her. She ain't worth your fretting."

She stared at his back as he walked outside. His last statement left her baffled. Why did he sound so bitter? As she mulled it over in her mind, the phone rang. She punched on the speaker phone.

"Hello."

"Hi, Sis, I'm almost there. Thought I'd get on the road as soon as possible, so didn't have a chance to call you."

"Great. See you soon."

Becky put on a fresh pot of coffee and placed Cory's favorite cookies on a platter. He arrived within twenty minutes and let himself in.

"Hey, I'm here."

They hugged.

"How's Susan?"

He made a circle with his arms and hands, forming a huge stomach, puffed out his cheeks, then waddled across the room. "Fat and miserable."

Becky couldn't help but laugh. "You're mean."

He slipped off his jacket and tossed it on the living room chair. "I know, we're both very ready for this baby."

"I'm sure you are." Becky changed the subject. "Have you had lunch?"

"Yes, grabbed a sandwich on the way."

"Let's have a cup of coffee and go up to Dad's office. I've got a lot to show you."

"Okay," he said, following her into the kitchen. "But before we get involved in those items, let me sign the trust papers so we have that out of the way; then I can concentrate better." He grabbed a handful of cookies as he seated himself at the table.

Becky placed the documents in front of him. After those matters were taken care of, they went upstairs to their dad's office, and Cory sat down at the desk and soon became engrossed in all the deeds and papers. He finally glanced up at his sister. "Appears to me, Dad had some sort of contact with Mom."

Becky nodded. "My thoughts, exactly. What I don't understand is, why he never mentioned it to us."

"We were just kids. And if Mom didn't want to come home, he wouldn't know how to break that kind of news." He flipped his fingers across the stack of documents. "But he somehow talked her into signing over all these deeds. How the hell did she expect to survive? Those houses would have given her a nice living. Why would she sign them over to him?"

Becky shook her head. "I really don't know. However, she actually signed them over to us; but we were minors. The rent payments went into a bank account in our names." She paced the floor. "It doesn't make sense, Cory. Dad made plenty of money to support us. Why would Mother sign over those houses, when she had no other income."

Cory rubbed a hand across his chin. "Dad might have agreed to pay her a healthy alimony." He threw up his hands. "We really don't know much about her or what she had."

"Mom told me after her high school graduation, she spent her days working at a piddly job at a candy shop while waiting for Dad to get out of college. So she didn't possess any skills. She didn't have any money, unless she received a bundle of cash along with the houses from her folks. Her parents were still alive when they married, so I'm assuming Mom lived at home until then."

"Boy, you sure know more than I do."

"She and I used to talk about girlie things, while you played in the dirt with your cars and trucks."

Cory grinned. "Yeah, I was just a snotty nosed little brother."

Becky reached over and gave him a playful jab. "Well, you've sure grown up to be a good-looking brat. I hope Susan realizes what a catch she has."

He blushed. "Thanks, Sis. You're not too shabby yourself." Cory pulled one of the boxes toward him. "Did you by chance find Mom's birth certificate?"

"No. I'd assumed she took it with her. Why?"

"I'm curious about the name of our grandparents. A private investigator might want to know her maiden name."

"Patterson."

Cory shot a look at her. "How'd you know? I don't remember it ever being mentioned."

Becky removed the love letters from the desk drawer. "I planned on keeping these myself."

Cory read through several of them. "She sure loved Dad when she was younger. It must have broken her heart when she caught him cheating."

"I wish I knew more about the other woman."

"Have you searched this room completely?"

"Not really, just the desk, and vault. The rest came from the briefcase and safe deposit box." She pointed toward the closet. "I found the valise buried in there."

Cory frowned. "Odd he'd hide it." He got up, crossed the room, stepped inside the small enclosure, and began knocking on the walls.

Becky followed him. "What are you doing?"

"Looking for a hidden compartment or wall safe."

"Why would he resort to those means, when he had a vault and a secure box at the bank?"

"I'm not sure, but I'm beginning to doubt our dear old Dad stood clean and straight."

He soon backed out, tripping over assorted items. "I don't think there's anything there, it sounds pretty solid. You might check it again when you get all this crap out ." Sitting back in the desk chair, he tapped his fingers on the surface. "When did you say you had the next appointment with Mr. Casey?"

Becky exhaled and waved a hand over the piles of paper. "I'm going to bundle all this stuff up and take it to him tomorrow. I have no idea what's important."

He nodded. "Probably a good idea."

"Did you think of any persons who might have known the folks?"

"Only Henry and possibly the Bradleys. You'd probably remember more than me."

"Glad you mentioned Henry. I asked him today about friends of the folks. He told me about the Bradleys. Then he said a weird thing."

"What?"

"Mother was not worth fretting over."

Cory grimaced. "You probably caught him off guard. We might have to talk to him again."

"I think I'll leave it to Mr. Casey."

"You're right. This whole thing has an air of mystery." He shifted in the chair and stared at his sister. "Are you prepared for what we might find out?"

She frowned. "What do you mean?"

"Mother could have been murdered."

CHAPTER NINE

Long after Cory left, Becky sat in her dad's chair staring out the office window. Her brother's statement about, 'murder' kept popping into her mind. Why would anyone kill her mother? She didn't have any money. As far as she could tell, no one would benefit by her death, except her father. Then he'd be free to do whatever he wished. Tears welled in her eyes. She couldn't believe her dad could do such a thing.

Shaking off the horrible feelings, she went downstairs and prepared a sandwich, then let Scruffy in for the night. Flipping on the television, she flopped down on the couch, but couldn't concentrate on any program. She finally turned off the tube and went to bed.

The next morning, Becky made an appointment with Tom Casey for eleven. She packed the extra items into a small duffle bag, then carried it along with the briefcase to the car. She hadn't slept well and her heart felt heavy. Maybe she should have left well enough alone. Too late now; she'd already paid the deposit.

Lugging the two bags up the stairs to the Private Investigators office, she almost stumbled into the small room.

Hawkman jumped up from his desk and relieved her of the burdens. "It appears you found more information."

"Yes, and I didn't know what to keep or toss. So I brought everything."

He grinned and placed the items on the desk. "Better safe than sorry. Have a seat and I'll get you a cup of coffee."

"Thanks."

After placing a mug of the steaming brew in front of Becky, he settled in his seat and pulled a yellow legal pad toward him. "I've done a couple of searches on your mother and found no record of her death. However, the only address recorded was the residence where you're living now. Which I thought odd if she'd started a life elsewhere."

Becky leaned forward. "What does it mean?"

He shrugged. "It could be a number of things, but right now let's concentrate on finding her."

She nodded, her expression solemn.

"I also did a search through the police records to check if a missing person's report had ever been filed."

Her eyes lit up. "Did you find one?"

"No. I checked the rest of the year from the time you told me your mother had left until five years later. I found nothing. Do you think your father might have known where she'd gone and made contact with her?"

"That's a possibility." She reached into the briefcase and pulled out the deeds of the property she'd secured with a rubber band. "My mother's signature appear on these. I have no idea if it's really hers or a forgery."

"Do you have a sample of her handwriting?"

She reached into her purse and took out the bundle of love letters. "I'm not sure how good of a sample these might be, as they're pretty old." Placing them in front of Hawkman, she bowed her head and almost whispered. "They're love letters she wrote to Dad before they were married."

He read through a couple, then glanced up. "May I make a copy of these for the purpose of comparing the calligraphy on the deeds to these letters."

"Sure."

He walked to the copy machine. "In fact, I'll make copies of the papers and documents I feel necessary to have for this case, and return the originals. I want you to keep them in a secure place, preferably in a safe deposit box at the bank."

She frowned. "Why can't I keep them in the vault at the house?"

"It's best you keep them stored away from the residence."

Becky stared at him. "Why? Do you suspect foul play?"

"We never know, so please do as I say." He sat back down at the desk, retied the bundle of letters and handed them to her, then slipped the copies into the file. He asked her more questions about her mother, then leaned back in his chair. He motioned toward the stack she'd brought in. "It'll take me a while to go through these items, so don't expect to hear from me for a few days."

"I feel bad bringing everything I found, but I got to the point where I wasn't sure what might have some value and what didn't."

Hawkman smiled. "It's better than throwing an important piece of information away. When I'm finished, I'm sure I'll have more questions. There is one thing I'd like you to do. Go to the rental agency handling these houses and have them furnish you with the names of the latest tenants. If they don't know your father has passed away, you'll probably need to show them a copy of the death certificate and the will putting you in charge. Also, don't tell them you've hired a private investigator. In fact, don't tell anyone. The fewer people who know, the better. Call me as soon as you have the information.

Becky stood. "I might just run by there today. I'm carrying a copy of the death certificate and will in my purse until everything is settled. Thank you, Mr. Casey. I'm relieved this is in your hands now."

"I'll keep in touch as I move along on the case."

After she left, Hawkman eyed the mound of stuff. He decided to look over the deeds first, and sat the two bags on the floor, then got comfortable at the desk.

He became engrossed with the information, and time passed. After several hours he stretched his arms in front of him and groaned at the stiffness he felt after sitting in the same position for so long. He stood and walked around the room for several minutes before pouring himself a hot cup of coffee. Staring at the documents, he picked up the pile and placed them on the copier. The deeds and contracts made with the renters puzzled him. They seemed out of the ordinary and he decided they'd be the first group to investigate. If Carole Simpson's signature proved to be authentic, it appeared Mr. Simpson had contact with his wife after she left the home. Why would she sign over those houses? It just didn't make sense.

After making the copies, he placed the originals into a separate folder to be returned to Becky. He sat back down and pulled another bundle from the valise and prepared to go through the next stack, when he noticed the corner of a small book had partially slipped out of an envelope and hung precariously in the air. He pulled it out and flipped through the pages, frowning at the content.

"What the heck is this?" he asked aloud. The entries were in a code he didn't find familiar. He assumed the person concocted it for privacy. Hawkman decided not to run it through the copier, but work on it from the original pages. He shoved it into his take home file.

He'd jotted down the addresses of the rentals along with the names of the people who had originally rented the places, and planned to drive by each of them before going home tonight. He stuck the list into his pocket. It might give him some idea about the occupants. Becky didn't recognize any of the renters, except the gardener, and didn't have a clue if the tenants listed were still living in the homes. He hoped she'd be able to get the names of the latest occupants from the rental agency without any problem.

Hawkman spent another hour sorting through the items and made a pile of small pieces of paper containing numbers or a word. He wondered if they had meaning, since Becky found them in the vault or briefcase. Otherwise, they'd have been tossed and not put away for safe keeping. He placed these in a folder with sides so they wouldn't slip out and get lost.

The afternoon waned into early evening and he decided to leave before dark so he could get a good view of the rental homes. He packed the items he hadn't gone through into a separate briefcase and decided to carry it all with him. Something in his gut warned him, he'd need to keep these files away from the office. Just like he'd cautioned Becky to put them into a safe deposit box away from her residence. His intuition usually proved right.

CHAPTER TEN

Hawkman took off and drove by the Simpson rentals. They were all in a range of approximately five miles from each other and he had no trouble finding the addresses, especially with the GPS. None of the homes were spectacular in appearance or very large. Two needed a gardner and a good paint job, and one appeared vacant. The others were well maintained, with mowed lawns, picket fences and trimmed hedges. But the home that caught his attention was the last one on the list and rented by the Simpson's caretaker, Henry Harris. The home appeared larger and groomed to perfection. Mr. Harris was a gardener, so it made sense.

A fairly good sized trailer sat in the side yard, bordered by the house, fence and carport. A large tree obscured most of it. Hawkman wondered how they ever managed to get it into the space. He could also see the roof line of a separate building at the rear of the house. Circling the block, he realized he couldn't get closer for a better view, because a large building sat behind the houses. The alley had been boarded up with a 'No Trespassing' sign nailed on each end. He parked off the side of the street and jotted down notes beside each of the addresses. Putting a question mark beside Mr. Harris' place, he decided to set up an appointment with him at the residence. He'd like a better look.

When Hawkman arrived home, Jennifer and her cat, Miss Marple, were busy at the computer center, so he waved and headed toward his office. He took the small book from his briefcase, flipped on the light and began studying the pages. It appeared to be a payment ledger of some sort. He checked the front and back, looking for a guide to the code. Finding none, he stood and searched through his small library on the shelves next to his desk. "Ah, here it is," he said aloud, pulling out a small book of "How to Decipher Codes".

Going through the index, he picked several subjects, read them, but found nothing faintly resembling the strange cryptography in the little journal. He exhaled loudly and set the two books aside. He figured he could eventually crack the code, if not, he'd get his friend who deciphered them as a hobby to help him out. But there might be the possibility of his finding a clue in the pile of stuff Ms. Simpson had brought. Just as he lifted his briefcase to the desktop, Jennifer popped her head in the door.

"Hi, how was your day?"

"Fine, busy. And yours?"

She smiled. "About the same. Are you working on the Simpson case?"

"Yeah, and it's intriguing."

Her eyes lit up. "Oh, tell me more." She stepped into the room and took a chair beside his desk.

"Not much to report. It's a cold case, some fifteen years old. Not sure if I'll be successful in finding this woman."

Her shoulders drooped. "Shoot, I thought you had some big news."

Hawkman laughed. "What's the matter, you stuck on one of your stories?"

She nodded. "Kinda. It'll come. Just thought maybe you could get me rolling again."

"Hopefully, I can give you some ideas soon."

Standing, she picked up Miss Marple and cuddled her close. "Guess we'll head for the kitchen. Hope a nice fat sandwich will satisfy you tonight."

"Sounds great. I want to see if I can make a dent in the items Ms. Simpson brought me today."

"I can see you've definitely got lots of work ahead." She moved out the door. "I'll bring your food in here."

"Thanks, hon. I'd appreciate it."

He opened his briefcase and pulled out the folder with the tidbits of paper Becky had thrown into the mess. He figured they had some sort of meaning or wouldn't have been in the safe. After he'd lined them up on his desktop, he picked up the small ledger and glanced through the pages. It appeared he'd found how to crack the code. Now to get the symbols and letters in order. He took a legal pad from the drawer and began writing. Then he took the ledger to his copy machine and ran off a print of the first two pages. He didn't feel he should deface the original and would decode it on the facsimile.

Jennifer brought in his sandwich along with a frosty beer. He gave her a peck on the cheek. "Thanks, hon. I couldn't live without you."

"I hope not," she said, grinning as she left the room.

Hawkman worked his way through several pages of the ledger and saw it take form as payments. Unfortunately, it hadn't mentioned a name so far, only totals and dates. He found the initials L. A. here and there, and felt this would fit into the puzzle somewhere. But right now he didn't have a clue. Placing the book, the small pieces of paper and his notes into a large brown envelope, he set it aside to work on later.

Digging deeper into the bag, he removed the bank statements indicating the money deposited into Becky's and Cory's account. He needed to find out when they were opened, what the rental charges were and if the payments had stayed the same throughout the years. He jotted down several questions to ask the next time he talked with Becky.

Finally, he flipped up his eye-patch, rubbed his eyes and glanced at the clock. "Good, grief," he mumbled. "One thirty AM already. I better get to bed." He stood, stretched, and turned off the light.

The next morning, Hawkman awoke to the aroma of coffee and bacon. "Man, it smells good in here," he said, strolling into the kitchen.

Jennifer smiled. "Thought the smell of food would set your senses on high. I have this feeling, even though it's Saturday, you're going to the office. And I didn't want you tempted by Clyde's wonderful donuts."

He laughed. "Now pray tell me what's the difference between, eggs, bacon, toast smeared with butter, and coffee compared to a couple of bear claws?"

She reached over and pinched his love handles. "Nutrition and calories."

"Okay, I believe you," he said, smiling as he slid onto the bar stool.

"You worked late last night; did you find out anything helpful?" she asked, setting a loaded breakfast plate in front of him.

"All depends if it will come together. I'm just scratching the surface, but there are lots of questions needing answers. What's frustrating is Becky and her brother were quite young when their mother left, so I'm not sure how much she really remembers, or what might just be figments passing through a young girl's mind through the years. Now that her father has died, makes it a bit hard to figure out the reasons behind the woman's leaving. I'm going to do a lot of interviewing of people who knew this couple. And I'm not sure how many I'm going to find still alive or in the area."

Jennifer sat down opposite him at the kitchen bar. "Sounds like it's going to be complicated and involve a lot of footwork."

He nodded. "It's going to be interesting, to say the least."

"If you need me to help, let me know."

Pointing his fork, he eyed her. "You'd love to get involved in this case, wouldn't you?"

Putting a napkin to her lips, she nodded. "It sounds intriguing."

"I might just take you up on your offer. We'll see how involved it gets."

"Fair enough."

Cleaning the last remnants off his plate with the corner of the piece of toast, he rose from the bar stool. "I better get rolling. I hope I'll be home at a decent hour tonight, but don't worry about making a big dinner. Leftovers will be fine. I'll give you a call if I'm going to be real late."

"Okay. Good luck in your search."

When he arrived at his office in Medford, he smiled to himself as he climbed the stairs. He could smell the wonderful aroma of baking pastries, but Jennifer told him right. With a full stomach, he didn't have the desire for a bear claw.

He put on the coffee pot and sat down at his desk. Picking up the phone, he dialed Becky's number and hoped she'd be home. When she answered, he punched on the speaker so he'd have his hands free to go through the items he wanted to talk about.

"Hi, Ms. Simpson, this is Tom Casey."

"Please call me, Becky."

"Okay, if it makes you more comfortable. I wanted to check and see if you got the information from the Rental Ease Company."

"Yes, I went by there after I left your office. I had them give me copies going back to when they took over the rentals. I have everything from who lived in the houses to how much they paid monthly."

"Fantastic. I need that data as soon as possible. Can I run by and pick it up?"

"Sure. I'll be home all day. I'm trying to clean up Dad's office before I have to go back to work on Monday."

"I'll come by within the hour and promise I won't stay but a few minutes. I'll bring you the originals I've copied, and pick up the documents you have. I hope you've made arrangements for a safe deposit box."

"I took care of getting one yesterday with my bank. I'll tuck everything away safely on Monday."

"Great. See you shortly."

CHAPTER ELEVEN

Hawkman arrived at Becky's within the hour. She met him at the door, and invited him into the living room.

"Have a seat and I'll get the documents. I want to talk to you about a couple of the people on the list."

He thought she appeared tired. Dark circles under her eyes made her seem much older, and her brown hair hung limp around her face.

"You look worn out."

She wrapped her arms around her waist. "I haven't slept well. I'm wondering if I'm doing the right thing in searching for my mother."

"If you want to call it off, just say the word."

Shaking her head, she threw up her hands. "No. I think I've got to go through with this, or I'll never be satisfied. It'll haunt me forever and I need closure." She turned and headed for another room. "I'll be back in a second."

Hawkman sat down on the upholstered floral couch and placed the two briefcases on the floor beside his feet. He glanced around the room and decided this area must have been off limits to kids play, because the furniture, even though outdated, showed no signs of wear. A large painting of a ship on the high seas hung on one wall, a small mirror hung beside the off center fireplace and a few framed pictures decorated the tables. He noticed one in particular of a tall man with two young children standing beside him. Becky's likeness in the girl, indicated these were taken many years ago with who he assumed to be their dad. The rest of the room lacked the knickknacks or personal things a woman might place in strategic spots. It had a comfortable feeling, but without much personality.

Becky soon returned. She'd combed her hair back into a pony tail, dabbed on a bit of lipstick and brushed some soft blush onto her cheeks.

"Boy, I did look awful," she said laughing. "I've been so busy, I hadn't taken the time to even check myself in the mirror.

Hawkman waved his hand. "You look fine."

"Thanks." She sat down beside him on the couch. "I want to show you the people I know who live in these houses." She pointed to the names. "Mr. and Mrs. Frank Bradley have been friends of the family as long as I can remember, the same as Henry and Lisa Harris. Dad hired Henry Harris years ago to take care of the grounds. I never liked him, because he frightened me when I was a little girl."

"Do you still feel the same way?"

"No. He's a strange man. Very quiet, but does his work well."

"Did Mr. or Mrs. Bradley work for your dad?"

"Not that I know. They'd get together for dinner or cocktails. Mrs. Bradley has always been the most outgoing. Frank does whatever she wants. I don't recognize any of the other names who lived in the houses before Mom disappeared. I'm not saying the folks didn't socialize with them, they may well have."

"Would your brother know them?"

She shook her head. "He's younger than I am, he wouldn't have a clue either. And, of course, I don't recognize the newer tenants." She held up a couple of pages and pointed out a column. "It appears Dad raised the rent a few times, but not by much."

"You did a good job on getting all this information. They didn't by any chance have forwarding addresses for any of the older names?"

"No, I asked. I thought it might be useful if we could locate them, but they couldn't help me out there." She flipped the paper over. "Oh, they did mention one of the houses is vacant right now. They're going to have it painted on the inside and are replacing some carpets. There is a person very interested in the place, so it should be rented by next month. Also, they informed me they're having the exterior of a couple of the houses painted and hiring a gardener to maintain the yards. So it does sound like they're doing their job."

"Have you viewed any of the rentals?"

"No. I guess I just haven't had the time yet with the funeral arrangements, and being the executrix of Dad's estate has kept me busy. Then to find out my brother and I are landlords has really been a surprise. We had no idea about these homes. I'm sure we'd have eventually found out."

"I can imagine the shock. I took a drive by them last night on my way home. They're all small but very good properties. I'd say the most impressive is the one where your gardener lives." Standing, he tucked the new reports into his briefcase and handed her the other. "I've made copies of all these items. There's a few I haven't finished, but will get them to you as soon as I can."

Becky took the bag. "There's certainly no hurry."

"As I promised I wouldn't keep you long, I'm going back to my office for the rest of the day. If you have any questions, just give me a call. In fact, you can reach me on my cell phone anytime. You did a great job on getting this information. This will help me tremendously."

Becky followed him to the door. Hawkman turned toward her before stepping outside. He looked into her soft hazel eyes. "Once I start asking questions, the news will ricochet all over the community that you've hired a private investigator to find your mother. Are you prepared for the impact?"

She frowned. "I think so."

Hawkman returned to his office, anxious to get busy on the information Becky had acquired. She'd gotten more than he'd requested, and he appreciated her insight into what things he needed. His biggest job would be locating the original renters of four of the houses. It seemed strange the two couples still in these places would rent all those years, and never make the effort to own their own homes. Of course, there were always circumstances forcing a person to lease instead of buy. Maybe he'd find out some of their motives.

He knew for a fact, rental homes were hard to come by in Medford. So he figured from the statement of the Rental Ease Company, the vacant dwelling would be occupied very shortly. Hawkman planned to talk with Henry and Lisa Harris first, then venture over to the Bradley's before searching for the others. It would be useless to talk to any of the other tenants, unless he needed to know how their payments were handled. But he figured the rental company took care of that aspect. And more than likely, Becky could find out all the information he needed.

Hawkman wondered how people were going to react to his questions about the Simpson's after all these years. It all depended on what they had to hide, if anything. He'd jotted down their names, along with the addresses, tossed the pencil aside and stood. "Right now is as good a time as any to start the ball rolling," he said aloud.

CHAPTER TWELVE

Hawkman stopped on the street in front of the Harris' and scrutinized the scene. The dwelling set back almost a half block from the curb, so he turned and drove into the long driveway. Not wanting to block any of the vehicles already there, he parked in the center, giving plenty of room for anyone to get by his SUV. He strolled to the front door and knocked. The yipping of a small dog announced a stranger at the door.

He could hear heavy footsteps clopping across a wooden floor, and a woman's shrill voice sounded through the walls. "Shut up, Sugar." When the door opened, Hawkman stood face to face with a very large female. Her face puffed out so much, her eyes looked like two little blue beads stuck in a hunk of clay. Short, dyed, red kinky hair hugged her head like a close knit stocking cap and a waistless muumuu dress fit over her large shoulders, draped across an ample bosom and flowed straight down to her slip-on house shoes.

"Yes?" she said.

Hawkman flashed his badge. "I'm Tom Casey, Private Investigator. Are you Mrs. Harris?"

Her face paled at the sight of the badge and a hand went to her chest. Beads of sweat immediately popped out on her rosy cheeks. "Are we in trouble?"

Hawkman smiled and shook his head. "No, I'm just here to ask some questions about the disappearance of Carole Ann Simpson fifteen years ago."

A wave of fear flashed across her face. She turned her head slightly and yelled over her shoulder, "Henry, get out here."

The small dog standing at her feet whined and backed away. Mrs. Harris reached down, scooped up the animal, held it close to her bulging bosom, and lovingly caressed the animal "I'm not yelling at you, my little sweetie."

Henry Harris walked up behind his wife. "What's the problem?"

She stepped back and pointed at Hawkman. "This is a private investigator wanting to ask questions about Carole Simpson's disappearance."

He glanced out the door with shadowed eyes. "Who sent you?"

Hawkman again showed his badge. "I've been hired by Becky Simpson to try and locate her mother."

Henry let out a sigh. "Invite the man in, Lisa. No sense in him standing in the doorway."

She backed out of the way and gestured toward the living room. "Come on in and have a seat. I'll leave you men to discuss this."

"I might need to ask you a few questions," Hawkman said.

"Couldn't tell you a thing about the woman; never met her."

Hawkman furrowed his brow in question. "Why not?"

"We weren't in the same class of people. Henry worked for Mr. Simpson. We didn't see them socially." She flipped her free hand in the air and lumbered out of the room, making cooing noises to the pup she had cuddled under her arm.

Henry Harris had large shoulders and a thick chest which tended to make his arms stick out from his side. He only stood about five foot seven, but didn't appear to have an ounce of fat on his body. His salt and pepper colored hair, which desperately needed cutting, stuck out in unruly curls from underneath the ball cap perched on his head. The skin on his face and arms had the appearance of rough leather. Hawkman assumed the man had done outside labor most of his life.

"Well, get on with your questions, I don't have all day," Henry said, plopping down on the couch and entwining his fingers together in his lap.

Before slipping into the large upholstered chair facing Mr. Harris, Hawkman reached into his pocket and flipped on the voice activated recorder. He would never be able to use the recording for anything but his personal use, but he found it a heck of a lot easier than writing everything down. "Mr. Harris, how long have you worked at the Simpson household?"

Henry shrugged. "Close to twenty five years."

"Is gardening your occupation?"

"Yes, I have about twenty some regular jobs in the area. Been with most of them at least ten years, others longer. When I was in desperate need of work, Mr. Simpson was kind enough to give me my start."

"So you knew Carole Simpson?"

He nodded.

"Could you tell me something about her?"

Hawkman noticed Henry clenched his hands tightly together until his knuckles turned white.

"Not much to tell. Nice enough woman. Kept to the house mostly when I worked outside. But when her favorite flowers, the roses, were in bloom, she'd ask me to cut her a bouquet each time I came."

"You never carried on a conversation with her?"

"I'm not much of a talker."

"Didn't you have some sort of opinion of her personality?"

"Not really. I minded my business and she minded hers."

"Did she and Mr. Simpson get along?"

He lifted his shoulders, and put his hands, palms up. "Who knows what goes on inside the walls of others. I seldom saw them together. Mr. Simpson was at work when I did my job."

"I see."

He pointed a finger at Hawkman. "As long as I do my job and my clients are happy to pay me, I don't pry."

Hawkman nodded. "I understand. You rent your home from the Simpson's, right?"

Henry's eyes narrowed. "What business is that of yours?"

"It's Becky and Cory Simpson's concern on when and how this came about. From the records we've found, this property belonged to the Patterson's, Mrs. Simpson's parents, and she inherited it at their deaths. It appears you've rented this property for close to twenty years. Who did you make the rental checks to when you first got the house?"

"You certainly know a lot about the past."

"It's my job."

He sighed. "When I first found the house, Lisa and I lived in another town. I wanted to get my family here, as this looked like a place I could bring in a steady income. I didn't have much money saved at the time, so made a deal with Mrs. Simpson, to pay her extra each month until I could get the first and last month's rent plus the damage deposit paid. She knew Mr. Simpson had hired me, so she felt pretty safe and agreed. But she told me the minute I slighted her, I'd be out on my butt."

"So you made your checks out to her?"

"No, she insisted on cash. And I always made sure she gave me a receipt. Then, a lawyer presented us with contracts when Mr. Simpson took over, which we signed and from then on out we sent the rent payments to the bank."

"Didn't you think this a bit odd, since I'm sure you'd heard Mrs. Simpson had disappeared."

He raised his eyes and stared into Hawkman's face. "Not at all; in fact, I liked it better, easier to keep track of your records. Mr. Simpson raised the rent a tad, but not enough to hurt us."

"So you started sending checks to the bank without question? Didn't it bother you there'd been no word of Mrs. Simpson's whereabouts or her demise?"

Henry glared at him. "Mr. Casey, my private thoughts are my concern, not yours. As long as I had a roof over my family's head and we weren't going to be evicted, I didn't question anything."

Hawkman stood and held out his hand. "Mr. Harris, I appreciate you seeing me. I may need to ask you more questions later. I hope you don't mind if I come by again."

"It appears you know as much as I do. Not sure what more I could tell you. I certainly have no idea where Carole Ann has gone."

Henry walked him to the front door.

When Hawkman stepped onto the porch, he pointed to the trailer. "My curiosity has the best of me. How in the heck did you get that trailer in there?"

Henry snickered. "More people have asked me. It's been there ever since we've lived here. They must have put it in before they closed off the alley, because there's no way anyone could get it out now."

"Do you use it for storage?"

"Nope, rent it. It's perfect for college kids, just like the apartments in the back."

Hawkman raised a brow. "You have rentals?"

"Yep. Three all together. Sure helps the income."

Hawkman left the premises and drove down the street. He parked at the side of the road, scribbled some notes, then placed a call to Becky.

"Hello, Becky, Tom Casey here. I just need to clear something up in my mind. Do you remember if your mother was referred to as Carole Ann or just Carole?"

He listened intently.

"Thanks, Becky."

He hung up and stared out the windshield. If Mrs. Simpson only allowed her friends to call her Carole because she didn't like her middle name. How come Mr. Harris, who stated he didn't know her well, and Mrs. Harris, who claimed they weren't in the same social circle, have the familiarity to refer to her as Carole Ann. Hawkman suspected dear old Henry knew more than he'd let on.

CHAPTER THIRTEEN

Hawkman pulled onto the road and continued toward Frank and Elma Bradley's place. Their house sat in a clump of slightly newer tract houses, with sidewalks and a curbed street. Their place didn't appear much bigger than the Harris home. The freshly cut lawn and pruned bushes gave him the idea these people had a certain amount of pride. He made his way up the sidewalk to the front door and rang the bell.

While waiting, he flipped on the recorder in his pocket. A short matronly woman not much over five feet with a deep dimple in her chin answered.

"Yes?"

"Mrs. Bradley?"

"That's me."

Hawkman introduced himself, and flashed his badge. "I've been retained to try and find the whereabouts of Carole Simpson. I understand you knew her many years ago. I'd like to ask you a few questions."

"Bet you've been hired by Becky Simpson."

"You're correct."

She waggled her head of white hair. "I had a feeling she would eventually want to know what happened to her mother. Such a fine young lady; I hate to see her go through all this agony. First, her mother disappeared and now losing her father. It's really sad."

A loud male voice echoed through the house. "Elma, who's there?"

She twisted her head around, then glanced back at

Hawkman. "Come on in, Mr. Casey. My husband, Frank, will want to meet you."

Hawkman followed her through the kitchen, which smelled of baked bread, into what appeared an enclosed back porch. Large windows covered one wall, giving a wonderful view of a well-groomed back yard. "Nice place. Did you add this room?"

"Yes, Mr. Simpson allowed us to do some remodeling at our own expense."

"Have you lived here a long time?"

"Close to thirty years. We rented from the Patterson's before they passed away."

"How come you never bought your own home?"

She let out a small sigh. "Just about the time we'd have a little cash put away for a down payment, some tragedy or incident set us back. Then Frank got hurt on the job and we decided to forget trying to own a home. We like it here and doubt we could afford to buy now with the heavy medical bills."

The room extended the width of the house, then cut to the left making it an 'L' shape. Mrs. Bradley went straight to the man in the wheelchair and pushed him toward Hawkman.

"This is my husband, Frank Bradley. Frank, this is Tom Casey, a private investigator hired by Becky Simpson to try and find out what happened to her mother."

Frank extended a trembling hand. "Nice to meet ya. I don't understand why Becky wants to find her. The woman never came back to see those kids. Hard to imagine a mother high tailing it out of town and leaving her children. Mighty shameful, if you ask me."

"Did you know Mrs. Simpson well?"

Frank pointed to his wife. "Elma probably knew her better than anyone around."

Hawkman turned and faced Mrs. Bradley.

She frowned and fingered a doily she had on the back of one of the chairs. "I met Carole before her parents passed away. She appeared very shy while single. After she married Al, she tended to come out of her shell, but still remained a very private person."

"Did she ever mention any marriage problems?" Hawkman asked

Elma shook her head. "No. After the children were born, her life evolved around them, especially Becky. She didn't seem to know what to do with a little boy, but she talked about them almost constantly. The only thing I remember her saying about Al was she wished he'd spend more time with Cory. We just assumed they were a happy family. Then the rumor hit town about him having an affair. It probably took about three months before Carole got wind of it. Suddenly, the next thing we heard, she'd disappeared."

"She should have hung around and confronted the whore," Frank grumbled.

Hawkman glanced at the man. "Who was the other woman?"

Frank raised his hands and slapped them down on the rests of his wheelchair. "Who knows?"

"Surely there were rumors."

"Maybe someone else can tell you, but we never heard. Maybe people didn't want to tell us, because we were their friends," Elma said.

"Speaking of others. Could you furnish me names of those who had a close association with Mr. and Mrs. Simpson during the years when Carole was still present in the household?"

Elma tapped a finger against her chin. "Gee, let me think. They had a housekeeper once a week. If I can remember her name." She snapped her fingers. "Marie Olson. I think she's still around, but I haven't seen her in ages. She's from England, has a wonderful accent." She lowered her eyes in thought, then glanced back up. "Oh, yes, Carole had a teenage girl, Robin Kregor, who used to baby sit on rare occasions. Of course, she's a grown women now. The last I heard she'd married a banker." She waved a hand in the air. "But my goodness, these things all happened years ago. I don't know where Marie is, but Robin lives in Medford in a mansion from what I understand." She furrowed her brow. "For the life of me I can't remember her married name."

"What about Al Simpson? Tell me a little about him."

"He made a good living," Elma said. "Loved those kids. I think it devastated him when Carole left."

"Yeah, only because he had to take care of the kids and hire some help. Face it, Elma, Al hated to part with his money," Frank snorted, then turned his wheelchair around and scooted into the other part of the room where he flipped on the television.

She shook her fist at him, then motioned for Hawkman to follow her back into the kitchen. "Sorry about my husband, but he's turned into an old grouch."

"Is it true about Simpson being tight with his money?"

"No more than any other man. We've all worked hard and scraped our pennies so we could buy groceries. Why should Al be any different?"

Hawkman nodded. "True. Did you notice a change in the Simpsons' relationship near the time Carole left?"

She frowned. "Now that you mentioned it, yes. We used to have dinner together at least once a week. About three months before all hell broke loose, it ceased. And from that time on, things just weren't the same. Al stayed pretty much to himself and took care of the children. He hired an older woman to come in every day when they got out of school. She'd fix dinner and stay until Al got home from work. He kept her on until his daughter reached the age of fourteen, then he let the woman go and had Becky take care of Cory."

"Do you remember the woman's name?"

"Carmella Jones. But she passed away a couple of years ago."

"Tell me how you felt when suddenly you were confronted with Al Simpson becoming your new landlord."

She shrugged. "I didn't feel good or bad. It seemed the right thing to do since Carole had disappeared."

"You mean you weren't disturbed when a lawyer turned up on your doorstep carrying a new contract?"

"Frank thought it a bit strange. But we don't understand the workings of the real estate business, so we kept our mouths shut. We sure didn't want to get evicted. Things have gone along smoothly. Just hope Becky doesn't want to sell the place."

"I have no idea what her plans are, but I doubt she'll do anything without contacting you." He handed her one of his business cards. "If you remember any other acquaintances of the Simpson's, will you give me a call?"

"Sure." She took the card, read it, then placed it on the kitchen cabinet.

"I really appreciate your time. I might need to question you again, if you don't mind."

"Not at all. We don't get much company nowadays. Nice to have someone different pop in now and then."

Hawkman touched the brim of his hat and made his way to the front door. Elma followed, and waved from the porch as he drove away. Flipping off the recorder in his pocket, he thought about the two families he'd interviewed. He'd kept the questions on the surface for now. Later he might have to delve deeper. Surprisingly, he'd gotten more out of Elma than he'd expected. At least a few more names he could add to the list. Even though the nanny had passed away, he might find some relatives that she'd talked to about the Simpsons.

The information he'd collected so far, left him wondering about the private lives of Carole and Al Simpson. Henry Harris seemed reluctant to admit he knew Carole better than he actually did, and Lisa claimed she'd never met her. It appeared Frank Bradley didn't care for her, but Elma liked the woman. Becky didn't seem to have anything but pleasant memories about her mother. If these two people were so happy, why did one find a lover and the other skip out? Something didn't jive.

CHAPTER FOURTEEN

When Hawkman returned to his office, he checked to make sure the names the rental agency had supplied were people who'd lived there at least six months before Al took over. He found it interesting: Marie Olson, the housekeeper, Carmella Jones, the nanny, and Robin Kregor, the baby sitter, all lived in those rentals at the time Carole Simpson had control.

He took out a couple of phone books from the desk drawer, one of the immediate area, the other covering Ashland. Starting with Medford, he decided to try and find the first name on the list supplied by the rental people: Roy Taylor. No one had mentioned him, but he found a listed number and jotted it down. On a separate piece of paper he wrote the housekeeper's, baby sitter's and nanny's names. Maybe it would jog Becky's memory. She hadn't mentioned any of these people in their conversations.

He continued to search the phone books and found a Kregor in Ashland. The deceased nanny, Carmella Jones, would be a hard one to track down, as the list of Jones extended for pages. He needed more information on her before even attempting to find any kin. Maybe Becky could remember something about the woman and her family. After finishing the list, he punched on the speaker phone and dialed the number of Roy Taylor in Medford.

A female voice answered. "Taylor residence."

Hawkman introduced himself.

"I've heard of you. Aren't you called Hawkman by the town's people?"

He laughed. "Yes. I'm searching for the Taylors who used

to live on Bradford Drive some fifteen years ago. Are you by any chance the Mary Taylor who lived there?"

"Yes. But why are you interested? Has a crime been committed in the area?"

"Not that I know about. I've been hired by Becky Simpson, the daughter of Carole Simpson. Becky would like to find her mother."

"Oh my, after all these years?"

"You rented from Carole before her disappearance. Is that correct?"

"Yes, then we decided to get out of there. We don't like scandal and decided the time had come for us to buy our own home."

"Could you enlighten me?"

"I'll try to remember. It's been a long time ago."

Mary went through the same story about Al having a lover and Carole leaving.

"We didn't know what to do with our rent, so ended up writing a check and took it to their house, where we deposited it in the mailbox. It seemed to work, until one day a lawyer came with a contract. They wanted us to lease for a minimum of two years, but we'd already decided to move, so we told him we'd only affix our signatures if we were free to leave without a penalty. They redid the contract, and kept it open ended, so we went ahead and signed. We didn't know how long it would take us to find a place and we sure didn't want to be on the street."

"I understand. Tell me, how well did you know Carole Simpson?"

"About as well as anyone knows their landlord. She always took time and chatted when she picked up the rent the first of each month. Oh, by the way, she always wanted cash. Then she'd ask if everything was okay. Sort of like a ritual."

"Did she ever speak of her husband?"

"No. She appeared happy, always smiling. Until the month before she disappeared. When she came to pick up the rent, she looked strained and told us she didn't have time to chat, but hoped all was well. That was the last time we ever saw her."

"When the scandal occurred, did you hear any gossip about who Al Simpson had taken as a lover?"

"No. I don't think anyone had the foggiest notion of who it could have been."

"How in the world did the rumor get started, if no one had seen him with a woman other than his wife?"

"I haven't a clue."

When Hawkman finished up his conversation with Mary Taylor, he sat for a moment thumping his pencil on the desktop. He pulled the contract for these people from his file and noted where it had been left open as she'd stated. Glancing at the copies for the others, he spotted where they'd all signed for two years or more.

Before calling more people, he punched in Becky's number.

"Hello."

"Becky, Tom Casey. Are you free this afternoon?"

"Yes."

"I've got some questions, I'll be by shortly."

Becky met him at the door, her expression full of concern. "Come in. I've never dealt with a private investigator before and I've worried ever since you called about what you'd discovered."

He smiled. "Nothing serious. Just some new names I've come across and hope you can help me with them."

"Let me get us some coffee and I'll see what I can do."

They settled in the living room, and Hawkman removed his notes from the briefcase. "Did you pay any attention to the names on those contracts?"

"No, other than the Harris' and Bradley's."

"Do you remember a Roy and Mary Taylor?"

Becky shook her head. "No."

"How about Marie Olson?"

"She sounds vaguely familiar."

"Your mother's housekeeper."

Her eyes lit up. "Yes, I remember the name now. Have you found her?"

"No, I wanted a little more information about these people before I hunted them down."

Becky grinned. "I hadn't thought about Marie in years. She used to try and sing opera as she worked. Mom and I always giggled behind her back when she hit a sour note."

"Did your mother tell you anything about her?"

"Not really, other than she came from the old country." Becky chuckled. "I never knew what she meant."

"Did Marie ever mention her family?"

"No, but she must have had a husband, as a man brought and picked her up."

"When did you last see Mrs. Olson?"

"I never saw her again after Mom disappeared."

"Did she appear old or young?"

"Oh, gee, being a kid at the time, I'd say old. But more than likely she would've been close to fifty at the time."

"Surely your dad hired someone later. You were too young to do housekeeping, and your dad had to work."

Becky scratched her head. "You're right, but she must have come while Cory and I were at school, as I never remember meeting anyone. I do recall wondering how the spot on the carpet suddenly disappeared, or how clean towels got hung in the bathroom. I never dwelled on it much, as I was too young to care. When I got into high school, Dad hired me to do the cleaning. He paid me enough so I could buy some stylish clothes and such."

"Okay, let's go to the next name I've come across. Carmella Jones."

Becky threw her hands in the air and laughed. "How could I ever forget Carmella. She was a hoot. Cory and I really loved her. She's probably the closest thing to a mother we had, once ours left."

"Tell me more."

"Dad had her come every weekday. She'd be here when we got home from school. The house always smelled wonderful with baked cookies, cakes, or just food. My stomach used to growl the minute I walked in the door. Even Scruffy loved her. He bounced around like crazy until she'd snap her fingers and point to his rug. She read us stories, giggling, laughing and pantomiming through the whole thing."

"Why did she quit coming?"

"Dad decided when I reached fourteen, I could take care of dinner and Cory. We really missed her."

"You know she passed away?"

Becky's gaze dropped to the floor. "Yes, two or three years ago. I went to the funeral. She'd suffered with cancer for years and it finally took her."

"Do you know any of her family?"

"She never married, but she had a stepbrother. I believe his name was Edward Barnett. He stayed with her during the last months. I'm not sure where he is now."

Hawkman jotted down the name. "Anyone else you can think of who had a close association with her?"

"No, with me still a kid when she left us, I didn't pay attention to who her friends might have been. Elma Bradley told me about her illness."

He nodded. "Do you remember a Robin Kregor your mom hired on occasions?"

Becky rolled her eyes. "Oh, do I. One wild young girl. She could hardly wait to get Cory and me to bed, then she'd be on the phone or have her boyfriend over. They'd smooch and make out on the couch for an hour, then she'd run him off before the folks got home. But that happened years ago. Robin's turned into a fine young woman. She married a banker here in town and has been an outstanding person in the community."

"What's her married name?"

"Robin Shepard. They live in a lovely home. I guess they have a bit of money." Becky looked up at him. "Are you going to question all these people?"

"If I can find them, yes."

She flopped back on the couch. "Oh, man, I'm going to be the talk of the town."

Hawkman stood. "You can stop any time. Just say the word and everything will come to a screeching halt."

She let out a sigh. "No, I want it to go forward. I just hope I haven't opened a big can of worms."

CHAPTER FIFTEEN

After Hawkman left, Becky drifted through the house in a daze. She hadn't thought about all those people in years. "Private investigators dig deep," she mumbled. And wondered if any information on her mother would ever surface.

She shook away the nagging thoughts and set up the ironing board in the kitchen. Her work clothes needed pressing and she'd better get to them. She only had one more day before hitting the nine to five routine.

While the iron heated, she glanced out the window and spotted Scruffy playing with a stick. She giggled as he threw it into the air, then attacked it like a pup when it fell to the ground. He'd returned to his playful self and it made her happy. Flipping on the television, more for background noise than anything, she proceeded to press her outfits for the coming week. As she hung the last garment and unplugged the iron, the phone rang.

She hit the mute button on the television, and picked up the mobile. "Hello."

"Becky Simpson, call off your private investigator."

"Who is this?"

Hearing the hang-up, she hit the disconnect button and stared at the phone.

Glancing at her watch, she decided to give Mr. Casey a call. She definitely didn't want this type of harassment. Having placed his number in the memory bank, she punched the button and waited.

"Tom Casey."

"Mr. Casey, this is Becky Simpson. I just received a disturbing phone call."

"What about?"

"They told me to call off my private investigator."

"Did you recognize the voice?"

"No."

"That's interesting, it's a little early in the game for this to happen. Did this go onto your answering machine or did you take the call?"

"I answered."

"From now on, here's what I want you to do. Don't answer until the person identifies themselves or you recognize the voice. Let the message be recorded, then we'll have a voice pattern."

"Could I be in danger?"

"I doubt it. If anything, they'll come after me. I'm the one doing the investigating."

"Does this type of thing happen often?"

"Only if I'm getting close to something. Right now, I wouldn't get too worried, just figure word is out you've hired an investigator. Some people get their kicks out of making threatening phone calls."

"I'm trying not to be scared, but I have to admit it spooked me."

"That's normal. The one thing I want you to do is be sure and get all those papers concerning your mother's disappearance out of the house Monday and into a safe deposit box."

"I'll get them to the bank first thing."

"Phone me if you get another call."

"Okay."

Becky hung up, and immediately let Scruffy in, then locked up the house. She knew with nightfall, every strange noise would set her nerves on edge, even though Mr. Casey had assured her they were probably after him.

Hawkman placed the receiver back on the cradle, then tapped the erasure of his pencil on the desk for several seconds. He didn't expect the harassing to start so soon. Of course, any person knowing he'd been hired could take advantage of the news. He pulled the file toward him and glanced over the names of people he'd interviewed. Everything he'd discussed was common knowledge, but possibly the idea of a cold case being revived, struck a nerve in one of them. Guilty people didn't like to be asked questions. Henry Harris seemed the most hostile. However, he had the feeling Frank Bradley had no love for Carole Simpson either.

At this early point in the investigation, he couldn't take this call to Becky too seriously. But someone might have been afraid he'd dig deeper, which he intended to do. This case intrigued him. He hoped Becky wouldn't get too frightened or disillusioned to keep him on the payroll.

He stood, lifted his cowboy hat off his head and ran his fingers through his hair. "If I don't get a haircut soon," he mumbled, "Jennifer's going to claim she's married to a mountain man." Gathering up the Simpson files, he tucked them into his briefcase, turned off the coffee urn and headed out the door. As he made his way down the stairs, he ran into Clyde, the donut shop owner.

"Aren't you staying open a little late?" Hawkman asked.

"Hi, Mr. Casey. Had trouble with one of my ovens and the repair man just left. Getting it fixed is going to cost a bundle." He shrugged. "But I can't afford a new one."

Hawkman frowned. "I'm sorry to hear such news, Clyde. Is there anything I can do?"

The baker shook his head. "Thank you, but no. I'll work it out; just bad timing."

"It seems rotten news never comes at a good time."

Clyde managed a forced grin. "You got that right."

Hawkman waved. "Try to have a pleasant evening."

The men moved in opposite directions toward their vehicles.

When Hawkman reached home, Jennifer sat in the chair overlooking the lake with her feet up, Miss Marple immediately jumped down from her lap and made a beeline for his boots.

He put his briefcase in the chair and picked her up. "Hey, why's your mistress not at the computer? Did she get writer's block?"

Jennifer smiled. "No, just taking a break. I got so tense working on one of my books it made my back tired, so I decided to try a different position."

He raised a brow in comic scorn.

She laughed. "Stop looking at me like that. It does help."

Strolling over, he planted a kiss on her lips. "I'm just teasing." He placed the cat on her lap. "I've got some work to do. Becky received a threatening phone call today, which sort of worries me."

Jennifer sat up in the chair. "My goodness, it seems a little soon in the case for those to start coming in."

"My thoughts exactly. It could be just a crank call. I'm sure it's all over town she's hired me. Some nut case grabbed onto it and decided to have a little fun."

"It certainly isn't amusing to be on the receiving end. What did they say?"

"Said something on the order of 'get rid of the private investigator'."

"I hope you assured Becky it wasn't directed toward her and you could handle it."

He nodded. "But not sure I succeeded. She sounded pretty nervous."

She sighed. "People can be so cruel." Rising, she stretched her arms above her head. "Are you hungry?"

"I'm not in the mood to eat right now. Don't fix anything special. A little later I'll have a piece of the roast we had last night."

"Good. I hoped you'd go for leftovers."

Hawkman picked up his valise and headed back to the home office. While waiting for the computer to boot up, he listened to the recorded conversations and took a few notes. He couldn't figure what caused enough anguish for someone to call his client. The stuff he'd talked about when interviewing friends of Carole Simpson, they knew by heart and he'd said nothing threatening to any of them. Maybe they were afraid of what he might find if he kept digging. People didn't realize threatening phone calls made him want to probe deeper. He removed the tape from his recorder and replaced it with a new one.

Then, he opened the phone book and searched for a Marie Olson. Finding three Olsons, he wrote down the names and addresses, then thumbed through looking for the name Barnett. He did find an Edward. The daughter of the Kregor's proved no problem to locate. Not only did he find Robin Shepard, but her husband and kids, all with different phone numbers at the same address. He bet the whole family had cell phones too. Tomorrow, he'd check out the new list of people.

He also needed to go through the financial reports Becky had supplied and see how they fit into the circle of things. It sure seemed odd that her father never told her about these pieces of property. Guess he figured he had more years to live. One thing about working for the Agency, you learned real quick. Today could be your last, so be prepared for the future. He'd seen guys in their late twenties set up their living trusts and wills. Good thinking on their part.

CHAPTER SIXTEEN

Sunday morning, before leaving for the office, Hawkman decided to see if any one of the Olsons in the phone book happened to be Marie or her relatives. Sitting down at the kitchen bar, he pulled the phone toward him, and punched on the speaker button. He struck out on the first two calls, being told they didn't know a Marie Olson. But on the third call, just as he started to hang up, a breathless woman with a thick British accent answered.

"Hello, this is Tom Casey, I'm a private investigator trying to locate Marie Olson."

"Well, I'm not sure I'm the only Marie Olson on the globe, but I'm one of them. What in the world do you want with me?"

"Are you the Marie Olson who did housecleaning for Carole Simpson about fifteen years ago."

"Yes. I just read Mr. Simpson had passed away. Are the children still around? Oh, what were their names? Goodness it's terrible getting old."

"Becky and Cory. Would it be all right if I dropped by and paid you a visit this afternoon? I'd like to talk to you about Carole Simpson."

"Sure, I'll be here all day."

"I'll try to make it about four o'clock."

"That'll be fine."

Hawkman hung up, relieved to know she still lived in the area. He decided to head out, which would put him in Medford about one thirty; a good time to pop in on the Shepard family, in case they went to church. He'd check with Robin about her folks, since they'd lived in one of the rentals when Carole had control. He'd found a Kregor in Ashland; might be her parents.

He'd prefer not setting up appointments, as people were better about supplying information when caught off guard. He understood why they didn't like to be called on at dinner time or too late in the evening. Grabbing the recorder, he slipped it along with the addresses into his pocket, and picked up the briefcase. He hesitated a moment, wondering if he'd need it. But on second thought, in case he wanted to look up any information, he'd have it at hand.

When he strolled into the living room, he smiled when he noticed how focused Jennifer appeared, staring at the computer monitor. He slipped up beside her and planted a kiss on her cheek.

Startled, she glanced up. "Oh, you're taking off already? Any idea how long you'll be gone?"

"Nope. So don't worry about dinner; I'll grab a couple of Subway sandwiches on my way home."

"Sounds great."

Once Hawkman rolled into Medford, he followed the instructions on his GPS to the Shepard's address. He soon found himself in front of what he considered, a huge two story mansion. "Glory be," he muttered, "who'd want to take care of this place?"

He parked in front and ambled up the winding sidewalk to the front concrete porch. The door appeared at least fifteen feet high by six feet across. The entry looked like a picture he'd seen in a Greek mythology book, guarded by two open mouthed yawning lions on each side. When he pushed the bell, he could hear chimes echoing throughout the house. A young woman in a white uniform answered.

"Yes?"

"I'd like to speak to Mrs. Robin Shepard."

"Do you have an appointment?"

"No, but please tell her I'm Tom Casey, private investigator, looking into the disappearance of Carole Simpson about fifteen years ago."

"Just a moment."

When she shut the door, Hawkman stepped back, flipped on the recorder in his pocket, then observed the expanse of the front porch and how it was walled in by decorative columns. A table with cushioned chairs and an umbrella graced one end. Potted plants were spaced along the sides. A palm tree, planted in a large ceramic pot, stood about eight feet tall, and dominated the opposite side. The door suddenly opened and a smiling woman poked out her head.

"Mr. Casey?"

Hawkman jerked around and quickly moved toward her. "Yes."

She held out her hand. "Robin Shepard. I've heard a lot about you. Please come in."

"I hope you heard nothing but good stuff."

"Very much so," she said, laughing softly as she led him into a magnificent living room, and gestured toward a large velvet couch. "Have a seat and I'll get some coffee."

As she left the room, clicking across the marble floor in her high-heels, Hawkman assessed her to be in the mid-thirties, very trim, with an expensive taste in clothes. Her blue silk suit accented her eyes. Her long blond hair pulled back with silver clips on each side, left soft curls swirling around her face. A very stunning and beautiful woman.

She returned carrying a silver tray with two mugs of coffee, a carafe, sugar and creamer. Hawkman looked at the cups in surprise.

"I didn't think a man your size would appreciate the dainty tea cups," she said grinning.

"Very thoughtful. Thank you."

"To tell the truth, I don't like them either. They're too small, and so thin they don't hold in the heat. I like a hearty mug myself."

Hawkman decided right then and there, he liked Robin Shepard.

She settled on a large chair, on the opposite side of a huge glass topped coffee table. Frowning, she glanced at him. "I'm surprised about the Simpson case being reopened."

"Becky Simpson hired me to find out what happened to her mother. She isn't satisfied with the fact that she never kept in touch. She'd like to know why."

Robin nodded. "I can understand; she needs closure. Especially, now that her father's passed on." She placed her cup on the table and folded her hands in her lap. "Now what can I do to help?"

Hawkman scooted forward, holding the mug with both hands, and observed her expression. "When you were younger, did you baby sit for the Simpsons?"

She blushed. "Yes, and I'm sure Becky told you I was quite a wild teenager. I'm not proud of those years."

He chuckled. "I don't think I'd worry about them. You just sowed your wild oats early."

Robin shook her head. "Boy, did I."

"Tell me about Carole and Al Simpson. What kind of a couple were they?"

She stood and wrapped her arms around her waist, then paced. "Strange."

Hawkman raised a brow. "What do you mean?"

"Mrs. Simpson appeared very domineering. I heard her more than once tell Mr. Simpson what she expected of him. And believe me she didn't say it kindly. On the outside, people thought them an okay couple. But she never showed any affection toward him. Once I saw him attempt to put an arm around her shoulders. She backed away and shot him a look that would have killed."

"Did she always act like this or was it after the rumor of his taking a lover?"

Robin waved a hand in the air. "After that rumor emerged, he couldn't even stand near her. In some ways she acted like a bitch."

"In some ways?"

"She treated me and the kids okay. Becky and Cory were the apple of her eye. Of course, if she'd ever known I'd had a boy over while taking care of the kids, she'd have had my head. To tell you the truth, she frightened me."

"You're the first one who ever revealed a negative side of Carole Simpson."

She shrugged. "Maybe others hadn't seen them when they weren't putting on a front. What happens inside a home is usually very private."

"Wonder why she let her guard down when you were around?"

"I haven't the vaguest idea, except she may have thought me too young to notice."

"It appears Mrs. Simpson befriended some of the people who lived in her homes. What's your opinion?"

She scoffed. "I don't know who told you that, but it's a bunch of hogwash. You couldn't be a day late with your rent or she'd threaten to evict. She even came by and picked up the money." She raised a finger in the air and waggled it back and forth. "And by the way, she preferred cash."

"What about the Bradleys? Weren't they good friends with the Simpsons?"

"Probably because Mrs. Bradley stuck her nose into everyone's business. Carole more than likely decided it best to befriend her than be an enemy."

"Tell me more about Al Simpson."

"I felt sorry for him. Carole nitpicked at him constantly. When they were getting ready to go out, whatever the man wore, she told him it didn't look good. I remember one night when she picked me up to baby sit, she sounded furious. I asked her what had happened. She told me he drove her crazy. He didn't know how to dress, or act."

"So you're saying she nagged him."

She threw up her hands. "Constantly. I baby sat quite a bit for her, and I never saw them act like a contented couple inside those walls. How they acted outside, I couldn't tell you."

"Where were Becky and Cory when these events took place?"

"They were usually playing in their rooms, waiting for me to get there. Once the folks left, I brought them downstairs before their bedtime and we'd play a game, watch television or have popcorn." She rolled her eyes. "Then, after I put them to bed, I had the house to myself. One night I caught Becky spying on me when my boyfriend came over. I told her if she ever told her mom, I'd probably never get to come back." She sighed. "I don't think she ever squealed."

"What about Henry Harris?"

"I don't know a lot about him. Very quiet man. His wife is not well liked. I believe her name is Lisa. I don't know it for a fact, but from the gossip grapevine I heard she told Carole off one month when one of their kids had to go to the hospital and they had to use the rent money to pay the bill. Carole approached them ready to evict, but that's one time Al stepped in and told her they needed time to get the money together. From what I gather, Mr. Harris saved Mr. Simpson's life at one time, and he vowed to always make sure Harris had a job. He's been their grounds man for as long as I can remember."

"You obviously heard about Mr. Simpson taking a lover, and that's what spurred Mrs. Simpson to leave. Did you ever hear who the other woman might have been?"

Robin sat back down in the chair and poured herself another cup of coffee. "Want some more?"

Hawkman placed a hand over the mug. "No, thanks. I'm fine."

"Just before the big ruckus about the lover erupted, I remember baby sitting one night and while talking to my boyfriend on the phone, noticed a piece of paper on the floor. Mrs. Simpson kept an immaculate house, so I had to be sure and not mess up anything. The writing on the note had a woman's name, then said something about meeting at eleven thirty the next morning. And it wasn't Mrs. Simpson's handwriting."

"How'd you know?"

"She left me instructions every time I took care of the kids. So I would have recognized it. I believe Mr. Simpson had written himself a reminder note."

"Did you think it odd?"

"I really didn't think too much about it at the time, as it could have been a business meeting."

"Do you remember the woman's name?"

"Yes. LaVonne Adkins."

"Did you know her?"

"No. Never heard of the woman. I asked my folks since they knew most everyone in the town, but they didn't recognize the name either."

"What did you do with the paper?"

"I put it back on the telephone table, where I assumed it had been. I had no idea if it might be important. And when the Simpsons came in, usually Mr. Simpson took me home. I noticed while gathering up my belongings, he searched around the area where I'd found the piece of paper. When he spotted it, he snatched it up and stuffed it into his pocket. And I swear he sighed in relief."

"Did the name ever come up again?"

"I heard it once more."

"When?"

"I hadn't taken care of the children for some time after the big rumor hit about Mr. Simpson's lover. I just assumed they weren't going out much. Then one night Carole called. Arriving at the house, I could sense the coldness between the two; they hardly spoke. While spreading my homework out on the kitchen table, I heard them arguing in the other room before they left. Carole said something like, 'I may not be your precious La Vonne, but I'm your wife, so act like it'." She waved a hand in the air. "Or something on that order. It really made me cringe. That's probably why I never forgot the name."

"Have you ever told anyone about La Vonne?"

"No. I didn't figure it was any of my business what these two had going on. I sure didn't want to be in the middle of it."

"You definitely remember a lot for so many years."

"Mr. Casey, you're the first person I've ever told. I never thought this day would come. But with a search on for Carole Simpson, I think you need to know as much as possible."

"I appreciate your frankness. There's one more thing: I'd like to speak with your folks. I know they lived in one of the Simpson homes for years. They're no longer listed as renters. Do they live nearby?"

"Yes, I finally got them into a lovely home in Ashland."

"Would they mind talking to me about their years knowing the Simpsons?"

She picked up a pen from a side table, jotted down their address and phone number on a pad of paper, tore it off and handed it to Hawkman. "I don't think they'd mind at all. In fact, I'll give them a call and let them know you might be down in the next day or two."

"I'd appreciate it."

Hawkman rose. "Mrs. Shepard, it's been a pleasure talking to you. And I want to thank you for all the information. It's already made my job a lot easier."

CHAPTER SEVENTEEN

Hawkman left the Shepard's residence, baffled by the alarming new information about Carole. Were people hiding the truth about the Simpsons because they didn't want to be disrespectful or were they concealing something else? Or did Mrs. Shepard just pull a good one? Why would she? The woman has nothing to gain from lying about her association with Al and Carole. This case has suddenly gotten very interesting.

He checked the clock on the dashboard, and would arrive at Marie Olson's early if he kept traveling. Figuring he'd used up most of the tape in his recorder, he stopped at the side of the road, retrieved a clean tape from his briefcase and replaced it.

When he parked in front of the address, he remembered driving by this house and thinking it needed a paint job and a gardener. Becky said this problem would be remedied soon. He made his way up the cracked sidewalk to the front porch and knocked.

A strange scraping sound met his ears as he waited. A woman balancing her tiny frame on a metal walker without wheels appeared and looked up at him with sparkling brown eyes. She smiled and pushed the screen door with the foot of her walker. Hawkman quickly assisted.

"Come in, Mr. Casey. I've heard you've done a lot of things in your lifetime. Is it true you were once a spy?"

"Many years ago."

She gestured toward the living room. "Have a seat. The patch over your eye tells me you've seen your share. I imagine you have a few scars on your body too."

Hawkman smiled at the woman's candid remarks as he took a straight back chair opposite the couch. "You definitely know more about me, than I know of you."

She chuckled softly. "It's a fun game for me to find out the history of people. And you have quite a past." She plopped down on the couch and let out a sigh. "It's such an effort to walk. These hips of mine have gone out on me and I don't have the money to get them fixed."

"That's too bad. Do you have someone to help take care of the house?"

She nodded. "Good neighbors. Since my George passed on, I've been stranded as I never learned to drive. He took me to all my jobs. Course, I can't work anymore. The good people around here take me to the grocery store, or call to see if I need anything when they go."

"I'm sorry about your husband."

She looked up at him, her eyes twinkling. "Don't feel sorry for me. I've had a good life and don't regret one day of it. Just hate the fact the body wears out. My brain is still working good. I can even use a computer." Pointing a crooked finger at him, she grinned. "Even looked you up and found out a little, just enough to be interesting. I have an e-mail address and play some of those stupid games. Pretty good at them too."

"Fantastic," Hawkman said. "I think it's great to keep your mind active."

"Now, ask me some questions about the Simpsons. I'll certainly answer the best I can."

"You did house work for Mrs. Simpson for several years, am I right?"

"Yes."

"Tell me about your employment."

"Very finicky woman. Wanted me to clean everything, but not touch anything."

Hawkman raised a brow. "How did you manage?"

"I sang a lot."

"I don't understand."

Her eyes flickered with mischief. "I couldn't carry a tune in a bucket, but if I could keep her and the daughter laughing, then I could clean without her noticing what I picked up."

"Did it work?"

"Most of the time, until Mrs. Simpson would get in one of her moods. Then she'd follow me around the house and spit out orders as if she were a general in the army."

"She obviously liked you, or she wouldn't have kept you on so long."

"I don't think that had anything to do with it."

"Really?"

"No one else would work for her. The reputation of her being cheap and bossy flew through the ranks of the women in my field. They all stayed clear of her. Many of them questioned why I stayed on."

"Why did you?"

Marie lifted her frail hands, then dropped them into her lap. "The time she wanted me fit in with my schedule and I needed the money."

"Did you ever get a raise or money gifts?"

She snickered. "Are you kidding. She and the Mister were so tight with their cash, they squeaked when they walked."

"Why did you quit?"

"I didn't quit, more like they laid me off. As I'm sure you know, Mrs. Simpson left the home when she found out the Mister had been seeing another woman. When I went to work at my regular time, I found an envelope attached to the door with my name on it. It had my pay for the day and a note saying I wouldn't be needed anymore. That was the last time I had any association with the family."

"Who picked up the rent?"

Marie threw up her hands. "A lawyer came by shortly afterwards with a contract for George and me to sign. I've sent my check to the bank ever since." She shifted her position. "I gather the two kids will take care of the houses now. I hope they let me continue to live here."

"I have no idea what the plans are for the property. Why didn't you ever buy your own home?"

She frowned. "We never had the money and our credit rating turned sour when we couldn't afford to pay some bills. So we just stuck it out here. We liked it; I still do. I wouldn't want to move."

"Did you know Mr. Simpson's lover?"

"No. It was a well kept secret."

"Can you tell me about any of the Simpsons' close friends?"

"I don't think they had many. Maybe Elma and Frank Bradley. And I know Mr. Simpson hired Mr. Harris and has had him for the yard work for years." She waved a hand in the air. "But they didn't get together socially, because Carole couldn't stand his wife."

"How come?"

She furrowed her brow. "I don't rightly know, except Carole said to me one day. 'I don't know how Henry can tolerate Lisa.' I never asked her why she said such a thing, I didn't think it my concern."

Hawkman stood. "Mrs. Olson, don't get up. I appreciate your time. If you think of anything else that might help me in the search for Carole Simpson, please give me a call." He handed her one of his cards.

She looked up at him with a puzzled expression. "You don't think she's still alive, do you?"

Hawkman shot a look at her. "What do you mean?"

"I figure Mr. Simpson murdered her, and buried her right there on the grounds."

He sat back down. "What makes you think such a thing?"

CHAPTER EIGHTEEN

Hawkman leaned forward, putting his arms on his thighs. "Tell me why you came to such a conclusion."

Marie shrugged. "Common sense. Carole Simpson loved her children, probably more than life itself. She wouldn't have taken off for any long period of time without making some sort of contact with those kids. Especially, the daughter."

"How do you know she didn't?"

"This is a close knit town and gossip travels. If Carole Simpson had tried to connect with her children, someone would have heard."

"So you don't think it could have been kept quiet?"

She shook her head. "And another strange incident that had me thinking about Carole being murdered. The Mister had the gall to take over her property as if he knew she'd never be back."

"That could have been a temporary setup for financial reasons."

"True, but it never changed after all these years. I think he killed her."

"Do others hold your same feeling?"

"Oh, sure. The whole town figured he'd done away with her, then buried her body in the rose garden."

"Did the police look into it?"

She looked up at him wide eyed. "Hell, no, they had no reason. No body was every found. They figured it was just a marriage gone sour and the woman disappeared into thin air. The police figured she'd eventually return. Time elapsed with no pressure to find her, so nothing ever came of it, like the whole thing just evaporated. I'm glad the daughter hired you.

Maybe we'll finally find out what happened to Carole Simpson. But I bet you won't find her alive."

Hawkman left Marie Olson's home, flipped off the recorder and drove toward town. A new twist had occurred and even though he didn't expect to find Carole Simpson alive, he didn't like the thought of murder. His next search would concentrate on LaVonne Adkins. He'd also hit the court house tomorrow and find out a little more about the property. He swung by the Subway place and picked up two pastrami sandwiches to go, then headed home.

Later that evening, Hawkman retreated to his office, booted up the computer and focused on the search for a LaVonne Adkins in Jackson county. He found several Adkins, but none bearing the name LaVonne. After expanding into Josephine county, he came up with the same results. Printing out the names he'd found, he leaned back and studied the list.

If this woman happened to be the lover of Al Simpson, he didn't expect her to be much more than an hour's drive from Medford. If Robin Shepard spoke the truth about the note she'd found years ago, a meeting at eleven in the morning between Al and LaVonne would indicate only a short distance drive, especially if Al were going to rendezvous with a lover. It would only make his wife suspicious if he left too early for work. And more than likely, Ms. Adkins had a spouse.

Tomorrow, he'd call the names, and maybe some clue would surface about this woman and why Al Simpson had her name. Lifting the eye patch, he rubbed his face and put the notes he'd written into his briefcase. Shutting down the computer, he stood, stretched and yawned. "Time to hit the sack," he mumbled.

Becky laid out the clothes she'd picked to wear for returning to work. She had mixed emotions about going back into the public arena. People would have heard about her hiring a private investigator to find her mother. How would she answer questions which were no one's business but hers and Cory's? She tapped a finger against her lips as she paced the bedroom floor, detouring around Scruffy as he followed her movements with his eyes.

Abruptly stopping, she pointed her finger at the dog. "Scruffy, I'll tell them I can't talk about a case in progress. It might jeopardize the search."

He responded with a sharp bark.

She laughed, bent down and gave the dog a hug. "You're a good listener. And you always agree."

Becky showered, dressed for bed, picked up the latest fashion magazine, then snuggled under the covers. Soon, she yawned, and turned out the light. She hadn't anticipated any trouble going to sleep, but found herself tossing and turning. Her mind wouldn't shut down. Memories of her mother kept creeping into her head. Had she done the right thing? In her heart, she knew she had. Then why did it bother her so much? Cory's words kept coming into her mind: 'Are you ready for what Mr. Casey might find?'

She pulled the cover over her head and tried to blank out all the negative thoughts from her brain. Suddenly, she heard Scruffy growl. Yanking the cover from her face she looked down at him. He stood facing the window, ears drawn back as he emitted a low grumbling from his throat. She shot a glance toward the glass. "What is it, boy? We're on the second floor, I don't see how anyone could be looking in the window."

The dog didn't move, but kept growling. Becky got up, and peeked out the window. Her breath caught in her chest as she spotted the silhouette of a man standing in the yard. She watched him move toward the house. Grabbing the portable phone she'd brought upstairs and placed on the bedside table, she prepared to dial the police when another figure emerged from the shadows. It appeared to be a woman. Becky watched as they walked to the street, and disappeared into the darkness.

"What the hell," she said aloud. Not wanting to turn on the lights, she threw on her robe, slipped on a pair of scuffs, then fumbled in the side table for the flashlight. Carefully, she headed down the stairs with Scruffy at her heels. "Who were those people and what were they doing in my yard at this hour?" she whispered.

Again Scruffy rumbled deep in his throat.

She put a finger to her lips. "Hush boy, they might come back."

A full moon ignited the yard, so from the front window she could see any movement as far as the road. She made her way to the kitchen and searched the side yard through the glass. No trace of any intruders. She knelt down in front of Scruffy. "Okay, boy, I want you to stick right with me. We're going outside. Those people could have left a bomb somewhere. It's up to us to find it."

Becky gnawed her lower lip as she opened the back door. She flipped on the flashlight as she stepped onto the grass. A cool breeze sent a chill down her back, but she continued inspecting the backyard shrubs, then examined the rose garden. Slowly she and Scruffy scanned their way to the front. She soon stopped and pushed the hair from her face as she examined the plants surrounding the porch. Finding nothing suspicious, she headed toward the back, when a sudden movement near the front door caught her eye. She illuminated the entry with a flash of light. Attached to the frame, a legal sized envelope flopped in the wind.

CHAPTER NINETEEN

Becky ran up the steps and detached the letter. She directed the beam of light onto the envelope. 'Becky Simpson' was spelled out in bold letters cut from a newspaper. She reached for the door handle and found it locked, so she gathered the front of her robe, held it high and darted around the house with Scruffy running alongside.

When they both were inside, she flipped on the lights and quickly checked the house, then bolted the door. Her hands shaking, she placed the flashlight and envelope on the kitchen table. It was too late to worry about smudging any fingerprints, but she'd be careful with the inside sheet. Grabbing a pair of tongs from the cabinet drawer she pulled out the paper and gently opened it. The message inside caused a knot to form in her stomach.

With the help of the nippers, she managed to slip the letter back inside the envelope without touching it. She glanced at the wall clock hanging over the sink and let out a sigh. "No sleep for the weary," she mumbled, and rose from the chair.

She wanted to call Tom Casey right now, but knew it would be in vain. Maybe she could get a couple hours sleep before daybreak.

The next morning, Hawkman left home early so he'd have time to stop by the office before going to the court house. He'd no more stepped into his office, when the phone rang. Letting the answering machine pick up, he dropped his briefcase on the chair but turned abruptly when he heard Becky Simpson's worried voice come over the line.

Reaching across the desk, he punched on the speaker phone. "Yes, Becky, this is Tom Casey, I just walked in the door."

"Oh, Mr. Casey, I'm so glad I reached you. I'm on my way to work, but would like to stop by."

"Sure, I'll be here for awhile."

Becky arrived within ten minutes, and immediately plopped down in the chair at the front of the desk.

Hawkman noted her nervousness. "Want a cup of coffee? Looks like you could use one."

"No, thanks. I've had enough to hold me for a month. I didn't sleep a wink last night."

He frowned. "How come?"

She related spotting the two strangers wandering in the yard around midnight.

"Did you recognize them?"

"No, they appeared as silhouettes, but I'm sure one was a woman."

She handed over the envelope. "They left this attached to the front door jamb. I'm sure my fingerprints are on the outside, as I wasn't thinking when I found it. But I didn't touch the inside sheet; I used a pair of kitchen tongs to remove it."

"Good thinking. And you're sure they're the ones who left this."

"Why else would they be lurking around my house at such an hour, if they weren't up to something?"

"Just making sure you didn't have other company during the weekend."

She shook her head. "No, I've been busy getting ready to start back to work today."

He checked his watch. "What time do you have to be there?"

"I have about thirty minutes."

Hawkman took a pair of latex gloves from the desk drawer and pulled them on. He then carefully removed the letter from the envelope, spread it out on the desktop, and read aloud.

"Drop case or someone dies." He glanced at Becky. "Pretty strong language."

She nodded. "I don't understand why someone doesn't want me to pursue finding my own mother. This really scares me."

"I understand. I must have touched a nerve with someone. Are you sure it was a man and a woman?"

"Yes. Even though they both had on long, dark colored coats, I could see the woman's legs and flat shoes when she walked. She also had a scarf draped around her head; the breeze picked up the ends and made them flutter. The man had on slacks and a hat."

"Did they resemble anyone you knew? Like Henry Harris and his wife?"

"No. The man was too tall and the woman too slim."

"When they left your premises, where did they go?"

She shook her head. "I don't know. They actually disappeared into the night. I watched for car lights, but never saw any."

Hawkman leaned forward, his arms on the desk. "I hope you're putting the original papers we've talked about into a safe place."

"I'm doing that today. I have them in the trunk of my car and plan to move them into the safe deposit box during my lunch hour."

"Good. I know it's frightening to receive such threatening notes, but I don't think they mean harm to you. They'll be coming after me real soon. But just to be safe, keep your doors and windows locked."

Becky sat up straight in the chair, her eyes wide. "I can't have you getting hurt, because of my wanting to find my mother."

Hawkman put up a hand. "It's part of the job. I've seen many of these missives. They're normally used to frighten away the intruder, which is me. Whoever wrote this figured you'd head straight to my office with letter in hand. Then they hoped I'd back off. What they don't realize, is private investigators are spurred on by such notes, because they figure they've hit a raw nerve somewhere, and it's in their blood to pursue. That is, unless you want to quit."

"No. In fact, it makes me very curious to know why someone doesn't want me to find my mother."

"Does the name LaVonne Adkins mean anything to you?"

She furrowed her brow. "No, I've never heard it before. Why?"

"She was mentioned. I wondered if she had any bearing on the case?"

"Just because I don't know her doesn't mean she didn't have some involvement with my parents."

Hawkman let the subject drop. "If you don't mind, I'll keep this note. I have a detective friend on the police force and I might ask him to check it for prints."

Becky threw her purse straps onto her shoulder. "Please keep it, I don't care to have it around as a reminder." She stepped toward the door. "I must get to work. Please call me if you find out anything."

He stood and walked her to the door. "I'll keep in touch. And you let me know of any more threatening calls or letters."

"Don't worry. You'll be the first to know." She stepped out onto the stairs and waved. "Thanks, Mr. Casey."

After Becky left, Hawkman scooted the note back into the envelope, slipped it into a plastic bag, and tossed the gloves into the drawer. He meandered over to the coffee urn and poured himself a fresh cup. Sitting down at his desk, he ran a hand across his chin, dropped the plastic bag with the letter into his briefcase, then flipped open the Simpson file and glanced through his notes. He hadn't had time to transcribe the tapes yet, but from what he remembered, nothing warranted the threats she'd received.

A man and woman delivering a letter at midnight and pinning it to the door baffled him. Becky figured the man didn't have the build to be Harris, and with Frank Bradley confined to a wheelchair, that pretty much knocked two couples out of the running for the midnight call. He hadn't met Robin Shepard's husband, but what stake would he have in the Simpson's lives? None of it made much sense.

He felt like he'd just scratched the surface and needed to do more digging. Removing the slip of paper Robin had given him with her parents' information, he punched the speaker phone and dialed the number.

A male voice boomed across the line. "Saul Kregor speaking"

"Hello, Mr. Kregor, this is Tom Casey, private investigator out of Medford."

"Yes, Mr. Casey. Our daughter told us you might be in contact."

"Would it be inconvenient if I dropped by this evening?"

"No problem as long as you don't come while I'm having supper. Don't like cold food."

Hawkman chuckled. "Understand. What's a good time?"

"How about six thirty?"

"Perfect. I'll see you then."

He hung up, slipped a fresh yellow legal pad into his briefcase and took off for the court house. When he arrived, he made it a point to greet the people he knew and those who'd helped him in the past. Things were much easier now as most records were filed into the computer system. Hawkman made his way to the small room holding five machines. He sat down at a vacant one, and removed the scratch pad containing his notes. Putting in the parcel numbers, he could trace the property back a good fifty years. He soon came across the transfer of the properties into Al Simpson's name. The lawyer handling the procedures came from the Howard Dimmer Law Firm out of Grants Pass, Oregon. It appeared Carole Ann Simpson had signed all the deeds, which seemed very odd to Hawkman, since they were dated a month after she disappeared. He searched through the data base to see if there'd been any objection to the hand-overs of these properties and there appeared to be none.

Hawkman also wondered why a law firm outside the county had handled the procedures. Not that it made any difference, but he figured he'd check out this firm and see if they were still around. If so, he might make a trip to Grants Pass.

He left the courthouse, assured the deeds had been recorded and appeared legal. Now to dig a little deeper. Going back to his office, he pulled out the calculator and the rental files on the Simpson properties. After a couple of hours working the numbers, he leaned back with a disgusted expression. "I must be getting rusty at math," he mumbled. "I can't get these rental payments to match up with the totals in the accounts for Becky, Cory and Maintenance." He searched through the pile of stuff and didn't find any other accounts tied to these transactions.

CHAPTER TWENTY

Hawkman finally closed the file, tucked it into his briefcase and prepared to leave for Ashland where he'd chat with the Kregors. He still hadn't balanced the figures and would call Becky tonight. Maybe another account had been set up and she'd failed to mention it.

He called Jennifer, but the answering machine picked up, so he left a message letting her know he wouldn't be home until ten or later. Pouring the rest of the coffee into his insulated travel cup, he unplugged the pot. He hoped he'd catch Clyde at the doughnut shop before he closed. A donut would taste mighty good.

Hurrying down the steps, he tried the bakery door and found it open. Clyde came from the back of the shop, smiling. "I see you're hungry."

Hawkman laughed. "Yep, have a late appointment and the ole stomach is going to make lots of noises if I don't get something into it."

Clyde glanced into the glass enclosed cabinet. "Not many choices left this late."

Scrutinizing the few scattered pastries, Hawkman pointed at the one remaining bear claw. "That will do the trick."

The baker lifted the delicacy with a square of wax paper and dropped it into a small paper sack, along with a stack of napkins. "There you go."

Hawkman paid the man, waved and headed to his 4X4. Tossing his briefcase on the passenger side, he placed his coffee cup in the holder between the seats, and climbed in. He'd no more settled behind the steering wheel and about ready to take a bite of the pastry, when he noticed an envelope stuck under the windshield wiper.

"What the heck?" he mumbled, opening the door. He had to step onto the running board, and stretch to pluck off the paper. Immediately, he became suspicious when he noticed the front of the envelope had 'Tom Casey' in cutout newspaper letters. It resembled the note left at the Simpson house.

He slit it open with his pocketknife, then reached into the back seat area and lifted the duffle bag of supplies to the front. Finding the small box of protective gloves, he pulled one on, then carefully removed the sheet of paper from its encasement. It read, 'Drop case or someone dies'. What he read didn't shock him, as it read similar to Becky's .

Tucking it into the plastic bag with the other one, he figured tomorrow would be a good time to stop by Detective Williams' office and see if his lab could run a fingerprint test on these two notes.

Just as he started his vehicle, he spotted the baker walking around the corner of the building toward his car. Hawkman shut off the motor and hopped out. "Clyde, gotta a minute?"

"Sure," he said, coming toward Hawkman.

"You spend a lot of time in the rear of your bakery tending the ovens." Hawkman pointed toward the large window facing the back. "Did you by any chance see any strange vehicle stop in the alley?"

"No. But usually I don't have time to watch such things, as I'm concentrating on the pastries." Clyde wrinkled his forehead in thought. "Why? Has something happened I should know about?"

"I received an anonymous letter on my windshield. Just wondered if you'd seen anyone unfamiliar."

"Sorry. Wish I'd been more observant."

"No problem. Have a good evening."

On the way to Ashland, Hawkman wondered if he'd find out anything different from the Kregors. Things had definitely taken a twist. He had no trouble finding the address and pulled in front of a lovely home, not a mansion like the daughter's, but plenty nice. They either hired a gardener or were people with a green thumb. The lawn appeared very lush, and the edges were trimmed to perfection. The bushes were pruned in rounded shapes and flowers bloomed in large attractive pots one on each side of the front porch. Quite a lovely sight.

Hawkman carried his briefcase to the door, flipped on the recorder in his pocket and rang the bell. A soft musical tune sounded and within a minute the door opened, revealing a big man almost six feet tall, with a rotund beer belly protruding over his jeans. A large belt buckle with a steer head, including the horns, poked into the man's lower gut covered by a tight western shirt. He had a round face with a ruddy complexion and sandy colored thinning hair. When he smiled, his eyes disappeared into small slits.

He held out a huge hand. "Mr. Tom Casey, I presume."

"That's me," Hawkman said, taking his hand.

"Come in." He gestured toward a neat room with an upholstered couch in earth colors, two matching chairs and a small oak coffee table. The walls were covered with pictures of family. "Mother, bring in some coffee. The private investigator's here," he called over his shoulder.

Soon, a thin woman waltzed into the room carrying a small wooden tray with coffee mugs and a plate of homemade cookies. She reminded Hawkman of Robin; same features but with a more mature look. Her short gray hair had curls on the top, but the sides swirled slightly toward her face, clinging close to the scalp. A touch of blush emphasized her high cheek bones and made her hazel eyes predominate. The straight legged jeans and silk blouse fit her to a tee. Probably a very pretty woman in her youth.

Once she'd placed the tray on the table and distributed the coffee and cookies, she held out a small dainty hand to Hawkman.

"Hello, Mr. Casey, my name's Frances. Robin told us you wanted to talk about Carole Simpson."

"Yes. I hope you've had your dinner."

She laughed, sat down on the edge of the cushion next to

her husband and gave him a playful slap on the knee. "Bet he told you not to interrupt his meal."

Hawkman chuckled. "Yes."

"No problem. We've eaten and the kitchen is clean. We're ready to talk." She reached for her cup and settled back on the couch.

"Tell me what you remember about Carole Simpson."

Frances took a sip of the hot brew. "Well, she and Al invited us to dinner a few times, but for sure we saw her the first of the month when she came by for the rent and boy, you better have it in cash or she'd hit the roof. When she picked up Robin to baby sit, she never got out of the car. Just tooted the horn."

"Why did she insist on cash?"

She shrugged. "Beats me, unless she'd had bad experiences with bounced checks. We always managed and didn't get the wrath we'd heard she could give out."

"Did you know some of the other tenants?"

"Not really, but Robin baby sat for the Simpsons quite often, and she'd tell me some of the things she'd hear."

"For instance."

"It appeared Carole liked our daughter and would unload her problems, as if a young girl could help. She'd tell her about the tenant she might evict, if they didn't get the rent to her with the late penalty. Naturally, Robin would come home and tell me all about it. So I kept up with the scuttlebutt pretty good."

"Did Robin like baby sitting for the Simpsons?"

"Kids that age don't tell you everything, only what they want you to know. I don't think she really liked Carole. She'd indicated several times the woman made her uncomfortable. But she never complained about the children. They were well behaved. It was about the only job a young girl her age could do to make extra money. So she was glad they called on her as often as they did."

"Mr. Kregor, what did you think of Al Simpson?"

He waved a hand in the air. "Call me Saul."

"Okay, Saul what did you think of him."

"Hardly knew the man. Like Francis said, we saw them a few times for dinner, but usually other people were there too. The house we lived in was once owned by Carole's parents. We lived there for about a year before they passed on and then Carole inherited the property and took over. The only time I met Mr. Simpson was after we'd heard Carole had left and were approached by a lawyer to renew the lease with Al instead of Carole. I thought this odd, because from the gossip we'd heard, Carole had only been gone a month and we'd heard nothing about her death, which is usually what happens when the spouse takes over the property."

"So this bothered you?"

"You're damn right it did. I tried to locate that lawyer's firm and couldn't find them listed anywhere in our area. I figured it was a scam. So I called and set up an appointment with Mr. Simpson."

"What'd you find out?"

"He assured me everything was legal and due to the circumstances of money being received, he'd had Carole sign over the property to him, so he could handle it."

"Didn't that sound odd to you when you'd heard she hadn't returned?" Hawkman asked.

"Not really. I figured the two must have agreed on those conditions and were still talking to one another or her name wouldn't have been on those papers. He assured me he'd sent the lawyer with the contracts, and everything was legal. It eased my mind tremendously."

"What did you think of Mr. Simpson when you met him. Did you feel he was on the up and up?"

"Hard to say. He didn't participate in any chatter, just the facts. He appeared busy and sort of rushed me out of the office."

"You lived in that Simpson house for several more years, right?"

"Yes. We liked the place and the location, but once Robin married and got into a higher crust of society, she thought we should move."

Hawkman faced Mrs. Kregor. "Frances do you have anything to add?"

"Robin didn't think the Simpsons were happily married, even before the rumor went out about Al having a lover. She swears she never saw any emotion between the two, and didn't blame him for finding someone else. They were like strangers passing in the same house. So I find it interesting Becky would try to find her mother after all these years. It looks like once she matured and realized Al cared about her and Cory, and knowing Carole never attempted to contact them, she'd get on with her life." She exhaled loudly. "I guess that's hard to do."

"Do you think Carole Simpson is dead?"

Saul and Frances exchanged glances.

"Yes," Saul said. "In fact, we have a feeling she's been murdered."

Hawkman sat forward. "What makes you think such a thing? And who would do it?"

Saul threw his hands in the air, then let them drop, slapping against his thighs. "The first person who comes to mind is Al Simpson, the betrayer. If so, he went to his grave with the secret. But I think Carole might have made life so miserable, he just did away with her. Unfortunately, the way the whole thing played out, the police never really got involved. And with no body, they finally just swept the whole thing under the rug and never pursued the case."

"Does the name LaVonne Adkins mean anything to you?"

Frances raised a finger.

"Robin found the name scribbled on a piece of scratch paper at the Simpson's home. She asked me if I knew the woman, and I'd never heard of her. Neither had Saul. So who knows what it meant."

"Do either of you know who Al Simpson's lover might have been?"

They both shook their heads.

Hawkman picked up his briefcase and stood. "I want to

thank you for your time. If you remember anything I might find of interest, please call." He handed them his business card.

On his way home, Hawkman pondered the interview. He'd not really learned anything new. But from all the conflicting views of Becky's mother, he concluded she appeared a complex woman. His next move would be a nationwide search for Carole Ann Simpson, or Carole Ann Patterson.

CHAPTER TWENTY-ONE

Hawkman left the Kregors and headed home. Since it was early evening, he decided to call Becky on his cell phone. She answered on the second ring.

"Hello, Becky, Tom Casey. I've been trying to get the bank account total to balance with the rental papers and am having a hard time. I'm wondering if there's another account you haven't told me about besides your's, Cody's and the maintenance ones?"

Hawkman gave her his full attention as he stopped at the light.

"Have you found a passbook or anything? Even an old one? There's bound to be an explanation for this discrepancy."

Turning onto the ramp, he merged onto Interstate 5 going south.

"There's quite a bit of money unaccounted for, so would you keep looking? In fact, you might even call the bank and find out if they have another account on file in your dad's name."

He kept his eye on the road as he listened.

"Get back to me as soon as you find out."

Becky hung up and sat for a few moments weighing the private investigator's inquiry. She knew there were no more accounts in her dad's name at the bank, as she'd already asked. But it didn't mean there weren't some in other institutions. However, she'd not found any passbooks or papers indicating any.

In the back of her mind, she thought about Cory looking for a secret spot in her dad's office closet. He'd found nothing.

When she finished clearing it out, she pounded on the walls also, but nothing sounded hollow like a hidden compartment.

"Maybe Dad used the money to live on; after all, he was raising two kids," she mumbled, as she halfheartedly strolled up the stairs.

She stopped at the office, went inside and circled the room. There were bookshelves she hadn't unloaded; possibly a cubbyhole was hidden behind them. Then she wandered into her dad's bedroom. The closet had been cleaned out and she'd found nothing resembling a vault in there either. She ran her fingers through her hair, flopped acros the bed, then turned on her back and stared at the ceiling. "Dad, how many secrets were you harboring before you died? The things I'm finding out scare me."

Grumbling, Becky got up and went downstairs. She let Scruffy in for the night, gave him some food, then fixed herself a bite to eat. The first day at work had worn her out and she really didn't want to look for more things. There were still a couple of drawers she hadn't cleaned out in her dad's office. She didn't feel he'd have thrown bank books into them, but she'd have a look. The thought visiting each bank in town and asking a bunch of questions, left a sour taste in her mouth. But since she'd gotten herself into this mess, she'd do it.

After cleaning up the kitchen, she and Scruffy went upstairs to her dad's office. The dog obediently sat on the rug and watched Becky open the drawers in the small dresser. The first one contained extra paper for the computer printer. The second one held odd pens, paper clips, stationary and envelopes. As she closed it, she heard something like paper crackling. She reopened it and ran a hand along the backside. Finding nothing, she slowly pushed it forward and heard the noise again. Feeling across the bottom, her hand hit an obstacle. Squatting on her haunches, she spied an envelope taped to the underneath side. She carefully pulled off the tape from each end and brought it out.

Taking it to the desk under Scruffy's keen eye, she sat down and turned the envelope over in her hand. The seal had not been secured and inside she found a small index card with numbers written across the middle. The way they were arranged, with an 'L' and a 'R' at the beginning of each digit, indicated they belonged to the combination of a safe. But they weren't in the same order as the vault she'd already opened. There were no other floor safes in the house. It had to be in the wall, but where?

Becky grabbed a dust cloth from the linen closet and decided no time like the present to start investigating. She started on the bookshelves and worked for a couple of hours dusting the tomes as she removed five to eight at a time, waxed the shelf, then banged on the wall. Half way down, she'd replace the books, and start on the next batch. After finishing the two longest shelves, she flopped down in chair and groaned. She'd found nothing. There were still three more shelves to go on the other side of the room, but they weren't as long. Suddenly, she jumped up and removed the pictures from the walls.

"Darn, nothing," she exclaimed, wiping off the cobwebs. "Oh, Scruffy, I think this is all in vain. I don't know why your old master has made everything so difficult."

The dog let out a short whine and dropped his head on his paws.

Becky laughed. "It's not your fault, boy. I have to vent to someone or go crazy, and you're available." She reached down and gave him a rub on the head.

He thumped his tail and gave a low woof.

She put a hand on her hip and glanced down at the dog. "I'd swear you understand every word I say."

Continuing with her job, she worked for another hour and finally slapped her hands to her side. "Well, Scruffy, I've examined every inch of these walls and there's no hidden vault. I think we'll call it a night. Tomorrow we'll start on Dad's bedroom. Something tells me there's a hiding place in this house. We've just got to find it."

Becky showered, decided what she'd wear to work, then went to bed. As she lay there staring at the shadows bouncing across the ceiling, she thought about her past and searched her memory to see if at any one time she suspected her dad of doing something sneaky. She wondered if she'd swept those types of memories out of her mind, for fear her dad might disappear?

Once she'd come to the conclusion her mother had left for good, her fears diminished as her dad took over the duties and her life proceeded on track. He always saw to it she and Cory had everything they needed. Her thoughts drifted into oblivion as sleep took over.

The next morning, Becky had to rush, as she'd overslept. She put Scruffy out for the day, and gulped down an instant breakfast. On her way to work, she slapped her forehead. "Oh my gosh, today is payday for Henry and I forgot to leave him a check."

When she arrived at her office, she quickly called the Harris household and reached Lisa.

"Lisa, this is Becky Simpson. I'm at work and completely forgot to leave a check for Henry. It's going to take me awhile to get used to the fact I have to do these chores, since Dad isn't here."

She listened for a moment, then said, "Thanks, Lisa. I'll drop by after work and leave the money. Please, give Henry my apology."

After hanging up, she took her check book and wrote out his pay so she wouldn't forget, then got busy with her job at hand. Her day passed rapidly, as they were getting ready for a big style show in a few weeks, and all the garments had to be specially tailored to fit the models. They would start rehearsing for the big event in another week, and all the loose ends needed to be tied together. Fortunately, the woman who took over while Becky had taken off, had worked hard and gotten everything rolling. Becky would make sure she got a bonus, even if she had to take it out of her own salary.

Later that evening, after a late night at work, Becky dropped by Henry's place to leave the check. When she reached the entry, Henry opened the door before she had a chance to knock.

"I'm so sorry I forgot to leave your pay. It's going to take me a while to get into the groove."

Henry stepped out on the landing. "I understand, Ms. Simpson." He took the draft, then glanced into her face. "Are you still searching for your mother?"

"Yes, I'd like to find out where she is."

Narrowing his eyes, he glared into hers. "Why don't you call it off. It's not going to cause you anything but heartache. You're probably not going to find her alive."

"I hope I'm prepared for any outcome," Becky stammered, taken aback by his bluntness.

He shrugged. "I feel sorry for you." Turning, he went into the house and slammed the door.

Becky almost lost her footing going down the steps. She quickly got into her car and headed home. Her mind reeled with Henry's words. When she pulled into the garage and got out, she could smell the freshly mowed grass as she bounded into the house.

Unzipping her dress as she dashed upstairs to her room, she could hardly wait to slip into something more comfortable. She dropped the garment to the floor, then kicked off her shoes and removed her pantyhose as she plopped down on the edge of the bed. Grabbing her robe from the chair, she stood and slipped it on, then slid into her house shoes. She gave a sigh of relief. "I must be getting older; there's nothing like a loose fitting garment after a tense day. And not only that, I'm beginning to talk to myself an awful lot." She laughed and glanced into the dresser mirror. "Oh dear, look at those crow feet." Brushing off the idea, she hurried downstairs to let Scruffy inside. After feeding the dog and fixing herself a bite, she headed for her dad's bedroom.

"Well, Scruffy, we'll try this room tonight and see if we have any success."

Becky brought the dog's rug from the office into her dad's bedroom and dropped it in the middle of the floor. Scruffy immediately sat down on his haunches and watched her start the tedious task of searching behind the pictures and books. She finished in about an hour, and flopped down on the edge of the bed.

"Scruffy, there's not a hidden cubbyhole in here. I guess I'm going to have to search some of the other rooms. I feel in my gut, there's more secrets concealed in this house. I just don't know where to look."

Becky had been asleep for several hours, when suddenly, she jerked up out of a deep slumber. "Oh, my! That's where it is!"

CHAPTER TWENTY-TWO

Hawkman stopped by the Medford Police Station and went inside. He strolled down the hall to Detective William's office and poked his head around the door. "I'm looking for the detective. Have you seen him?"

Williams glanced up and laughed. "My word, have I aged that much since I last saw you?" He stood and extended his hand. "Good to see you. Come in and have a seat. I need a break."

"Does the paperwork never end around here?" Hawkman asked, as he pulled a chair up to the desk.

The detective massaged his wrist. "It gets worse by the day." He leaned back in his chair. "You look mighty fit after your last case. Those guys were in for the kill. Sure glad you got through it okay."

"Thanks. They had their sights on taking me out, that's for sure."

"So to what do I owe this visit? I know you don't just drop by to say hello."

Hawkman smiled. "You're right." He pulled the plastic bag from his pocket and placed it on the stack of papers. "If your lab guys have time, wonder if they'd run a fingerprint scan on these two notes? Tell them not to bother with the outside of the envelopes as they've been handled by me and my client. But the inside sheets might provide some prints."

"Sure, we're not real busy right at the moment, so I'll see what I can do. What does this concern?"

"I've taken on a cold case. Helping a woman find her mother after fifteen years."

The detective slapped his forehead. "Have you lost your mind?"

"Probably. But it's proving to be very interesting." He pointed to the bag. "Those are two threatening notes. One placed on the front door of my customer's house, the other put on my windshield."

"You must be getting close to something. Do I know the person you're looking for?"

"Carole Ann Simpson."

Williams tapped his temple. "Doesn't ring a bell. Any relation to the Al Simpson who just passed away?"

"Yes. His wife. The daughter wants to know what happened to her mother." Then Hawkman gave him a run down of the particulars.

"Sounds mighty complicated. I should look in the archives and see if the case is still open."

"I don't know if the police ever got involved. I couldn't find anything about her disappearance in the files or newspapers, nor could I find a missing person report. People I've talked to said a body was never found, so it just faded away as another woman who left her husband."

"Sure sounds fishy."

"It's moving in that direction for me too."

"If it gets into something more complicated than a missing woman, give us a call. We'll be glad to help out."

"Thanks. I might end up needing the police. Right now I'm not sure." Hawkman stood and cleared his throat. "I won't keep you from your work."

The detective grinned. "You're very considerate."

"Say, if you ever take a day off, Jennifer and I'd like to have you out for dinner."

"Speaking of your pretty little wife, how's she doing?"

"Great. She's still in remission,and keeps me hopping."

"Good news. Give her my regards. I might just surprise you one of these days and take you up on the invite."

Hawkman left the station and drove to his office. While the computer booted up, he fixed a pot of coffee, then sat down at his desk and searched for the Howard Dimmer Law Offices in Grants Pass, Oregon. He examined the archives back twenty years and found no such law firm. Checking the contracts, he made sure he had the spelling right. He went through several attorney directories and their records from the surrounding counties without finding either the lawyer or the firm. After expanding to the national level, he'd just about given up when the name, Howard Dimmer, Attorney at Law, popped up in Indiana, Hawkman jotted down the name and phone number.

Tapping the pencil erasure on the paper, he wondered if this lawyer happened to be in debt to Al Simpson. A man coming all the way from Indiana could rack up quite a bill for such a minor job. It didn't make sense, unless Al Simpson had something to hide.

Becky, jolted out of a dead sleep, rubbed her eyes and glanced at the lighted clock on her bedside table. "Five in the morning," she gasped. Then it suddenly dawned on her why she'd awakened. The dream had really happened; she'd just forgotten about it.

One night, as a little girl, she'd taken ill with a fever and upset stomach. She'd gone to her dad's bedroom in tears, but couldn't find him. Calling his name softly, she started down the stairs, clutching the bannister as she felt dizzy and her head hurt. She walked into the living room where he stood near the wall with his hands on the picture of the large ship on the sea. He must not have heard her until she was practically beside him, as he jumped and almost dropped the painting. "What is it, Becky?" he'd asked sharply.

Forgetting her sickness for a moment, she'd asked him what he was doing. She remembered he told her the picture hung crooked and while trying to fix it, the wire slid off the nail. He'd told her to go back up to her room and he'd be up in a moment. She remembered he never moved the frame away from the wall, but held it tightly in place.

Becky grabbed her robe and hastened downstairs to the living room. Scruffy followed at her heels. Stepping upon the couch, she pulled the corner of the large picture forward, so she could see underneath. She sucked in a deep breath when she spotted the round indentation. Struggling with the heavy painting, she finally removed it, placed the bottom edge on the floor and leaned it carefully against the overstuffed chair. When she glanced back at the wall, the silver colored metal disk glistened from the lamp light. A small black dial, resembling a one-eyed monster glared at her.

Becky dashed upstairs into her father's office, yanked open the safe, and grabbed the odd code she'd found taped to the bottom of the drawer. Running back downstairs, she stood on the sofa, her knees resting on the back as she worked the knob. She heard the tumblers fall into position when her fingers dialed the last number. Giving the lid a slight tug, it easily swung open.

She removed the contents and sat down on the couch. Her heart thumped as she fingered the papers. Opening a large brown envelope, she put a hand to her mouth, "Oh, my God."

CHAPTER TWENTY-THREE

Hawkman thought about doing a genealogical research on Howard Dimmer's name. But it wouldn't do him a lot of good since he didn't know the maiden names of the women involved in the case except for Carole Simpson. Dimmer could be a brother, uncle or a relative of sorts to any of the people involved. It gnawed at him that this man was somehow connected to the disappearance of Carole Simpson. But how?

He glanced away from the monitor and realized the sun had already set. Checking his watch, it astonished him to see the time. He'd continue his search later and sent the link to himself, in case he had time tonight to get on the computer at home. Shutting down, he locked up the office, and left.

Nightmares of the Simpson case flooded Hawkman's mind and he didn't sleep well. He soon gave up around six o'clock and quietly slipped out of bed so as not to wake Jennifer. Miss Marple, their Ragdoll cat , followed him out of the room. When they reached the kitchen, Hawkman pointed a finger at her. "Now, look little 'Miss Nosey', I'm not giving you a treat at this hour in the morning. You've put on some weight and I'm not sure that's good for you. Your mistress is going to have to limit the number of snacks she lets you have. And I'm certainly not going to be fussed at for giving you extra stuff."

He put on the coffee pot, as the cat wound around his ankles. "No, loving me up isn't going to help."

The kitten finally stuck her nose in the air and marched into the living room where she jumped into his chair and curled into a furry ball. Hawkman chuckled, as he went to the sliding glass door and went outside on the deck. He checked his falcon,

Pretty Girl. She gave him a good scolding, as he replenished her food and water.

"I know, I know, you want to go hunting. Soon, I promise." He jerked around when Jennifer came out in her gown carrying his cell phone.

"A call for the private investigator."

Puzzled, he put the phone to his ear. "Tom Casey."

After hanging up, he walked back into the house, his brow furrowed.

Jennifer stared at him with concern. "I figured the call was important. I didn't think Becky would call at this hour unless something had happened."

"She wants to meet me in the office at eight. Said she'd found something of interest."

"Didn't she give you a hint?"

"No, but I have a feeling she found another account, as I couldn't get the books to balance and talked to her about it. And whatever she's found has disturbed her very much." He gave Jennifer a squeeze. "By the way, I'm sorry my phone woke you. I certainly didn't expect a call at this hour."

"It's okay. I'm glad I answered."

"I appreciate it."

"I'll be anxious to hear her news."

He grinned. "I'm sure you will." He headed for the bedroom. "Guess I better get a move on it. I don't have much time."

As he headed out the door, Jennifer handed him a yogurt and plastic spoon. "Here, maybe this will keep the grumbling of your tummy down, so you're not tempted by Clyde's fattening donuts."

Hawkman laughed loudly as he jumped into his 4X4. Driving to Medford, he found himself anxious to know what Becky had discovered. Arriving at his office fifteen minutes before the appointment, he put on the coffee pot, then pulled the Simpson file from his briefcase. He'd no more poured a mug of the hot brew than a knock sounded on his door.

"Come in."

Becky poked her head around and smiled meekly. "I'm so sorry for calling you so early. I'm sure I woke your wife."

Waving her off, he said, "No problem. We were both up," he lied. He motioned toward the urn. "Want a cup?"

"Yes, please. I've been awake most of the night and need my fix."

"Have a seat." He turned and poured a cup. When he set it in front of her, he noticed her gnawing her lower lip. "Have you discovered something upsetting?"

"Yes. It's very disturbing. I'm finding more than I'd anticipated about the actions of my father." As she spoke, she emptied a brown legal sized envelope onto the desktop.

"Where did you find these things?"

She told him about discovering the combination taped to the underneath side of a drawer, then about her dream. I know it sounds strange, but the memory had tucked itself away in my brain and it all flooded forward. "Sure enough, when I checked behind the big picture, I found the wall safe." She pointed to the items. "This is everything I pulled out of there."

Hawkman picked up the bank passbook and opened it. His gaze riveted on the name, LaVonne Adkins. He glanced at Becky. "You're sure you've never heard of this woman?"

She shook her head. "Never, until you asked me about her earlier."

"Does the name Howard Dimmer mean anything to you?"

She frowned. "Wasn't he the lawyer who delivered the contracts to the renters.

"Yes. But had you ever heard the name in your youth?"

"I sure don't recall it."

"You have no kin by that name?"

"I have few relatives. My Mother was an only child and her parents died before I knew them. When I was in my teens, I remember my Dad mentioning his brother had been killed in an automobile accident. The only time I remember him talking about his past, was one Memorial Day when we went to the parade. He stood and saluted the flag. Later, he told me he'd gone into the service shortly after high school because his folks couldn't support him. He never spoke about his people, so I don't know if he had a happy childhood or one wracked with pain. I've never even seen a picture of his parents." She took a tissue from her purse and blew her nose. "I'm sorry, I didn't mean to go off on a tangent. Back to your question. I know of no one by the name of Dimmer."

"What about any of the people we've talked about. For instance, the Harris family or Bradley's? Do you by any chance know the wives' maiden names?"

"No, I really didn't get close to any of my folks' friends." She shrugged. "Big age difference."

Hawkman smiled. "I understand." He shifted in his seat. "I do find it odd that no one knows of this LaVonne Adkins. I've done a search and can't find any listing. There's a couple of Adkins I'm going to question, but I've found no record of her personally."

Becky took a deep breath. "Well, you're going to find more shocking news in those papers." She again pointed at the stack. "There are letters to my Dad telling him she's pregnant. If he doesn't want his name smeared all over town, he'd better see to it she receives a thousand dollars a month."

Hawkman's mouth dropped open. "You're kidding."

She reached over and handed him several long white envelopes from the stack. "She explains it all in these. I'm assuming she got an abortion or maybe gave the baby up for adoption, just from the way she wrote. But she still had him over a barrel. So I think that's why you couldn't get the books to balance. Part of the rental money was going into a savings account for her. As you can see from the passbook, it appears my dad had his updated ever so often, so she was pulling the money from the account. And this has been going on all these years. Her last withdrawal looks like it took place about a month before he died."

Hawkman glanced at the passbook again. "Okay, here's what I want you to do. Go to your bank and tell them you want the full amount of the rental fees put into your and Cory's account. You don't want the extra funds transferred anymore.

You want everything in one spot now. Just act like you've known all along what's been going on. You're the executor of the estate and I don't think you'll have any trouble. I doubt your dad let the bank know that the funds were being transferred into a joint account. He probably just gave them his name and this number." He pointed at the top of the passbook.

Becky pushed her hair behind her ears as she reached into her purse for a pen. "I better write that number down. I'm sure they'll need to know."

"Good idea." He handed her a pen and pad of paper. "If they happen to ask if there was another name on that account, just tell them, not to your knowledge. Your dad was the holder, so he had control. You might have to sign a paper or two, but that's okay. It then puts you in full authority. If they ask for the passbook, tell them you haven't located it yet, but your dad told you about the account before he passed away."

"What if they give me static about this?"

"Call me. We'll work it out. I have a lawyer friend, if we need one."

"Have you read the rest of these papers?"

"Yes."

"Any other shocking news?"

She tried to smile. "No. It mostly deals with the blackmail and what she expects. It gets a little nasty."

"I'll make copies and get the originals back to you in a day or two."

After Becky left, Hawkman sat down at his desk and proceeded to open the rest of the letters. He made copies of all the items, then sat down at his desk to study them.

They were all written to Al in ink. He wondered if Mr. Simpson had responded. He read each one carefully and noted Becky made a good analysis. The girl pretty much threatened him in no uncertain words about the pregnancy, writing she'd ruin his good reputation if he didn't pay her.

Then he raised his brows as he noticed the name LaVonne was signed several different ways. Once it had a capital 'V', another time with a little 'v', and stranger yet, another spelling with the space between the La and Vonne. Wouldn't the girl know how to spell her own name?

Hawkman quickly put all the letters in front of him and analyzed the penmanship. He soon came to the conclusion, they were all written by the same person. But this person's name wasn't LaVonne Adkins. This was obviously an alias the pair had decided upon in case someone managed to get a hold of the correspondence.

Also the letters indicated the girl would get rid of the baby, but Al would have to pay for her trip out of state. She didn't mention whether by adoption or abortion. Then Hawkman noticed an erasure mark on one of the letter's signatures. He held it up to the light and could see she'd almost signed her real name. What he could make out shocked him.

CHAPTER TWENTY-FOUR

Hawkman thoughtfully folded the letters and returned them to their envelopes. He couldn't prove anything yet, so would keep his suspicions to himself until he had more evidence. But this information he'd discovered definitely helped him with the case. One never knows when a break might occur. Now he needed a plan on how he could trap this person.

As his mind churned, the phone rang, and he punched the speaker. "Tom Casey."

"Detective Williams. Thought I'd let you know I got the fingerprint report back on those two notes."

"So, what'd they find?"

"Nothing. Looks like your perp used gloves. There were some smears, but nothing my guys could identify as a finger mark."

"Doesn't surprise me. I pretty much suspected those results."

"I have the notes in my office, so any time you want to pick them up is fine. If I'm not here, have the gal at the front desk come and get them. I'll have the letters in a brown envelope on my desk with your name on it."

"Thanks, Williams. I really appreciate your help."

"No problem. Any breaks on the case?"

"Possibly, but I'm keeping my mouth shut until I have more proof."

Williams laughed. "I take it, you're being a bit cautious."

"You know how it goes."

"Right on. I'll see ya soon."

Hawkman hung up and turned back to the Simpson file. He took his calculator and figured out the math on the rentals, then added what the figure would be if a thousand dollars had been removed each month for fifteen years. The total balanced.

He then jotted down some questions he needed to ask Becky. Maybe he'd drop by this evening after she got home from work. Turning to his computer, he decided to run the names Bradley and Harris through a genealogical search. Knowing this would take some time working through the family trees, he settled comfortably in his chair and proceeded.

It took him a couple of hours to get through the Bradleys and he found no mention of anyone's name being Dimmer. Elma's maiden name turned out to be Smith, but none of her sisters married a man named Dimmer and none of the brothers married anyone with such a title.

He changed over to Harris and after an hour's work, he sat up straight as Lisa Harris' maiden name floated in front of him. "Dimmer!" he exclaimed out loud.

Quickly searching the rest of the family tree, he discovered her brother's name was Howard. Hawkman flopped back in his chair. This certainly threw a new light on things. However, maybe he should have expected this turn of events. Al Simpson had been good to Henry Harris, repaying him for saving his life by making sure the man always had a job to support his family. Henry in turn offered the services of his brother-in-law. Made sense. But why put Grants Pass, Oregon, on the contracts? Maybe Dimmer thought about starting a business there, but discovered he couldn't make a decent living in a small town, and moved out before he registered the law firm.

The way things were shaping up, he had several families involved with Al Simpson. Now to find the one who knew the whereabouts of his wife. And Hawkman figured one of these people could tell him.

He glanced at his watch and decided he'd see if Becky had gotten home from work.

Punching in her number, he only had to wait two rings. He made arrangements to drop by within the hour.

When he arrived at the Simpson home, he spotted Becky clad in jeans and sweatshirt, running around the front yard, throwing a stick for a canine to retrieve.

"Hello, Mr. Casey. Meet Scruffy, my dad's mutt. Since I've taken him over, he seems to like me okay."

"Nice looking pooch." The dog bounded toward him, wagging his tail, with the small limb in his mouth. Hawkman took the branch and tossed it high into the air. The dog jumped up and caught it. "Hey, good boy."

When the animal ran to Hawkman again, Becky intervened. "Okay, Scruffy, enough. You go play by yourself. Mr. Casey and I have business to take care of."

They walked up the porch steps as Scruffy watched with forlorn eyes and dropped the stick from his mouth. Before they disappeared inside, he picked up the toy and shook it.

"Can I get you something to drink?" Becky asked as they entered the living room.

"No, thanks, I'm fine."

Becky pointed to the wall safe. "There's where I found the hidden vault. I haven't rehung the picture yet. It's pretty heavy."

"Would you like me to help you?"

"That would be great."

Hawkman lifted the picture to the wall as Becky fingered the wire and got it over the hook.

"Thank you. I really didn't like the safe exposed, but I couldn't manage by myself as the wire kept slipping from my grip."

"It's a big picture. Always easier to get them down, but awkward for one person to hang."

She motioned toward the couch. "Have a seat."

"Were you able to get to the bank today?" Hawkman asked.

"Yes. Surprisingly, I had no trouble getting the whole payment put into Cory's and my accounts. I thought for sure I'd be barraged with questions. I only had to sign a couple of papers."

"Good. I'd like to know more about Henry Harris. You said your dad felt indebted to him because he'd saved his life. Could you tell me about the incident?"

Becky exhaled. "I don't know. It happened years ago. I just remember when Dad hired him, he told Mother he wanted to make sure this man always had a job. He owed him."

"You mentioned you didn't like Henry Harris."

"I didn't then and I'm not fond of him now, especially after taking his paycheck to him last week."

Hawkman raised a brow. "Oh. What happened?"

"In so many straightforward and ugly words, he told me to drop the search for my mother."

"Why don't you fire him?"

She bowed her head. "I can't. It would be going against my father's wishes. The man meant something to Dad." She wrung her hands. "I just couldn't do it."

"Have you noticed other strange behaviors in Mr. Harris?"

"I don't know how significant this might be, but shortly after the funeral, Henry came to do the lawn. I happened to look out the kitchen window which overlooks the side yard. Henry stood at the opening of the rose garden holding his hat over his heart as if in prayer, then he placed his hat back on his head and crossed himself."

"Has he ever done this before?"

"I truly don't know. Maybe he does it every time he weeds that patch of land. Mother loved that section with the flowers, and I just surmised it reminded him of her."

"When I talked with Mr. Harris, he gave me the impression he didn't know your mother well."

Becky frowned. "Really. That seems odd. Mother used to have him come in for a cold drink and cookies almost every week. I could hear them talking in the kitchen."

"Do you remember any of their conversations?"

"No. I was too young to care."

"What about Lisa Harris?"

"I know Mother didn't like her, but I don't know the reason."

"So this couple never showed up at your house for dinner or any type of social gathering?"

"Not to my knowledge."

"What about Francis and Saul Kregor?"

"Robin's parents?"

"Yes."

"Now, I do recall them coming to the house a couple of times. Mother would pick Robin up about an hour early so she'd have time to get ready without us underfoot. Then Mr. and Mrs. Kregor would take their daughter home when they left ."

"Were your mother and Francis Kregor good friends? For example, did they talk on the phone or see each other often?"

"My mother didn't have any intimate friends. She seemed pretty much a loner. The only people surrounding her were Dad, Cory and me. Sometimes I'd see her staring out the window, as if she were daydreaming. Now that I'm older, I look back on those moments and think she must have been very lonely."

"After your mother disappeared, did you notice any different behavior in your father?"

Becky crossed her legs and folded her arms around her waist. Her eyes glistened in the light of the lamp. "Strange you'd ask me such a question. What bearing does it have on the disappearance of my mother?"

"I have to try every avenue. Right now I'm clueless where your mother might be and I need to ask all kinds of things. You obviously saw a change in your dad."

She blinked back the tears. "Yes, and even as a little girl I didn't like it. He seemed happier or relieved. I'm not sure which. It bothered me for a long time; then the feeling subsided as time passed."

"Did your dad continue to have friends over, or did he ever go out in the evening?"

"Sometimes he'd be gone overnight on business." She shrugged. "Anyway, that's what he told us."

"Who stayed with you and Cory when your dad took these trips?"

"He used a professional baby sitting service when he'd go. Someone different showed up each time, sort of like a one-night stand. We never saw them again."

"Did this happen often?"

"No. I'd say maybe three or four times. And Dad never had people over for dinner, since he didn't cook much. Even when we had Carmella taking care of us, he didn't. Some of the neighbors would occasionally bring us casseroles, which I thought very nice. But those lovely gestures soon ceased."

Hawkman looked thoughtful for a moment and remained silent.

"Something bothering you?" Becky asked.

"Yes. If your father had a lover, as many say, you would have thought he'd have been away from home more often."

CHAPTER TWENTY-FIVE

The next morning, Hawkman again rose early and headed for Medford. He planned to hit the Harris' home soon after Henry left for work. As far as he knew, Lisa didn't have a job and she was the one he wanted to question. When he pulled around the corner going toward their house, he slowed and drove past the residence to check for Henry's truck loaded with his yard tools. He'd noticed the time he came before, Harris had parked the vehicle at the side of the garage on a concrete slab, shaded by a canopy.

"Good," Hawkman mumbled under his breath, " Henry's apparently gone to a job." He made a U-turn, parked in front of the house, flipped on his recorder and went up the narrow sidewalk. When he knocked, he heard the yipping of the little dog and the heavy footsteps of Lisa Harris.

When she opened the door, dressed in a sack dress and thongs on her feet, she frowned. "Oh, it's you again. Henry's gone to work."

"This time I came to speak to you."

"I don't know a thing about Carole Simpson."

"What about your brother, Howard Dimmer?"

Lisa's face paled. "Is he okay?"

"As far as I know. "

She scowled and put a hand on her hefty hip. "Why do you want to know about him?"

Hawkman concluded the questions would have to be asked while he stood on the front stoop, the sun beaming on his back, and a screen door between Lisa and himself. "He lives in Indiana, right?"

"Yeah."

"Did he ever have a law firm in Grants Pass?"

"It fell through, so he left the area and went straight to Indiana."

"Before he moved, he worked up the contracts for Mr. Al Simpson to take over his wife's property, right?"

She shrugged and looked at the ground. "I don't know nothing about the legal jargon. He and Henry talked business all the time."

"But you do know Mr. Simpson hired your brother?"

"Yeah."

"Did Henry talk Howard into giving Mr. Simpson a good deal?"

"Like I told you, I don't know the details, you'll have to talk to Henry."

"Why did your husband feel so beholden to Al Simpson?"

"Henry always liked him, because he got him a lot of jobs." She wrinkled her forehead, making her beady eyes almost disappear. "I don't like all these questions."

Hawkman ignored her comment. "How did your husband save Mr. Simpson's life?"

She backed up, and pulled the screen door tight. "What does that have to do with the disappearance of Carole Simpson?"

"It might have a lot to do with it."

"In that case, you better talk to Henry," she retorted, and slammed the wooden door in Hawkman's face.

Walking back to his vehicle, Hawkman flipped off the recorder. How did the act of saving a person's life get so shrouded in secrecy? This seemed odd to Hawkman. Especially since it happened long before Carole Simpson disappeared. When he pulled away from the house, he spotted Lisa staring out the window, holding her mangy little yippy dog. At least he now knew Howard Dimmer belonged to the Harris' family.

The next person on his agenda, whom he hadn't interviewed yet, was Edward Barnett, the stepbrother of Carmella Jones. He'd done his research and discovered the man resided in a retirement home outside the city limits. When he called

Barnett and explained his mission, they made an appointment. Hawkman doubted the man could tell him much, but maybe he'd remember bits and pieces of conversation with Carmella about the Simpson family.

He arrived at Vista Manor and parked in the lot next to the large one story building. The grounds were stunning; even a running fountain graced the front between the two entries. A high wall encased the back area. Hawkman wondered what it hid.

He meandered up to the front desk occupied by a young woman in her late twenties or early thirties. The extended sides of the desk were manned by nurses, busy charting and using the computer. He asked the directions to Edward Barnett's room.

The receptionist smiled. "He occupies one of the cottages, number one forty six, but I doubt you'll find him there. He maintains the back area grounds and is usually trimming or cleaning out the flower beds from daylight to nightfall." She pointed to a large glass double door leading outside. If you'll go out that way, you'll probably find him pruning something."

"Thank you," Hawkman said, touching the brim of his hat.

He strolled down the hallway, taking in the occupants' rooms where doors were ajar. It impressed him. Very clean, nicely decorated, with a sense of happiness displayed by laughter ringing through the halls.

Walking out on the patio, it amazed him to view the numerous tables with colorful umbrellas extending down the length of the building. This place covered many acres of land, surrounded by the tall barrier he'd observed when he arrived. Cottages were scattered on the outskirts, and a row of golf carts lined one side. Hawkman assumed people living in the far houses could ride them home and back, in case walking any distance presented a problem.

He glanced around the scattered flower patches, sewn in between curving sidewalks throughout the lovely landscape. Hawkman noticed a man clipping dead flowers and throwing them into a small wastebasket sitting on the concrete. He assumed this might be Mr. Barnett, flipped on the recorder in his pocket and approached the man.

"Mr. Barnett?"

The gardener glanced up, smiled, placed his pruners in the belt he had around his waist which carried several small garden tools, took off his gloves and extended his hand. "Mr. Casey, I presume? I've heard about you. You're definitely not hard to spot with your eye-patch and cowboy hat."

"My trademarks," Hawkman laughed, as the men shook hands.

Barnett pointed to a vacant table. "Let's go over there so we can talk in the shade. I'll get us something cool to drink. You like lemonade?"

"Yes, sounds very refreshing."

They settled at the table, each holding a large glass. Barnett adjusted the umbrella so they were completely protected from the rays of the sun. Then he removed his straw hat and ran his fingers through thinning gray hair.

"Gets warm while I'm in the direct sunlight."

"This is quite a place. I've never been out here before," Hawkman said.

"I could never afford it, if they didn't let me garden to pay the expenses. My sister left me a little bundle, but I knew it wouldn't last my lifetime, although it really helps."

"What made you decide to live here?"

"I have some health problems which require twenty-four hour attention. This place guarantees I'll get the care I need, and so far they haven't disappointed me. Great staff."

"Good to hear. As I told you on the phone, I'd like to ask some questions about the Simpson family. Your sister took care of the children after their mother disappeared. I don't imagine you know much about them, but I've been told you stayed with Carmella during her last months and maybe she commented about the family from time to time."

"Carmella was a wonderful woman. Even though we weren't blood kin, we got along marvelously, and I never thought of her as anything but a true sister. When she got ill, I wanted to be with her. I truly believe it helped prolong her life a little longer."

Hawkman noticed the man's blue eyes twinkled when he spoke of his sister. "You must have loved her a lot."

"I did. She got me through a lot of turmoil as I grew up. We had a rough family life and we clung to each other for support. She never let me down."

"Mr. Barnett, did she ever speak to you about the Simpsons?"

"Please, call me Ed."

"Okay, Ed."

"Yes, she did. It upset her very much when Mr. Simpson let her go. She couldn't imagine how that little girl, I believe her name was Becky, could ever do the jobs expected of a grown woman. She tried to talk some sense into the man, but he told her he couldn't carry the expense of a nanny any longer. But she didn't believe him."

"Why not?"

"She said he made plenty of money and then he took over all of the rental properties belonging to his wife. Carmella believed he didn't want to share the love of the children with her."

"You give the impression Carmella didn't care for Mr. Simpson."

Ed shook his head. "No, she didn't like him, but she loved those kids. She said, Mr. Simpson never complimented her on the work she did with the children, and believe me she did a lot to keep that little girl and boy happy. I know my sister. She wanted to help those little ones get over the loss of their mother. But she told me he appeared aloof and he didn't like it when Becky and the little boy showed any affection toward her. "

"What made her think such a thing?"

Barnett shifted his weight and took a swig of lemonade. "Sis said, he'd remove the children from her embrace and tell them, 'Ms. Jones is here to take care of you. Not to be your mother.' This just killed my sister."

"Did she ever witness Mr. Simpson with another woman?"

"No. She even doubted the rumor."

"Did she ever state what she thought happened to Mrs. Simpson?"

He nodded. "Yes, she believes Mr. Simpson murdered her and buried her in the rose garden."

Hawkman stiffened. "Why did she think there?"

"One morning on arriving at the household a little early, she noted the gardener, I believe his name was Harris, working over the ground with a heavy rake. She went into the kitchen and watched from the window. A mound about the size one would expect a body to be under, protruded and he proceeded to smooth it out flat."

CHAPTER TWENTY-SIX

Hawkman stared at him for a moment. "It could have been a pile of top soil, or fertilizer."

Ed shrugged. "I agree with you. After the doctors treated Carmella with heavy doses of chemotherapy to battle her cancer, her imagination tended to take over. She babbled about the Simpson children days at a time. It got to the point where I didn't know what to believe."

"Do you remember when she told you about the mound of dirt?"

"It had to be after she got so sick and needed my help. We kept in close contact by phone and letters. But I hadn't seen her personally for years."

"Did she ever mention the Simpsons when she wrote or talked to you?"

He gulped down the rest of his cool drink, then nodded. "Constantly. Her letters were filled with tales of those two kids. But I assumed it a pretty normal thing, since her daily life evolved around them for close to three years."

"What about Al Simpson? Did she talk about him?"

"Not a lot. As I said, she didn't like him. However, she did think he cared for the children. So she tolerated the man's strange behavior." Ed scratched his head. "You know, I think she did mention that mound of dirt in one of her letters."

This piqued Hawkman's interest. "I don't assume you have those letters?"

"As a matter of fact, I have every one she wrote."

"Are they handy?"

"No. I have them in one of the boxes stored at my cottage. It'll take me a few days to go through them and find the right one. But I can sure do it, if you're not in any hurry."

"I'd really appreciate it." Hawkman handed him a card. "Give me a call when you've found them." Then he stood. "I better not take any more of your time, I'm sure you've got work to do."

Ed stuck the card into his pocket, then picked up his hat from the table and pushed it onto his head. "I enjoyed our visit. I'll get back to you on those letters."

"Great." Hawkman started to walk away, then turned. "Thanks for the cool drink."

Harris gave a wave, then collected the glasses and carried them toward a two way window at the side of the building.

When Hawkman reached his vehicle, he noticed the sun had moved and his SUV no longer sat in the shade. He unlocked the door and stood back for a moment to let the hot air escape. On his way back toward the city, he decided to swing by Becky's place and take a closer look at the grounds around the house. He didn't think she'd mind.

The front yard didn't have a fence across the face; instead it ran down each side of the property to the road. The enclosed area extended from the sides of the house and across the back. He opened the gate and Scruffy came charging around the corner, barking fiercely.

"Hey, Scruffy, don't you remember me?"

The dog immediately quit growling and wagged his tail.

As Hawkman strolled through the backyard, it impressed him how the dog wouldn't venture near the roses. He picked up a ball he found on the grass, and deliberately tossed it into the flowered area. The dog stopped at the perimeter of the rose garden and whined.

"You're a very well trained animal," Hawkman said, as he retrieved the ball and pitched it elsewhere. Scruffy brought it to him within a few seconds. Observing the grounds, he noted the rose bushes were planted in a semicircle, with a large opening in the middle and plenty of space between each bush. There had definitely been some planning of this garden. A small, white, recently painted, round wrought iron table and matching chair were placed in the middle.

The plants had been trimmed to perfection with new growth apparent. It wouldn't be long before dozens of flowers bloomed. Hawkman didn't know much about roses, but he could tell they were tended regularly. He walked through the center, and noted the softness of the ground. The soil had been turned over many times to get such a texture.

Scruffy waited for him as he walked out. Hawkman gave him a rub on the head. "Okay, boy, one more throw and I'm outta here." After throwing the ball, he headed for the gate. He'd just raised his hand up to grasp the handle, when it suddenly flew open. Henry Harris, hoe in hand, glared at him with his almost black eyes.

"What the hell are you doing sneaking around here?"

"For your information, Mr. Harris, I'm not sneaking. And if it's any of your business, I came to play with Scruffy." Hawkman brushed past him with a smirk on his lips.

"Mr. Casey."

Hawkman turned. "Yes?"

"I'd appreciate it if you didn't bother my wife any more."

He walked up to Henry and stared down into his face. "How did you save Mr. Simpson's life?"

"Henry narrowed his eyes. "It has nothing to do with the disappearance of Mrs. Simpson."

"I don't know what you're hiding, but I'm going to find out one way or the other. And if it means questioning Lisa, I'll do it."

The gardener stomped into the side yard and slammed the gate.

Henry leaned against the fence, took off his hat and wiped his forehead with the back of his arm. "Nosey private investigator," he hissed.

Scruffy with the green tennis ball in his mouth, stood looking at him with his tail wagging slightly.

The gardener pushed on his hat, and looked puzzled, then glanced back at the gate. "Did he really come to play with you?"

The ball dropped from Scruffy's mouth and he let out a woof.

"Sorry, boy, he's left."

Henry proceeded toward the entry to the rose garden and stopped abruptly. The boot marks in the soft soil, told him Mr. Casey had done more than play with the dog. He dropped the hoe to the ground, and brushed away the spider webs as he examined between each bush. Standing, he breathed a sigh of relief when he saw no sign of any deep disturbance to the soil, and appraised the healthy bushes. "It won't be long, Ms. Carole. All your favorites will be in bloom and dispersing their aromas throughout the yard." He removed his hat, crossed himself, picked up the garden implement and headed for another part of the yard.

CHAPTER TWENTY-SEVEN

Hawkman pulled around the corner and hopped out of the SUV. Praying the dog wouldn't catch his scent, he quickly hoofed it back to Becky's house. He found a small slit in the fence where he observed Harris standing on the outskirts of the rose garden with his hat over his heart, mumbling incoherently. After the gardener made the sign of the cross, and moved out of sight, Hawkman hurried back to his vehicle.

While driving to his office, he still couldn't believe someone had buried Carole Simpson's body in the rose garden. It just seemed too risky. But considering Henry's behavior along with Becky's story of observing him conduct the same ritual, and Ed's story of his sister seeing the dirt mound, made him wonder. Yet, each of these had a very normal explanation of why they happened. So far, his day had proven quite interesting, and a bit baffling

Parking behind the donut shop, he pulled his briefcase from under the passenger seat, and went up the stairs. While fingering his keys to find the right one for the office, he stepped up on the last rung, and felt an object under his boot. He glanced down to see he'd stepped on a paring knife with a broken tip. His gaze drifted up the door and taped across the center, a white envelope rippled in the breeze with 'Tom Casey' pasted across the front in cutout newspaper letters.

He leaned over the bannister and scanned the alley, but saw nothing out of the ordinary. In case there'd be fingerprints on the knife, he unlocked the door, slid the briefcase inside, then picked up the blade by the blunted end, carried it inside, and deposited it into a plastic bag.

Slipping on a pair of latex gloves, he opened the unsealed envelope and removed the sheet of paper. Sprawled across the page, glued on letters spelled out the words: "You don't listen. Now you've gone too far."

Hawkman put the note in another bag and stored the items inside his briefcase. He then scurried down the steps to the bakery in hopes of catching Clyde before he closed up shop. Relieved to find the door still open, he went inside, as the bell jingled warning Clyde of a customer.

"I'm closed. No more pastries until morning," a voice called from the back.

"It's Tom Casey, I need to talk to you a moment."

Clyde hurried forward with a towel thrown over his shoulder, and his hair covered in a fine flour dust. "Sorry, I can't see who's here. I only hear the bell."

"Just wondered if you'd seen anyone going up to my office today?"

"No. My shop sits back too far, and the stairs aren't visible." He frowned. "I hope no one broke in."

"Nothing like that. Thanks, Clyde. Sorry to have bothered you."

Hawkman went back to his office and punched in Becky's number. She obviously hadn't gotten off work yet. So he left a message. "Becky, Tom Casey. I need to talk to you. If it's all right, I'll drop by this evening. Give me a call when you get home. Thanks."

She returned his call within thirty minutes, and Hawkman made arrangements to see her immediately.

Becky met him at the door. "Hi, Mr. Casey, I saw you drive up. It always worries me when you want to talk in a hurry."

"I'll get right to the questions I need answered." He sat down on the couch, removed his recorder from the briefcase, flipped it on, and placed it on the table. "Hope you don't mind, I'd rather use this than take notes."

"I don't mind. In fact, it's a great idea." She took the chair opposite him.

"One thing I've never bothered to ask, and thought I'd run across it in my investigation, but haven't. What did your father do for a living?"

"He worked for the Rogue Valley Freight Company, started out as a dock hand and after several years, moved into a manager position, where he stayed until retirement. It wasn't a glamorous job, but he knew it inside and out. It brought in a decent living, and he seemed satisfied."

Hawkman nodded. "Have you received any more threatening phone calls or notes?"

She stared at him with a questioning expression. "No. But I have a sneaking suspicion you've received some."

"You're right, I have. So don't let your guard down and stay aware of everything around you. Let me know immediately if you think you're being followed, and keep all important papers in the safe deposit box at the bank. I don't mean to frighten you, but the notes are menacing."

"I think I've really stirred up a hornet's nest."

"Tell me more about Robin Kregor Shepard. Have you seen her much?"

"Not really. We speak if we happen to run into each other on the street. She's in quite a different league than me." She put her finger on her nose and pushed it up. "You know, high society."

Hawkman smiled. "I guess her husband being in the banking business does put her in a class of her own. By the way, do you recall when she married?"

"Oh, geez, she's been married a long time. I'd say ten or twelve years ago."

"Do Robin's parents have money?"

Becky shook her head. "Not to my knowledge. But that really doesn't mean they don't."

"Do you know if Robin's husband was wealthy when they married?"

"It appears that way. They bought the mansion right off the bat."

"How did she meet him?"

She shrugged. "I haven't the vaguest idea."

"What's his first name?"

Becky tapped her finger on her chin. "I believe it's Doug."

Hawkman changed the subject. "Shortly after your mother disappeared, do you recall any truck coming and dumping soil or fertilizer on the grounds?"

She furrowed her brow. "What an odd question?"

Hawkman nodded. "I know, but do you remember any such thing?"

"Henry will periodically have a load brought out from the local nursery. He then takes the wheel barrow and dumps mounds of it over the ground and in the rose garden. Then he spends a couple of days raking it until it's level. But I don't remember any specific time; maybe every six months or once a year. I lose track of such a schedule."

"Has he always done this?"

"Yes. I even remember mother not letting us play on the lawn for a few days until the smell subsided." She tilted her head. "Why is this important?"

"I've interviewed people who feel your mother is buried in the rose garden."

Becky gasped and put a hand to her mouth. "Oh, my God! That means they think she's been murdered."

"True. I've come to the conclusion we're dealing with a sinister act. Whether it's murder, I can't be sure. I'm obviously getting close to finding some answers or these messages wouldn't be showing up. From what I've learned, the love your mother had for you and Cory would have driven her to contact you some way. And she never did. So I honestly don't think your mother's alive."

Tears welled in Becky's eyes. "I think I've known it all along, just didn't want to admit it." She raised her head defiantly. "If she was murdered, I want you to find out who killed her."

"Many think your father's guilty. I have my doubts, but can't be sure just yet. A few leads have popped up, but I'll keep those to myself until I have more proof."

Becky took a tissue from her pocket and blew her nose.

Hawkman bowed his head. "I'm sorry to cause you this pain."

She waved a hand. "I hired you to find my mother. You're doing your job. My brother, Cory, even warned me I might not like what we discover. He's right, I don't like it, but I want to know. So please hang in here with me."

He nodded. "I will as long as you want. The police might be drawn into the case, because I can't handle it alone if it involves murder."

"I understand." She sucked in a deep breath. "Do whatever is necessary. Now more than ever, I need to know what happened to my mother."

CHAPTER TWENTY-EIGHT

Becky stood at the entry, hugging herself as she watched Tom Casey drive away. She stared into space long after he'd disappeared down the street. Slowly closing the door, she went to the kitchen and gazed out the window, then went out the back where Scruffy met her with the ball in his mouth. She gave him a rub, took the toy and halfheartedly tossed it into the yard. While the dog scampered after it, she strolled to the side of the house and stood at the opening of the rose garden. Then she stepped inside the circle.

Scruffy sat on his haunches on the outskirts with the ball in his mouth, his tail thumping the ground, as he watched his new master walk around the plants, touching several of the buds.

She glanced at the dog. "Is she here, boy?"

He dropped the ball from his mouth and gave a couple of barks.

A shadow loomed across the ground and Becky whirled around. Her hand went to her throat. "You scared me, Henry. I didn't even hear the gate open."

"Sorry, Ms. Simpson, didn't mean to startle you. I didn't expect to find you out here in the garden. I'm sure you realize the flowers are not ready to cut."

"Yes, I know. It won't be long though. They're loaded with buds." She stepped out of the circle of bushes. "There seems to be a lot of spider webs. Should you spray?"

"They get the bugs that eat on the plants. They do more good than harm."

Becky nodded. "I see your reasoning. She glanced up at him, puzzled. "By the way, what are you doing here so late?"

He pointed to an implement resting against the fence. "I forgot my hoe and I'll need it in the morning."

Picking it up, he left the yard as silently as he'd entered.

When Scruffy moved alongside her, she knelt down and put an arm around his back. "He's a strange man. How I wish you could talk. I'm sure you'd answer a lot of my questions. One thing I'd like to know is, who taught you not to go into the rose garden? Dad or Henry? Of course, I can understand why they wouldn't want you in there digging up the soil to hide a bone." She stood, picked up the ball he'd dropped and tossed it toward the fence.

Becky played with Scruffy until the sun dipped low in the sky, and the breeze turned nippy. "Come on boy, you've worn me out; let's go inside."

Once she'd eaten dinner and fed the dog, she settled in the living room to watch a few minutes of the news. "Oh, shoot," she said, slapping the couch arm. Scruffy raised his head from the rug and perked his ears.

"I forgot to get the mail. Let's walk down to the box. I'm expecting some bills and need to get them paid."

After she and the dog returned, Becky placed the mail on the coffee table, made herself a drink, then sat down and fingered through the letters. Her heart sank as she came across an envelope with her name scrawled across the front in glued-on print. There was no address, nor a stamp. Someone had obviously placed it in her box after the mail had been delivered. Tom Casey had informed her no fingerprints were found on the other note, so she didn't take any precautions, as she figured this one would be the same. She flipped up the flap which was only pushed inside, and pulled out the sheet of paper. When a dried rose slipped from the folded sheet, and fell onto her lap, she sucked in a deep breath. Placing the crumbling flower on the table, she opened the single sheet. Pasted across the paper in print similar to her name, it said: 'Your mother is dead and buried. Let it go or else!'

Becky reached for the phone, then gave it a second thought and put it back on the cradle. I won't bother Mr. Casey with this tonight. There's nothing he could do about it at this hour, and he's got enough on his mind at the moment.

Before heading home, Hawkman had an idea and quickly drove by his office.

He booted up his computer and looked under the City of Medford's Public Works and after much searching finally discovered the waste pickup days under Rogue Disposal. After looking up the address he had in mind, he smiled to himself. Their trash would go out tonight, in time for the Friday morning pickup.

In the small cabinet under the coffee urn, he'd stored disguises he might need for surveillance. He found an old floppy hat and a ratty long coat. Looking in the mirror, he checked to insure the wide brim drooped down enough to cover his eye-patch. The coat hit below his knees. He now resembled a bum, perfect for what he had in mind.

Night had fallen before he left the office. He hid the briefcase with the Simpson file under the passenger seat of his vehicle, then drove away. When he reached his destination, he parked around the corner, pulled on a pair of gloves, removed a large plastic bag from the duffle case he kept in the back, folded it under his arm, locked up the SUV, then walked down the sidewalk with a heavy limp. As he passed each group of trash cans, he made it a point to open the lid and glance inside. When he reached the one he wanted, he dug into it a little deeper. Finding several items he thought might be of interest, he shoved them into the plastic bag. Suddenly, the front porch light came on. Hawkman quickly moved down the street, and turned the corner.

He glanced back and saw a man stuffing another load of garbage into the can.

Hawkman walked around the block and returned to his vehicle. Once Inside the SUV, he went through what he'd taken from the can, and decided he had enough to satisfy his hunch. But he had more investigating to do, because the things he'd found wouldn't hold up in a court of law. Now he had to prove these people were guilty of murder.

When he arrived home, he found Jennifer watching a movie on the television with Miss Marple in her lap. "Hi, Hon, sorry I'm so late, but had to do some sleuthing."

She eyed him strangely. "I can tell you right now, I don't like the hat or coat. Makes you look like a street person. Miss Marple doesn't like it either. She hasn't moved from my lap, and she's usually right at your feet."

He laughed. "Exactly how I wanted to appear." Shedding the garb, he rolled it up and placed it on the cabinet. I'll take this outfit back to the office. I might need it again."

"What in the heck were you doing? Raiding trash cans?"

He shot a look at her. "Are you psychic?"

Jennifer rolled her eyes. "What else would you do in such a garb?" Then she grinned. "Did you find a clue?"

He shoved his chin up in an arrogant manner. "Sure did."

This really piqued her interest. She put the cat on the floor and crossed the room. "Well, where is it?"

"I left it in the 4X4. Didn't think you'd be too happy having trash in the house. And I sure didn't want you to throw it away, if you got up before I did. I guess you want me to go get it?"

"Yes, otherwise I won't sleep a wink wondering what you found."

He grinned and picked up the disguise. "I'll take this out and bring in my garbage sack."

When he returned, Jennifer stood at the kitchen counter, tapping her foot. "What took you so long?"

"I wanted to get these notes out of my briefcase."

Her eyes twinkled. "I love this suspense."

He held up his hand. "I'm not going to tell you whose trash can this stuff came out of just yet. But, I promise I will eventually."

"Darn. You do this to me all the time."

"I know, but I have my reasons."

He placed the plastic bag on the counter, then slipped on a pair of latex gloves. "Don't touch these items. I'm not sure we'll find any fingerprints on them, since they've been smudged in the debris, but you never know." He carefully removed a newspaper and opened it.

Jennifer's eyes grew wide. "Oh, my gosh! Letters have been cut out of the printed pages."

Then he took some tongs and removed a pair of protective gloves. "I'm afraid they've used these, so I doubt we'll find prints on the paper, but you never know, we might luck out. And of course, I can't be sure the letters on the notes Becky and I received came from these newspapers." He opened one and compared the print. "Boy, it sure looks like the same font and ink. But I'm going to have Detective Williams' lab men check to make sure."

Jennifer touched his sleeve. "You took a big chance on getting these. Did anyone see you?"

"Hey, hon, it's the exciting part of my job. Someone did flip on an outside light, which gave me plenty of time to amble down the block before a person came out carrying another bag of trash. I don't think he paid any attention to me, as I stayed well hidden in the shadows of the trees lining the street."

He folded the papers, and slid them into the plastic bag, along with the gloves. "I'll run these by the police station in the morning."

"That's it? You're really not going to tell me any more?"

He smiled and shook his head. "Nope, I've still got plenty of investigating to do before I can come to any conclusions. None of this stuff will hold up in court by itself."

She sighed and went back to her chair. "Oh, darn. I missed the ending of the movie." Punching off the television, she headed for the bedroom. "Now, without any answers or conclusions," she threw up her arms, "I'll probably have nightmares."

Hawkman chuckled as he watched her march down the hallway.

CHAPTER TWENTY-NINE

Early the next morning, Hawkman stopped by Detective Williams' office and found him curled up asleep on the small sofa in the corner. He decided not to wake the man and quietly backed out the door. About the time he turned to leave, he heard a voice holler.

"Get your butt back in here."

Afraid the detective might yell again, Hawkman hurried back into the room. "I figured you'd been up most of the night and didn't want to bother you. I have a feeling you need all the rest you can snatch."

Williams wiped his face with a hand towel. "Yep, we had a gang of kids go wild last night. Had a time rounding them up. Finally got the bunch into the station and booked every one of the little snots. I don't know what's gotten into young people. They think they can do anything they want. In fact, it's a bit scary to see what we're going to have to deal with in the future." He poured two cups of coffee and placed one in front of Hawkman. "So what can I do for you today?"

"After the night you've had, I almost hate to ask."

The detective shook his head in the air. "Hey, this is my life. Yesterday was just a bit busier."

Placing the plastic bag on the desk, Hawkman explained the contents. "What I'd like for your lab techs to do, is find out if the letters in the note compare with the newspaper print. I think they do, but I'm not an expert, so I'd like your boys to see if they match."

"Shouldn't be a problem. Any hurry?"

"Think they could get it done by the first of next week?"

Williams nodded as he opened the sack and glanced inside. "I'll sure see what I can do. What about these gloves?"

"Is there a possibility prints can be lifted from the inside? I have a feeling they were used to cut out the letters so no fingerprints would show up on the paper."

"I'll see what they can come up with. Also I'll have the latex checked for ink smudges and such."

"Wouldn't hurt." Hawkman stood. "I'll get out of here in case you have a few more minutes to finish your nap."

The detective grimaced. "My brain is rolling now. Sleep is out of the question."

"Hope your weekend isn't too hectic. I'll talk to you on Monday."

Williams waved as he walked out of the office.

Hawkman drove away from the police station and headed toward the end of Main Street where he pulled into the parking lot of the People's Bank of Medford. He didn't do his banking here, so when he got inside, he studied the layout before proceeding. Not seeing any executive offices from the lobby, he strolled up to the teller's window. "I'd like to speak with Mr. Doug Shepard."

The young teller appeared a bit shocked when she looked up at Hawkman. He smiled to himself, as he'd encountered this reaction many times, especially with young women. Something about the eye-patch threw them off guard.

"Uh, do you have an appointment?" she stammered.

"No, but I think he'll see me." He handed her a business card.

After reading the title, she dropped her pen on the counter. "I'll check if he's available."

She returned in a matter of minutes. "He'll see you now." She walked to the end of the counter. "Please come around here and I'll take you to his office." Tapping in a code, she lifted the end flap, then led Hawkman down a small hallway.

A few steps behind her, he reached into his pocket and flipped on his recorder. She lightly rapped on a door with the words, President: Douglas Shepard, printed across the center. When it swung open, a man of six foot or more, dressed in a very expensive deep blue Italian suit, greeted him with a big smile and held out his hand.

"So you're the private investigator, Tom Casey?"

"Yes."

After they shook hands, he stepped back and motioned for Hawkman to come in. "Have a seat." Then he closed the door in Ms. Collin's face. Moving behind a gigantic oak desk, he flopped down in the leather chair. "My wife tells me you're searching for Mrs. Carole Simpson."

"That's right."

"So to what do I owe this visit, as I know nothing about the woman? Never met her or the family."

"No, I didn't expect you did. But your wife knew them."

Mr. Shepard changed his position, pulled a cigar out of a humidor and lit up. "Care for a smoke?"

"No, thanks. Isn't it against the law to smoke inside a public building?"

He puffed on the stogie for a few seconds, then waved the smoke away. "This is my private office and I'll do what I damn well please." He took another drag and looked Hawkman in the face. "Yes, my wife knew the Simpson family. I don't think she cared too much for the adults, but thought the kids were okay."

"So she has talked to you about them?"

"Yes, especially since you came into the picture." He placed the cheroot on the edge of an ashtray and folded his hands on the desktop. "Why does this daughter, I forget her name, want to find her mother? Surely Mrs. Simpson is dead, since she hasn't contacted those kids in all these years."

"I don't ask my clients why they want a search done. Becky Simpson hired me to locate her mother and my job is to do just that, even if it means we find her grave."

Mr. Shepard nodded. "I can understand your position. So what is it you want with me?"

"I need to fill in some blank spaces and am hoping you can help me. How long have you and your wife been married?"

He looked at the ceiling, closing one eye. "Aaah, thirteen years."

"Robin must have only been about nineteen?"

"Yep, grabbed my pretty little lady soon after she got out of high school."

"I understand you were just out of college and landed a job at this bank. So you were a few years older than her."

He chuckled. "You might say I had a silver spoon in my mouth. My grandfather served as the president here. He taught me the ropes and I moved right into his position within three years after he retired. I've been running a very profitable bank since then."

"You live in a very impressive home. I understand you and Robin moved into it shortly after you married. How'd you afford it at the time?"

Shepard narrowed his eyes. "You sure know a lot about our life?"

"It's my job."

He nodded. "I see. Fortunately, Robin had a little nest egg she inherited from her grandparents and we were able to put a down payment on the house. Then I got a loan, which wasn't hard to do with dear old grandpa at the reins." Then Shepard frowned. "What does this have to do with the Simpson case?"

Hawkman leaned forward, placing his arms on his knees. "I'm questioning everyone who knew or had any connection with the Simpsons."

"I'm not sure how my finances are anyone's business but mine."

"Any information helps."

Shepard glanced at his watch. "I hate to draw this conversation to a close, but I have a meeting in about five minutes."

Hawkman stood. "Thanks for talking to me. I appreciate it." He left the bank, flipped off his recorder, and headed for the barber shop. He arrived just before the noon crowd hit. "Hi, Mr. Barker, looks like I got here in the nick of time."

"Well, hello Mr. Casey, long time no see. And, oh, my goodness it looks like no one else has cut your hair either. Bet your pretty little wife has been giving you heck to get that wool cut."

Hawkman chuckled. "I think I'm treading on thin ice." He removed his hat and eye-patch, then sat down in the chair.

The barber draped the cloth around his neck. "Understand you're in charge of finding Mrs. Carole Simpson?"

"News travels mighty fast in this town. Who told you?"

"Elma Bradley brought Frank in for a haircut and their whole conversation evolved around you and the case."

"Did they give any opinion on whether they thought it a good idea or not?"

"They think it's bad to dig up the past. They feel it's going to cause problems for Becky Simpson."

"Why? She just wants to find her mother."

"All the old timers think foul play was involved in the disappearance of Mrs. Simpson."

"Looks like they'd want to find out."

"I think they're afraid it might somehow involve them, as you've been asking questions all over town."

"If they have nothing to hide, they shouldn't feel threatened."

"Exactly what I told them. But Frank ranted on and on. Says you're going to stir up a bumble bee hive."

"Let's hope they don't get stung. I'm not going to let anything stand in my way."

The barber chuckled as he brushed the cut pieces of hair from around Hawkman's neck. "I've got to say, getting that mop does wonders for you."

Hawkman laughed and glanced in the mirror. "Yeah, I don't even recognize myself. Not sure that's a good thing or bad." He paid, gave the man a hefty tip, slipped on his eye-patch, pushed on his hat and left.

Thinking about the conversation with the barber, he almost missed the turn to his office. He parked in the alley and headed up the stairs. It eased his mind not to see any more notes taped to the door. After opening the windows, he put on the coffee pot, then noticed the blinking red light on the answering machine.

When he punched it on, Becky's shaky voice came over the line. "Mr. Casey, this is Becky Simpson. Yesterday when you came by, I hadn't picked up my mail, and when I finally got around to it, I discovered a note, much like the earlier one, except I found the wording a little stronger. Someone other than the mailman delivered it, as there was no postage affixed. I'll bring it by your office when I get off work this evening, between five and six. If you won't be there, please give me a call on my cell phone." She recited the number. "Thanks."

Hawkman didn't like those notes going to Becky. He'd hoped, whoever was doing this, would concentrate on him. They appeared to be bolder and more dangerous than he originally thought. He figured the time had come to tighten the circle, but would first review the note she'd received. Then over the weekend, he'd make a couple more visits.

Just as he took a sip of coffee, the phone rang. He punched up the speaker phone. "Tom Casey, private investigator."

"Hello, Mr. Casey, this is Edward Barnett, Carmella's brother."

"Yes, Mr. Barnett, how can I help you?"

"Remember, I told you over the years, I had a bunch of letters from my sister?"

"Right."

"Well, I didn't sleep a wink last night, because after I found them, I started rereading and couldn't believe all the information she packed into them, so I ended up reviewing the whole batch. I think you'll find them rather interesting."

"When's a good time for me to drive out?"

"I'm heading into town in a few minutes to pick up some garden supplies. If you're going to be in your office, I'll drop off the box."

"Great. I'll be here."

Within thirty minutes, a knock sounded on Hawkman's door.

"Come in."

Ed Barnett stepped into the room. "Hi, Mr. Casey. I've got several errands to run, so can't stay."

Hawkman took the shoe box. "I'll get these back to you as soon as I go through them. Is it okay if I copy what I need?"

"Sure. And no hurry in returning the letters. I read enough last night to keep me for awhile."

"Appreciate your dropping these off. I'll stay in touch. And by the way, keep this to yourself. I don't know yet what you've read, but I have a feeling it's pretty potent stuff."

"You got that right. Don't worry, my lips are sealed."

After Ed left, Hawkman opened the box, removed the letters and sorted them by date. As he began reading the oldest, his brows raised. "Good Lord!"

CHAPTER THIRTY

*Hawkman read for a couple of hours, then flipped up his eye-*patch and rubbed his eyes. He glanced at his watch and realized Becky would be here shortly. After piling the letters back into the shoe box, he scooted it to the side, then pulled the yellow legal pad toward the center of the desk. He read through the questions he wanted to ask her.

When Becky arrived, she immediately handed Hawkman the note. "These are making me very edgy."

A dried rose slid into his hand when he opened the sheet. He arched his brows. "Did this come with it?"

"Yes. After you told me people believed my mother might be buried in the rose garden, the display of such a symbol made me very uneasy."

He nodded after reading the inscription. "I can understand why you're feeling skittish. It seems they're hitting us both. I'd hoped whoever is doing this would have targeted me, and left you alone."

She frowned. "How many have you received?"

"Enough for me to try and speed things up a bit, before they get bolder."

Her body stiffened. "What do you mean by 'bolder'?"

"I'm not sure, but be very careful and aware of what's going on around you. Keep an eye on your rearview mirrors and note any strange cars. Let the dog stay inside at all times, and make sure all the doors are locked. It's best to keep the windows downstairs closed."

She put a hand at her throat. "You're scaring me."

"That's my intention. Someone is feeling pressured. And when you corner a wild animal, it can become quite dangerous."

"Do you have any idea who's doing this?"

"I have my suspicions, but no proof yet."

"Couldn't you give me some hints?"

"No, because if I'm wrong, then I've planted a seed in your mind and you'd never trust the person again. It won't be long before the top blows."

Becky wrung her hands. "This is really getting more complicated than I ever expected."

Hawkman leaned forward. "Could you get out of town for a week or so?"

She shook her head. "Out of the question. I had to get the estate settled after dad passed away, and used up all my vacation time."

"Is there a chance your brother could stay with you?"

"No. He and his wife are expecting their first baby within the next few weeks."

He picked up a pencil and wrote on the paper. "I've got some men I might hire to keep an eye out on you and your place. I'll let you know, so you won't be alarmed at a strange vehicle in front of your house."

Becky frowned. "Mr. Casey, do your really think it's necessary for me to have a bodyguard? I think I can take care of myself."

"Do you know how to use a gun?"

She shrugged. "Well, no, but my dad always kept a shotgun in the closet, and it's still there."

He pointed a finger at her. "Don't even think about it. It could be more dangerous to you than an intruder." He scribbled some more notes on the legal pad. "I'll know within the next couple of days whether we'll truly need a surveillance crew.

"I wish you'd tell me why you're so concerned. After all, I'm paying the bill."

Hawkman drew in a deep breath. "Yes, you have the right to know. I've come across some clues indicating your mother was definitely the subject of foul play. And I'm convinced the murderer is still alive and lives in this town. I just need a little more time to collect the evidence and confront my suspect. "

Becky stared at him with fear in her eyes. "You aren't going to try and do this by yourself, are you? Shouldn't the police be involved?"

"I'll bring the police in when necessary. I've talked with the detective, and he's ready when I am."

She slumped back in her chair, and put her hands on her face. "I had no idea it would come to this."

"Neither did I, but we're too far into it to back off now."

Becky nodded. "I know. It's just hard to absorb."

"You stay alert and cautious. If anything out of the ordinary happens, call me, night or day."

She stood. "Okay. I think I better go. I want to get home before dark, and I need to stop at the grocery store."

"Before you leave. Tell me, do you have a neighbor by the name of Mavis Watkins?"

"Yes."

"How long has she been there?"

"Forever. But she has always kept very much to herself. Even to this day, I seldom see her outside."

"Is she married?"

"Widowed."

"How old is she?"

"Probably in her eighties."

"Does she appear to be alert?"

"I spoke to her shortly after Dad passed away. She seemed very sharp." She frowned. "What in the world would Mavis have to do with this whole mess?"

"Neighbors see a lot. I'll check her out and see if she's the nosey type."

"Oh, my," Becky mumbled as she left the office.

Hawkman felt rotten because he'd scared her so badly. But things were getting tense, and he knew he had to make her observant of details. He eyed the box of letters Ed had dropped off. He'd only read about half of them and already it appeared

Mr. Barnett had brought him a gold mine. Making copies of the originals, he secured them with a rubber band and planned on finishing the rest at home tonight.

After turning off the coffee urn, he wrapped a piece of twine around the box of letters and stepped out into the darkness. He climbed into the 4X4, situated the box and briefcase on the passenger seat, then turned the ignition. As he backed up, he knew something was terribly wrong. He threw on the brake, jumped out and immediately spotted the problem. "Damn!" All four tires were flat. Hitting the fender with his fist, he took a flashlight from the glove compartment, knelt down and examined each tire. Yanking the cell phone from his belt, he called a tow truck. "Hey, Max, bring me stems for four tires and your compressor. Some idiot decided to play games with my SUV."

While waiting for the service, Hawkman examined the area, looking for any clues indicating who might have done this, but found nothing. He lifted the hood, and ran the bright beam over the engine. Satisfied no tampering had been done, he slammed it back into place.

He called Jennifer and explained his dilemma. "Don't wait up for me, I have no idea how long this will take."

The tow truck finally arrived, and a big burly man with unruly blond hair, blue shirt and matching pants, stepped out of the cab. "Hey there, Mr. Casey. Haven't seen you in awhile. Course, I'm not a guy most people want to see too often." His beer belly rolled with laughter as he bent down and examined Hawkman's vehicle. "Guess you can count yourself lucky they didn't slash 'em. This shouldn't take long. Got all we need right here in the truck to get you rollin' again."

After two hours, Hawkman paid the tow truck driver, then climbed into his 4x4 and headed down the highway. Until he solved this case, he vowed not to park in the alley again. The front lot would be much safer.

By the time he arrived home, Jennifer had retired, but left on the kitchen light. A note on the cabinet told him she'd placed a foil covered plate of food in the refrigerator. He removed the cover, zapped the dinner in the microwave, grabbed some utensils out of the drawer, then balanced it all on top of the box of letters. Gingerly picking up his briefcase, he moved slowly back to his office. The plate started to slip when he stepped into the room, but he quickly dropped the briefcase on a chair and caught it with his hand. Breathing a sigh of relief, he placed the dish on the desk and started to sit down when he realized he hadn't brought a drink. "Shoot," he mumbled as he went back to the kitchen and snatched a cold beer. All that trouble and he had to make two trips any way. Settling into his chair, he dug into the pile of unread letters as he munched.

Soon, he pushed the empty dish away, but couldn't keep his gaze off the written sheets. Several hours later, he read the last one, flopped back in the chair and rubbed his hand across the stubble on his chin. "Mr. Barnett, you've just unleashed a bomb."

CHAPTER THIRTY-ONE

Hawkman intended to get up early, but not retiring until three in the morning, he figured he had a good excuse for sleeping until eight. He rolled out of bed and hit the shower. The smell of bacon frying swirled around his nose, and made his mouth water. Hurrying, he threw on a clean shirt, pulled on his jeans, and headed for the kitchen.

Jennifer stood by the stove, draping the crispy pieces across a paper towel. She glanced up and smiled. "Your reward for getting a haircut."

He laughed. "I promise to get one more often."

"Why did someone flatten all your tires? That doesn't sound good in my books. What will they do next?"

"I'm getting close to something. And I can guarantee you, I'm keeping a wary eye on things."

"How come you didn't get to bed until the wee hours of the morning." She placed a plate of bacon, eggs and toast on the counter.

He slid it toward him. "You remember me telling you about Carmella?"

"Yes." She sat down opposite him with her breakfast. "The woman who took care of the Simpson children when they were young. And has since passed away."

"Right. Her stepbrother, Ed Barnett, lives out at the Rogue Villa Manor and I'd talked with him several days ago. He brought me a batch of letters Carmella had written him after she'd been dismissed by Mr. Simpson." He raised his fork in the air. "I tell you, Hon, the stuff she wrote would curl your toes. Carmella had an uncanny sense of what was going on, and many of her accusations make a lot of sense, but I've got to verify her claims."

Jennifer had a bite of food half way to her mouth, but set it back down. "I hope you're going to tell me."

"Can't."

She narrowed her eyes. "Oh, you're so frustrating. You tell me just enough to really get me excited, then you stop. It's not fair."

He nodded. "I know, I'm mean. Eventually, everything will come out, I promise."

After breakfast, Hawkman left for Medford. Instead of going to his office, he drove toward Becky's house. When he arrived in the area, he parked in front of the neighbor's. He hoped he'd find Mavis Watkins at home this Saturday morning. He pushed the bell, heard the chimes ring, and a small voice calling, "I'm coming, hold your britches."

Several seconds later, a woman with crisp styled silver hair, neatly dressed, but bent with osteoporosis, opened the door halfway. She adjusted her glasses over her pale blue eyes and stared up at him.

"My goodness, you're tall."

He smiled. "My name's Tom Casey." He held out his private investigator shield toward her. "Are you Mavis Watkins?"

She took the identification and held it close to her eyes. "Yes, I'm Mavis."

"I'm working for your neighbor, Ms. Simpson."

"Why in the world would Becky hire a private eye?" she asked, handing back his badge.

"She wants to find her mother."

Mavis placed a hand over her mouth. "Oh, dear, I wondered when this day would come." She moved back, opening the door wide, and gestured. "Please come in."

Hawkman stepped inside. "I hope I'm not intruding."

"No, I don't have a thing planned," she said, leading him into the living room. "Make yourself comfortable. I hope you like tea. I have a pot simmering and was about to have a cup myself."

"Yes. It sounds very refreshing."

"Good. I'll be right back."

Hawkman surveyed the furnishings, and decided to sit on the couch.

When she returned carrying a tray with a very steady hand, he stood to assist, but she shook her head. "No need to help me. I'm in very good shape except for this danged ugly hump on my back. That's what I got as a result for not drinking my milk when I was a kid. Couldn't stand the taste of it then and still can't down a glass today. Have to take calcium pills now."

"You have a lovely home. How in the world do you keep it so neat?"

She wrinkled her nose. "Tried a couple of house cleaning services, but they just smear around and made things worse. So I fired them and clean it myself."

"You do a beautiful job."

"Thank you. I do have a gardener, can't do that work, too hard." She took a sip of tea. "Aah, perfect. Now what do you want to know about Carole Simpson?"

Hawkman took out his recorder. "Would you mind if I used this? It's much easier than taking notes."

"I don't mind at all. In fact, I've been wanting to unload my heart for years."

"Why haven't you talked before?"

She shrugged. "No one asked. You're the first."

"If you'll just state your name and that you've given permission to record your statement, then we'll proceed." He flipped on the instrument and set it on the table.

After an hour and a half, Hawkman left Mavis Watkins' house. He checked the side and rearview mirrors to make sure he wasn't being followed, then did a couple of switch backs to make certain. When he felt safe, he went immediately to his office, locked the door, then set up the computer to burn a CD of the recording. Once done, he gathered Carmella's letters and left again. These items were much too valuable for him to carry in a briefcase. Heading straight for the bank, he stored one copy of the recording and the original letters in his safe deposit box, and would take the rest home to store in the gun vault. What he'd learned from Mavis Watkins, combined with Carmella's letters, would crack this case wide open.

Hawkman now had enough ammunition to attack the suspects. It would be dangerous, as the news would travel fast to all those involved. He'd better make some plans for Becky's and Mavis' houses to be watched for the next forty-eight to seventy-two hours until he could wrap up all the loose ends.

Sitting in his 4X4, using his cell, he contacted Kevin Louis and Stan Erwin, two retired police officers who helped him out on occasions. The men would set up a schedule so both residences would be under twenty-four surveillance, starting tonight. He then notified Becky and Mavis, describing the men's vehicles so it wouldn't alarm them to have a strange car or truck parked in front of their home.

Once Hawkman had those two jobs out of the way, he turned on the ignition and headed for the Harris'. He'd like to speak with Lisa alone, but at this point, he didn't really care, because he planned on talking to Henry also. When he stopped in front, he noticed the gardener's parking spot stood vacant. He strolled to the door and knocked. The yippy little dog barked furiously until Lisa hushed him.

When she saw Hawkman, her eyes narrowed to small slits. "What do you want? I thought Henry told you not to bother me anymore."

"I'm a private investigator. And I don't cotton to threats."

She arrogantly threw back her head. "Well, I don't have to talk to you." And she put her hand on the door as if to slam it.

"I think you'd better, or I'll call in the police to interrogate you. They won't be as polite."

Her hand dropped from the door. "What do the police have to do with it?"

"You lied to me, Lisa. You said you didn't know Carole Simpson. How's that possible, when she stayed for over a month in your rental house."

A flash of fear crossed her face. "I don't know what you're talking about."

"Sure you do. When Carole left her husband, she told you to kick out your renters, because she was going to take up residence in the little house in your backyard." He pointed at the trailer next to the house. "And she planned on fixing that up for the children."

Lisa turned pale and grabbed the door jamb. Beads of sweat popped out on her forehead. "I don't know where you heard such a ridiculous rumor."

"It isn't gossip, Mrs. Harris. Those words came from Carole Simpson."

Her eyes grew large, she gasped, grabbed her chest and her knees buckled. Hawkman flung open the screen door, but couldn't catch her before she collapsed to the floor. He quickly called the emergency number. An ambulance arrived shortly and the paramedics worked over her for several minutes. Her eyes rolled back in her head and she groaned, but they couldn't get the woman to regain consciousness, so they rushed her to the hospital.

Hawkman went back to his vehicle. He didn't believe Lisa Harris' condition was life threatening. She did not do well under pressure and the little scene he'd just witnessed was no more than a ploy to avoid his questions. He'd expect a visit from Henry Harris as soon as he learned about his wife's encounter with the horrid private investigator.

CHAPTER THIRTY-TWO

Hawkman drove away from the Harris' home. Making sure no one trailed him, he made some unexpected turns, then finally headed for the Rogue Villa Manor. He found Edward Barnett in the back area clipping rose bushes. When Hawkman approached, Ed greeted him with a big smile.

"Hi, Mr. Casey. Didn't expect to see you so soon."

"Do you have a minute?"

He pointed toward a shaded area with a table and benches. "Sure do. Let's go over there out of the sun."

Ed grabbed some lemonade, and they strolled toward the cooler spot. "Did you have a chance to read Carmella's letters?"

"I read them all, and they were packed with information."

Ed shot him a puzzled look. "Really. You didn't think they were just a woman's ramblings?"

"No. I talked with Mavis Watkins, the lady Carmella mentioned in the letter as Carole Simpson's only friend."

"Oh, yeah," he nodded. "I remember the name. So what'd she have to say?"

"I can't reveal the information yet. But I figured I better store the letters in a secure place, so I've put them in my safe deposit box at the bank. I'll get them back to you as soon as this case is finished."

Ed scratched his head. "Wow, they're hotter than I thought."

"Have you told anyone about these?"

He shook his head. "Nope. Didn't have any reason. No one even knew I had a sister where I lived."

"Just as a precaution, I want you to be careful. Be aware of the people around you, and if you're in town, make sure you're not being followed. If anything unusual happens, call me immediately. Do you have a cell phone?"

He pointed to his belt. "Yep. Keep it with me all the time, in case I need to call a doctor."

Hawkman handed him a business card. "Call me day or night if you see any suspicious activity or you feel like you're being watched."

"Hey, I feel like I'm involved in a murder mystery."

Standing, Hawkman patted him on the arm. "You are, Mr. Barnett. You are."

Ed's mouth dropped open as Hawkman walked across the grounds toward the doors.

When Hawkman arrived at his office, he parked in the front lot, hurried up the steps, locked the door from the inside, and slid his briefcase into the leg area of his desk. The thought had entered his mind to add the copies to the safe deposit box, but decided he might want to refer to them. He'd just keep a close eye on the precious items. Picking up the coffee urn, he took it to the bathroom, dumped the black liquid down the drain, and rinsed it out. He'd just plugged it in to brew a fresh pot, when a loud pounding sounded on the door.

It didn't take much for him to guess Henry Harris stood on the other side. He reached up to his shoulder holster, loosened the flap, turned on his recorder, threw the dead bolt and wrapped his hand around the knob. When he swung open the heavy metal door, Henry's scathing stare latched onto Hawkman's.

"I'd like to come in, Mr. Casey!"

"Of course." Hawkman stepped back, gestured toward the chair in front of his desk, but kept his gaze riveted on the man. "Have a seat."

Henry sat down and clenched his hands in his lap.

Hawkman crossed over to the coffee urn. "Like a cup?"

"No."

He poured himself a mug, then moved to his chair. "Is Lisa okay?"

"Yes, she just had a panic attack, and is home resting."

"If my questions caused such a reaction, I must have hit a nerve about an incident she didn't want to talk about."

"You frightened her." Harris stood. "I just came by to tell you not to approach my wife again or I'll call the police and report you as harassing her."

Hawkman leaned back and pointed a finger. "Mr. Harris, sit down and listen to me."

"I have nothing more to say to you."

Pulling his gun from the holster, he placed it on the desk. "I said, sit down."

A flash of fear crossed Henry's face. "What are you going to do, kill me if I don't?"

"No. I want you to know I'm serious. You and your wife have been lying to me all along. I don't like liars. So, I think we'd better talk."

"I don't want to discuss Carole Simpson. I had nothing to do with her disappearance and don't want to get involved."

"I'm afraid you're already in pretty deep, but I'm willing to listen to your side of the story."

Henry took a deep breath, and flopped down in the chair. "Okay, what do you want to know."

Hawkman returned the pistol to his shoulder holster and leaned forward. "When Carole Simpson left her husband, she came to your place and told you she wanted to stay in the rental house in the back. Is that right?"

The gardener nodded.

"Tell me about it."

"You must realize I cared about the Simpsons. I would have done anything for either of them. But when she asked me to kick out my renters in both the house and trailer so she could use them, it upset me. It meant I wouldn't be able to meet my monthly bills. At that time I'd just gotten started in my business and didn't have a lot of clients. The rentals helped me keep my head above water."

"Did you refuse her request?"

"I tried, but she said since she owned the home, she'd have me evicted and use my place instead. It didn't leave me much choice."

"I'm confused as to why she wanted the trailer."

"She said she wanted to fix it up for the children."

"Did she?"

"No."

"Why?"

"I'm not sure."

"Did Mr. Simpson know Carole had taken up residence at your place?"

"Yes."

"Who told him?"

"I did."

Hawkman would have sworn the man's eyes glistened with tears. "Explain."

Henry cleared his throat. "Al came home early one day while I was mowing the lawn. He called me inside and asked if I'd seen his wife. I couldn't lie to this man who'd helped me so much."

"So after you told him, what happened?"

"He came to see her several times."

"How do you know this?"

"He sometimes parked in front of my house, and I recognized his car."

"How long did he stay on these visits?"

Henry shrugged. "I'd say not more than thirty minutes each time, but I only saw him in the evenings when I returned from work."

"Did Lisa ever see Mr. Simpson come by?"

"Yes. He and Lisa's brother went in to see her one day. They had the papers for Carole to sign over the property."

"Did Lisa and Carole visit during the day?"

"Never. They didn't get along."

"How many visitors came to see Carole while she lived at your place?"

"None that Lisa or I saw.

"Did you say Mrs. Simpson stayed there for a month or more?"

"Yes. I don't remember the exact dates."

"Where did she go after she left the apartment?"

He shrugged. "I don't know. She just disappeared one day, and left some of her belongings."

"What do you mean?"

Henry screwed up his mouth. "It looked like there'd been a struggle. One of the chairs had a broken leg, and there was stuff strewn all over the floor. Her clothes still hung in the closet, and she'd left her make up kit in the bathroom. It appeared she left suddenly."

Hawkman frowned. "You never heard any noises or screams?"

He shook his head. "Nothing."

"Did you call the police?"

"No, I called Mr. Simpson."

"How come?"

"If I'd called the police, what would I have told them? They'd have thought me crazy."

"So how did Al take the news?"

"He told me not to worry, Carole Ann was fine, but she wouldn't be coming back. He'd pick up her belongings and car within the next few days. I just figured they'd patched up their differences."

"How could she have left without one of you seeing her. You said her car was still there, so she had to leave with someone out the front. It's the only way out."

"Not back then. The alley was open until they constructed the big building. The City had to block the ends, because people were using it at a shortcut to get to the next street."

"So why didn't you come forward and tell your story when Carole Simpson never showed up again?"

He shook a finger at Hawkman. "Look, Mr. Casey, I've told you more than I should. The police never got involved with Carole Ann's disappearance. I figured Mr. Simpson knew her whereabouts. It just wasn't any of my business."

"How come you had the privilege of calling Mrs. Simpson, Carole Ann? I understand she hated her middle name and insisted she be called only Carole."

"Remember, I've known them for many years. Mr. Simpson always called her Carole Ann, so I just naturally picked it up."

"What do you think happened to Mrs. Simpson?"

Henry stood. "If you really want to know, I think Al Simpson killed her. Maybe unintentionally, but I think she's dead and buried in the rose garden."

"Why the rose garden?"

"Because several days after we discovered her gone, I went to take care of the Simpson's lawn and found a pile of fertilizer dumped inside the ring of roses. I usually ordered this kind of stuff for the grounds, but I'd not requested this load."

"Do you know who did?"

"Yes. I questioned Mr. Simpson and he'd seen a sale ad in the paper as quite a big savings."

"So what seemed so unusual?"

"The load is normally dumped in the front and I wheelbarrow it to the back."

CHAPTER THIRTY-THREE

Henry Harris grasp the door knob. "I've told you much more than I planned. I must say you're a good interrogator. Now, I hope you will leave my wife and me alone."

"I can't promise."

The gardener grimaced, then closed the door behind him.

Hawkman picked up a pencil and tapped the eraser on the desktop. He wondered if Mr. Harris' tale held much truth.

Suddenly, he heard the sound of gun shots coming from the parking lot. He dropped to the floor, drew his gun, then crawled to the window. After a few seconds, he cautiously peered out the corner of the glass. Below he could see a crowd gathered around a slumped body. Holstering his weapon, he dashed out the door, charged down the steps, two at a time, and ran to the fallen man.

"Someone call 911," he yelled, as he knelt beside the gardener. Hawkman quickly checked Henry's pulse and found him still alive. He noted blood running from his head, upper arm and leg; the chest area appeared free of injury. But he didn't dare move or turn him over, as a bullet could have hit his back and lodged inside the man's body. Hawkman quickly scrutinized the head injury, and cut away the shirt from the bleeding arm. Seeing both were just flesh damage, he concentrated on the leg area where he noted steady bleeding had saturated the pants. Henry let out a groan when Hawkman put pressure on the wound to slow the flow of blood. He glanced up at the crowd. "Did anyone see who did this?"

A burly looking man in a tee shirt and baseball cap stepped forward. He pointed toward one of the entries leading into the parking lot. "A white van drove in there and raced through the lot. I heard the shots, but it sped out the other exit so fast I didn't have time to see the guy firing, or the license plate." Then he motioned toward Henry's vehicle. "He was just stepping up on the running board to climb into the cab and the shots knocked him down. I'd say he was mighty lucky for backing into the parking place because his truck door took a hit." He pointed at the hole in the metal. "Probably saved his life."

Sirens blaring, the ambulance and police rolled to a halt beside the body. Detective Williams jumped out of one of the patrol cars and dashed to Hawkman's side. "When this call came through, I recognized the address, thought it might be you."

Hawkman stood and stepped out of the way of the paramedics. "It could well have been. This man's involved in the Simpson case and had just left my office."

"We're definitely encompassed now. Looks like you've just opened a case that should have been solved years ago."

"Without a body or any complaints from family, the police had no reason to get involved."

"After we talked about the missing woman, my curiosity got the best of me. So one afternoon, I went over to the building where we store old records, and weeded through the year you told me all this happened. I didn't find a thing on Carole Ann Simpson. You'd have thought someone would have filed a missing person report."

Hawkman hooked his thumbs in the front pockets of his jeans. "Strange isn't it?"

"Yep, mighty weird." Williams gestured toward the figure on the gurney, just as the paramedics slammed the doors. "What's his name?"

"Henry Harris. The Simpson's gardener"

Williams jerked his head around. "You're kidding."

The ambulance rolled toward the street with their lights flashing. Once they hit the traffic, the sirens sounded.

The detective gave orders to the officers to question the people who witnessed the episode, then turned toward

Hawkman, "Meet you at the hospital." He jumped into the patrol car with his assistant and they drove away.

Hawkman dashed up to the office, washed the blood stains off his hands, grabbed the briefcase and headed out the door. He jumped into the SUV and squealed out of the parking lot. When he got to the hospital, Detective Williams sat in the waiting room. Hawkman walked over and stood in front of him. "How serious are Harris' wounds?"

"Don't know yet. But the paramedics don't think they're life threatening."

"Has anyone contacted his wife?" Hawkman asked, as he paced in front of the detective.

"Yeah, she should be here any minute." Williams glanced up at him. Would you light somewhere; you make me nervous."

Hawkman grinned. "Sorry. Got a lot on my mind."

"Yeah, I gathered. You not only have an attempted murder on your hands, but now you have to cope with the cops. Any ideas who did this?"

Shaking his head, Hawkman sat down next to the detective. "I have an idea or two, but I'm not really sure about anything. Got more probing to do."

"Is the younger Miss Simpson in danger?"

"Could be. I've got my men watching her place and the neighbor's around the clock."

Williams frowned. "What's a neighbor got to do with this mess?"

"She's lived there forever and told me about a lot of happenings that surrounded the Simpson house some fifteen years ago."

"How come she's just telling about it now?"

"No one ever asked back then."

The detective grimaced. "Not good news for the department."

"It's not your fault. You weren't in charge at that time. Just one of those episodes that got swept under the rug."

Both men looked up when they heard Detective Williams'

name called over the intercom. He got up and hurried toward the two people standing in front of the receptionist's desk. Hawkman immediately recognized Lisa Harris hanging on the arm of another woman he didn't know. He decided to hang back and let the officer handle this situation; he didn't need Mrs. Harris having a panic attack in the hospital lobby.

"Who would shoot my husband?" Lisa cried in a shrill voice, as the detective approached.

Williams put up his hands to calm her. "Mr. Harris is going to be all right. Let's go sit down until they call us." He took her elbow and guided her toward a row of isolated seats.

When they moved out of Hawkman's hearing range, he watched Lisa's body language, and could almost tell her responses as the detective asked her pertinent questions. Lisa Harris did not seem dumb, but appeared oblivious to what went on right under her nose. Hawkman suspected she actually told the truth to the best of her knowledge. A very poor witness.

The intercom again boomed the detective's name along with that of Lisa Harris. The woman who'd accompanied her remained seated as the two headed toward the desk. Hawkman also wanted to get in on the initial questioning of Henry, so he rose from his chair and followed. It appeared Lisa didn't sense his presence until they scurried onto the elevator and she turned around.

Letting out a gasp, she put a hand to her mouth. "What the hell's he doing here?"

"You know Mr. Casey?" Williams asked.

"Yes. He's harassed me continuously." She glared at Hawkman with narrowed eyes and shook her fist in the air. "This is all your fault."

Hawkman remained silent.

"Calm down, Mrs. Harris," the detective said. "Let's talk to your husband before putting the blame on anyone."

When they entered the room, a nurse and doctor stood at Henry's bedside. The doctor held out his hand. "Detective Williams, I'm Doctor Calgary. We have a victim with three gunshot wounds. The head, shoulder, and lower leg. His injuries are not life threatening and he should have full recovery.

We extracted one bullet from the leg and have it for your investigation."

"Thank you. Is Mr. Harris feeling well enough to talk?"

"I doubt he'll be coherent for a few more hours. They just brought him up from the recovery room and he's still groggy."

Lisa waddled up to the side of the bed and stared at her husband's bandaged shoulder. "How long will it before he can garden again?"

The doctor gawked at her like she'd just come from another planet. "Probably six to eight weeks, maybe even longer."

"Oh, my. We won't have a paycheck coming in for two months. We'll starve."

The doctor shook his head and walked out of the room.

CHAPTER THIRTY-FOUR

Lisa twisted her head around, and fastened a stare on Williams and Hawkman. "I'd appreciate it, If you two would give me a few minutes of privacy with my husband."

Williams raised a hand. "No problem, Mrs. Harris. But I don't think he's up to answering questions." And they headed for the door.

"Wait!" she called. "I need to get my husband's truck. Do either of you know where it is?"

Hawkman turned and faced her. "Yes. I'll be glad to drive you over." He glanced at Williams. "That is, if the police are through with it."

"Why would they want his pickup?" she growled.

Williams interrupted. "I'm sure my men are through examining the vehicle and the area, so I'll make sure you can take it home." He moved forward and pointed at Henry. "You better first check and see if he has the keys."

She pulled open the drawer next to his bed, examined the small closet, then raised her arms and dropped them to her side. "His clothes aren't here. What do I do now?"

Williams spoke with firmness. "Just relax. He might have had them in his hand when he fell. I'll find them for you."

She breathed a sigh of relief and sat down in the chair next to the bed. "Thanks."

Before the men could get out the door, she called to them again. "Would you tell Ida May she can go home. I'll call her later."

"Will do," the detective said.

As they walked down the hall, Williams gave a whistle and glanced at Hawkman. "I think she's right at the edge of having a breakdown. She's a nervous wreck."

Hawkman nodded. "I agree, or else that's her nature. She's had the same attitude ever since I met her. Her dog's got it too."

The detective threw back his head and laughed. "They say a pet takes on the characteristics of its master."

Hawkman nodded and chuckled.

"I'm going to hunt down Mr. Harris' clothes and see if his truck keys are with them. If not, I'll call my men to see if they happened to find them. Why don't you go down and tell the poor lady who brought the bag of nerves to the hospital, she can leave now."

"I can do that. How long will you be staying?"

"Until I can talk to Mr. Harris. After you've taken his wife to the truck, come on back and we'll see what we can get out of him."

The detective located Harris' clothes and the only thing they had in the vault was the man's wrist watch and billfold. He contacted his men, found they'd finished the examination of the area, and one of the officers had found the truck keys on the ground next to the vehicle. Williams released the pickup, then gave instructions for one of the men to wait for Hawkman and Mrs. Harris with the keys.

They met back at Henry's room, where Mrs. Harris hadn't moved from the chair, but tapped her foot in an irritable fashion. "Well, did you find them?"

Williams handed her the bag of clothes, and the smaller sack of personal items. "I signed these out for you. You'll have to bring Mr. Harris fresh clothes when they discharge him. These have been cut away, so they're really no good."

Her mouth dropped open. "Why in the world did they have to cut up a perfectly good pair of pants and shirt?"

Hawkman ran a hand across his mouth, stifling a grin. "To keep from injuring the victim, it's easier to cut away the garments."

She stood and turned the pockets of Henry's pants inside out, then glanced at the detective with an agitated expression. "The keys aren't here."

"One of my officers found them beside the pickup. He'll be waiting for you."

She stuffed the pants back into the plastic bag, lumbered past the two men toward the door. "Well, let's go, Henry hasn't said a word."

Hawkman shrugged and followed her out.

When they reached Hawkman's office parking lot, Lisa spotted her husband's truck, and scrutinized the area. "What the hell was Henry doing here?"

"He came to see me." Hawkman pointed toward the donut shop. "My office is above the pastry store."

She narrowed her eyes and gave him a murderous look. "Someone probably followed him over here. If my Henry dies, I'm holding you accountable."

"What does Henry know that would endanger his life?"

"Probably a lot," she mumbled.

A patrol car sat next to the Harris vehicle. As soon as the officer saw them, he jumped out and approached the SUV.

"Hello, Mr. Casey. Here are the keys to the pickup."

"Don't give them to him; give them to me," Lisa snapped, holding out her hand.

She yanked the key ring from the young man and proceeded to slide out of the 4X4 before Hawkman could get around the vehicle to hold open the door. "These are the most horrible cars in the world," she complained. "They're too high off the ground. A person could kill themselves just getting in and out." Her feet finally hit the ground and she let out a loud groan. "I've probably injured my insides." She staggered toward her husband's truck, then let out a yelp. "Oh, my word, there's a hole in the door. Henry's not going to be happy about this."

"It probably saved his life," Hawkman said, as he took the keys from her hand, unlocked the driver's side and helped her inside. "I'm assuming you've driven this truck before?"

She rolled her eyes. "Many times. Stand back, I'm going home." Slamming the door, she started the pickup and drove away.

He watched until she turned the corner and disappeared from sight.

"Man, she's something else," the young officer said, as he climbed into the patrol car.

"Yep," Hawkman said, strolling back to his SUV.

He arrived back at the hospital and entered the Harris' room to find Williams nodding in the chair. His head jerked up each time his chin hit his chest. Hawkman quietly slipped into a chair against the wall, knowing the detective needed any nap he could catch.

Thirty minutes passed before the nurse came in to check on her patient. "Mr. Harris, it's time to wake up." She fiddled with his covers, and gently tried to move him.

He finally sputtered a few words of profanity. "My arm and leg hurt like hell."

"If you'll wake up, I'll give you something to help." She glanced over at the detective, who'd come alive, and winked.

"Okay, I'm awake," Harris groaned.

"You have some visitors who'd like to talk to you. I'll be back in a few minutes with medication to help the pain."

Henry blinked several times and gazed at Williams. "Who are you?"

The detective stood and took a step closer to the bed. "Hello, Mr. Harris. I'm Detective Williams from the Medford police. Someone shot you and we're trying to find out who. You have any ideas?"

Harris shook his head. "No."

About that time, Hawkman moved to the foot of the bed and Harris' eyes grew wide. "What's he doing here?"

"You were shot outside my office. By the time I got to you, the perpetrator had disappeared. Who knew you were coming to see me?"

"I didn't tell anyone. I just decided to come at the spur of the moment."

"Has anyone threatened you?"

Henry swayed his head back and forth very slowly. "No."

"Do you know anyone who drives a white van?" Williams asked.

"No."

"Did you ever think about filing a missing person report on Carole Simpson?" Hawkman asked, shifting closer to the side of the bed.

"Yes, but I never did."

"Did you discuss it with anyone?"

"I don't know. Probably several people. We were all concerned, but no one had the guts to do it."

"Who's 'we'?"

"Bradleys, Carmella Jones, Kregors and probably a couple more. I can't think good right now."

"I didn't think you people socialized."

"We weren't close friends. Just knew each other on sight. We were all worried, but to tell you the truth, most of them were frightened of Al Simpson. They figured he'd evict them. And no one wanted to lose their home. I knew he wouldn't kick me out."

"Because you saved his life?"

"Yeah."

"How'd you save Al Simpson's life?"

"I don't want to talk anymore. Could one of you get that nurse back in here. I need a pain pill."

CHAPTER THIRTY-FIVE

Hawkman and Williams left the room and went to the parking lot.

The detective leaned against his car. "I don't get it."

"What's that?" Hawkman asked.

"Why he wouldn't tell us how he saved Al Simpson's life."

"He avoids the answer every time I ask. You'd think a man would be proud of the fact he saved a person from death." Hawkman rubbed the back of his neck. "I have a suspicion it involved something shady."

"Yep, it appears as such. But what?"

"I wish I could tell you. It occurred long before Carole Simpson disappeared."

"Really? So you don't think the incident is involved in the case you're working on?"

Hawkman shook his head. "No. Henry's been in the picture as long as Becky can remember. And oddly enough, she doesn't care for Harris, but won't fire him. She says it was her dad's wish to see to it the man always has a job."

"You mean he never told his daughter how the man saved his life?"

"No."

"These are a bunch of strange people you're dealing with," the detective said, shaking his head as he climbed into the patrol car. "We'll keep an eye out for the white panel truck. Let me know if anything pops up."

Hawkman held up a hand. "Wait."

Williams rolled down the window. "Yeah?"

"I wonder if it would be a good idea to have an officer guarding Harris' door? He'll probably only be there tonight, but the assassins know by now they didn't get him, and may try again."

The detective looked pensive for a moment. "You're probably right." He glanced at the officer driving the patrol car. "Jim, I want you to stand guard duty. I'll get some one to relieve you in a few hours. Hawkman can drop me off at the station."

He and the officer climbed out of the car. Williams followed Hawkman to his vehicle and the policeman headed for the hospital entry.

Once they were in the SUV and driving toward the station, Hawkman glanced at the detective. "I think you made the right decision. This man may be our only clue to Carole Simpson's disappearance. Somebody doesn't want him talking."

"You think he killed her?"

At first, I thought so, but not after today. I think he knows who did, and that's why someone's after him.

"You have any ideas?"

"I've got a few suspects in mind, but need to weed them out. I'll let you know. There is one thing you could do that I can't."

"Oh, yeah, what?"

"It'll probably take a subpoena. I'd like to find out how LaVonne Adkins retrieved money from a bank account."

"Who's this woman? Is she connected to this case?"

"Yes. It's a long story, and I'm sure she used an alias. And if I'm right, she never appeared in person to do a withdrawal."

"I'll need the account number and name of the bank."

"It's at the office. I'll give you a ring as soon as I get there."

I won't be able to get on it until Monday, that is, if nothing major happens in the city."

"That'll be fine. Thanks, I appreciate it."

Hawkman dropped Williams off at the front of the station, then pulled into one of the parking slots and put a call into Kevin, who had the surveillance duty at Becky's house. "Hi Kev, how's it going?"

"Nothing suspicious so far."

"No white vans?"

"Are we supposed to be looking for a special make?"

Hawkman quickly related what had happened during the afternoon. "So keep an eye out for such a vehicle."

"That's quite a story. Wonder if they were after you?"

"I don't think so. I feel Henry Harris was definitely the target. He knows more than he's telling. And it goes way back, making this case very difficult to crack."

"I'll pass the word to Stan when he relieves me."

"Sounds good. I'll check in with you periodically. Anything occurs, let me know immediately."

"Will do."

Hawkman hung up and pulled onto the street. Since Robin Shepard didn't live far from the police station, he decided to drive by. In fact, he'd also swing by Bradley's. Approaching the Shepards' mansion, he noted the garage door opening, as a sleek pearl colored BMW turned into the driveway. He slowed, then pulled to the side of the road and reached into the glove compartment to pull out a pair of binoculars. The light in the garage made it easy for him to focus on the subject. As she stepped out of the driver's side, he noted she had her blond hair tucked under a bright red hat, and wore a white dress with some sort of a black design, cinched at the waist by a red ribbon belt. Her high heeled shoes matched her headgear. She opened the trunk while a couple of kids climbed out of the back seat and gathered around her as she handed them packages to carry inside.

Soon the garage door slid down, and Hawkman dropped the glasses from his face. The three car garage appeared vacant except for the Beamer. Douglas obviously wasn't home.

He drove away and headed for the Bradleys'. Circling the block, he noted no white vans in the vicinity, and eased by the house. The windows glowed with lights, and all looked peaceful.

Hawkman drove to his office, and immediately called the detective, giving him the name of the bank and number of Al Simpson's and LaVonne Adkins' joint account. "I'm sure you've run a check on the car rental agencies to see if anyone had rented a white van."

"Yep. And I just got the report that one of my officers discovered where a privately owned place rented one during the time frame of the shooting. Unfortunately, the company washed, and vacuumed it, then turned around and rented the vehicle again within a few hours."

"Who leased it?"

"A man called Alex Short. I'm sure it's a fake name. He paid cash, so we have no other information."

"I thought they were required to take down the data from the driver's license or credit card."

"Normally, yes. But this is some rinky, dink operation. More than likely, they were slipped cash under the table. I have a feeling this company's going under. Too many infractions on the books."

"It sure isn't helping us; that's for sure."

"I'll see what I can find out about this account. Hopefully, I'll have better luck, and get back to you Monday afternoon."

"Sounds good."

Hawkman had no more than hung up when it rang, he punched on the speaker. "Tom Casey."

"Hello, Mr. Casey, this is Becky."

"Everything okay?"

"Yes. After all, I have a bodyguard right outside."

"Don't let those guys bother you. They're for your protection."

"I have to admit, it does make me feel better. I'm sorry to call you so late, but I just heard from Lisa Harris."

"What did she want?"

"She screamed at me about her husband getting shot outside your office, and demanded I fire you immediately."

"Is that what you want to do?"

"Of course not. I'm just amazed someone would go after Henry."

"I'm trying to find the answer myself."

"Why would he hold back information?"

"Because he knows his life is in danger. The person who did away with your mother is alive and living nearby. They're keeping a sharp lookout on the people who know anything and will dispose of them if they talk."

Becky gasped. "How many are involved?"

"Right now, your guess is as good as mine. But I suspect four or five. So be careful what you say to anyone. I'm sure the word will get around with Henry in the hospital, and those who are guilty will clam up for sure."

"What about my neighbor, Mavis?"

"My men are aware of her involvement and are watching her too. In fact, they may follow you, so don't be alarmed if you see them tailing your car. You'll recognize their vehicles."

"Oh, dear Lord. If this doesn't come to a conclusion soon, there could be a blood bath of innocent people."

CHAPTER THIRTY-SIX

Hawkman hung up after Becky's call, and suddenly detected the low rumble of an idling engine. He knew the small shopping center had closed for the night. Why would someone be in the area now? He flipped off the lights, moved to the side of the window and studied the parking lot.

Sounds can be deceiving, especially if you're not paying attention. Not wanting to turn the lights back on, he pulled his gun from his shoulder holster, and picked up his briefcase from the desktop. He opened the door a few inches and frowned at the full moon. The brightness of the night wouldn't make it simple for him to slip out undetected.

He crouched, eased out the door, then closed and locked it behind him. His pistol poised, he practically crawled down the steps, hiding below the banister and keeping an eye on the alley. When he reached the ground, he quickly twisted behind the staircase next to the donut shop. He stayed close to the fronts of the stores and made his way in the shadows until he came in line with his SUV parked under the light. "Not good," he said under his breath.

He searched the lot and spotted a car sitting at the far end under a large oak. He swore he saw a movement on the driver's side. He glanced up at the sky and noticed a large cloud about ready to drift in front of the moon. It might at least distract the person long enough for him to get to his vehicle. And to think he thought parking under the street light would be safer. So much for hindsight.

The minute the sky blackened, Hawkman made his move and dashed for his vehicle. Fumbling for his keys in his pocket, he finally got the door unlocked and thanked himself for adjusting the interior light so it wouldn't go on. He threw the valise onto the passenger side and jumped in, revved up the engine and screeched out of the lot. The parked car threw on its headlights and pursued.

Hawkman decided his cowboy hat might prove to be a perfect target. He snatched it off his head and tossed it onto the seat. Scrunching down so he had some protection from the head rest, he drove one-handed toward the freeway, his other gripping the weapon. He didn't like the idea of being in a residential area in case a gun battle insued. Keeping the figure in the car in his sight through the mirrors, he noticed a hand coming out the window, and prepared for the shot.

He felt the impact on the frame of the vehicle and decided now was the time to call 911. Giving his location and destination, he described the car and reported its make. Another shot rang out, shattering the back window. He feared if they hit the tires or gas tank, he might be in a bit of a pickle. Driving erratically, he hoped to distract the shooter from hitting any vital area. Suddenly, the car sped up and rammed his rear end, sending him swerving dangerously close to a big tree. He managed to correct the steering and only scraped the front right fender without an impact.

He continued driving when another shot rang out as the vehicle bashed into the SUV again. Hawkman wondered what kind of front grill could take those hits without crinkling? About the time he could see the freeway ramp in the distance, he heard sirens in the background. Glancing into the rearview mirror, he spotted the car veer to the left, and almost turn over as it made a sharp turn around a corner. When he got within a block of the ramp, he could see where a patrol car had blocked the entry. Hawkman pulled to the shoulder, while another police vehicle with sirens blaring pulled alongside.

The officer jumped out, his gun poised and ran toward him. "You okay?"

Hawkman holstered his pistol, and climbed out. "Yeah. Did you get the guy?"

"Unfortunately, we didn't even see him." He eyed the broken glass on the SUV. "But I can certainly see the damage he caused."

Hawkman reached into the cab and grabbed his hat. "I didn't want to call in until the guy fired the shots. He might not have done anything, which would have been a waste of your time. Unfortunately, it proved to be too late."

The police took the report and asked what kind of car the shooter drove.

"A light brown Hummer. It had a front end on it like a tank. I concentrated on staying on the road. Couldn't read the front license plate, it was all bent. But it shouldn't be too hard to track down. There aren't that many Humvees around."

The officer glanced up from writing. "You'd be surprised how many are up in the hills. People keep them at their ranches to climb around the steep inclines. And unfortunately, they seldom buy them in this area."

Hawkman raised a brow. "Really? Interesting to know. I figured they were pretty expensive."

"They cost the bucks, but it's amazing how many people purchase them on time, just for the prestige of owning one."

Hawkman examined the back of his vehicle and decided it had too much damage to risk driving home. He called a tow truck to take the SUV to the garage. When they reached the mechanics, naturally everyone had gone home and the place had locked up for the night. Hawkman used his cell phone to have a rental car delivered to the station. While waiting, he unloaded the SUV and placed his things on the concrete. He kept a wary eye out for the Hummer, but saw no sign of it.

The car rental agency finally arrived with his vehicle, a bright red Buick LaCrosse.

He sure didn't like the color, but signed the papers, then piled his gear into the trunk and slipped into the driver's seat. It had been a long day and he could feel the fatigue setting in as he drove toward home. Jennifer wouldn't believe what he'd experienced.

Hawkman turned off toward Copco Lake, went over the railroad tracks and let out a groan as he spotted what looked like the Hummer parked in the driveway near the old stagecoach station. He quickly removed his cowboy hat and tossed it on the seat. They wouldn't know the car, but they might recognize his silhouette.

Driving by at a normal speed, he passed, then kept an eye on the rearview mirror to see if they followed. If they had, he would have called the police. He breathed a sigh of relief when it didn't pull onto the road, but he didn't like the fact, if this was the same vehicle, they knew where he lived, and probably figured on running him off the road on one of the steep inclines. He pushed the accelerator a little harder; the sooner he got past the sharp curves, the safer he'd feel.

When he finally reached his driveway without incident, he pulled into the garage, grabbed the briefcase, and hurried to get inside the house. Once in the kitchen, he checked out the window to be sure no one had followed. At this time, he wasn't sure what to expect, but he knew they were after him.

He went through every room, checked the windows, drew the drapes, secured the laundry room door and locked the slider. Once he had everything covered, he opened the lid of the alarm box in the coat closet. Not realizing he'd awakened Jennifer, he stepped back after setting the controls and almost jumped out of his skin.

"My gosh, don't walk up on me like that. You scared me half to death."

She frowned. "What's happened? You wouldn't be taking all these precautions if you hadn't had a close call."

"Yeah, a little incident occurred today."

"I don't believe it was little."

He twisted his hand back and forth. "Well, maybe medium."

"Hawkman, it's past midnight. Don't play games with me."

Putting his arms around her, he pulled her close. "I'd love to do just that."

She gently pushed him away and gave him a tiny smile. "Quit changing the subject. We can play games later." Cocking her head, she gave him a quizzical look. "Where's your hat?"

"In the car."

"Car?"

"It's a long story and I'm beat. You sure you want to hear about it tonight?"

"Yes. I'll get us a glass of wine and you can tell me the whole saga."

"Wine? Why wine?"

"It will relax you and it's good for the body."

He took a sip of the dark mixture and smiled. "Hey, this isn't bad at all."

They settled in the living room and by the time Hawkman finished his story, Jennifer had scooted to the edge of her seat, giving him her undivided attention. "I don't like the way this case is going. It's becoming right down dangerous."

He nodded. "Yeah, I know. It worries me. I'm just praying my guys stay alert in front of Becky's and Mavis' house. I don't want these killers to go after them. They're much more vulnerable."

"Didn't you tell me you had some good ideas about who murdered Carole Simpson?"

"Yes."

"Why haven't you gone after them?"

"I hoped to get a few more facts, but I think you're right. It's time to tighten the noose."

CHAPTER THIRTY-SEVEN

Monday morning, when Hawkman reached the office, he called Detective Williams on the speaker phone. He told him the story about how the rear end of his SUV got busted and how he thought he'd later spotted the Hummer parked in a driveway on his way home. If it was the villain, he apparently didn't recognize the rental car and never pursued.

"The report came across my desk this morning. I hoped you'd call. You okay?" Williams asked.

"Yeah, just a bit rattled."

"I can understand. We're keeping our eyes out for the Hummer. Also, I'm getting ready to go talk to the bank. They might let me see those records you wanted without a subpoena. I'll let you know."

"Good. Right now, I'm going to go do a little digging in the dirt. Are your lab guys available if I come across any bones?"

"Just give me a ring and we'll be there in a flash."

"Thanks. Talk to you later."

After hanging up, Hawkman punched in Becky's cell phone number. She answered quickly.

"Hello, Mr. Casey. I'm almost afraid to ask what you need."

"I won't keep you long as I know you're at work. But I'm going to start pushing hard. They're coming after me with both barrels. I got shot at several times yesterday."

"Oh my Lord, were you hurt?"

"No. But it's time to put on the squeeze and I need your permission to do some digging around your rose garden."

Becky sighed. "Do you really think my mother's buried there?"

"I'm not sure, but it's time to find out. Things are getting too dangerous, and I need to bring the killers to the front."

"Of course, you have my okay. There's a small shed in the corner of the yard full of garden tools. I'm sure there's a shovel."

"Thanks. I'll keep you posted."

Hawkman had an errand to run first, and surveyed the parking lot from the window, then quickly checked the alley as he went down the stairs. Seeing nothing suspicious, he hopped into the rental car and headed for the courthouse. He again greeted familiar faces, then made his way to the computer room. Taking a vacant machine, he put in the information and waited patiently as it fed into the data base. Soon, what he needed popped up on the screen. He jotted down the facts, which verified his suspicions.

He drove back to the office and changed into an old pair of jeans and boots he kept there for dirty jobs, then stuffed leather gloves in his back pocket. On the way to Becky's house, he remembered when Henry, hoe in hand, caught him in the side yard the day he went over to examine the area. He thought it a bit odd since the Simpsons' had all the gardening tools on the property. Of course, he mustn't be too judgmental; people tend to have favorite implements.

When he arrived at the house, he chatted with Stan who had the morning shift.

"Hey, where'd you get the new set of wheels? Nice car."

Hawkman laughed. "Yeah, I guess. If you like to stand out in the crowd." He gave a quick rundown of the last evening's events, then told him of his plans to dig up the rose garden. "It might be a long shot, but I've got to see for myself."

"Want some help?"

"No, you stay right out here. Keep an eye out for a Hummer and a white van. Whoever is after us, is dangerous. And I sure wouldn't want anything to happen to Mavis."

"Kevin and I decided to work together. He's in town keeping an eye on Becky while she's at work and I'm watching

Mavis. We've taken money out of our own pockets to have a colleague of ours take the graveyard shift while we catch a few winks."

"Hey, that's good of you guys. I appreciate it very much. This case is getting sticky and it's going to pay to keep an eye out on these gals."

"That's what we thought."

"Well, I better get to my job, I'll talk with you later."

Scruffy greeted Hawkman at the gate with a ball in his mouth and bounced around like a young pup. "My goodness, boy, someone fed you jumping beans for breakfast," Hawkman said, chuckling, as he walked toward the small shed at the corner of the yard.

It didn't surprise him to find the tools neatly arranged along the walls. He immediately spotted the hoe Henry had carried in that day. The man appeared definitely worried about something. But why would someone try to kill him if he'd been the murderer of Carole Simpson. Things just didn't fit.

He put on the leather gloves, then placed a short and long handled shovel into a wheelbarrow and rolled it to the rose garden. He removed the small round table and chair from the center and placed them on the outside of the ring. Scruffy sat on the edge of the garden watching.

Hawkman rested the long handled shovel against the table, took the short one and began lifting the soft soil from the center of the plot, turning it over slowly. The hours ticked away as the dirt pile grew and the hole became wider and deeper. He tried to spare the bushes any damage, but it might be impossible as the plants were old and the roots had entwined around one another. Scruffy soon moved to the shade of the tree, but kept an eye on the progress, sometimes cocking his head back and forth. When the dog bounced in front of him and a shadow suddenly crossed the area, Hawkman looked up to see Becky standing there, gnawing on her lower lip.

"I had to come by on my lunch hour to see if you'd found anything."

He wiped the sweat from his brow and took a gulp of the bottled water he'd brought. "Nothing so far. I'm trying not to injure the rose bushes, but they may suffer some shock with the exposure to their root base. The ground gets harder the deeper I dig."

"Please, don't worry about the plants. If they're concealing a body, I could never look at the flowers in the same light again."

The gate slammed and a voice boomed. "What the hell's going on here?"

Becky jerked around to find Henry, his arm in a sling, coming toward her. "What are you doing out of the hospital?"

"They released me today." He stepped forward and glared at Hawkman. "I asked a question."

"I don't have to answer, Mr. Harris. Ms. Simpson owns this property, not you."

Henry turned toward her and waved his good hand at the dirt pile. "Why are you letting him ruin the rose garden? It will take me months to get the bushes back in shape."

Becky took him by his good elbow and led him toward the gate. "Mr. Harris, you go on home now. I'll take care of this situation."

He yanked away from her. "You don't know what you're doing."

She looked him in the eye. "Yes, Mr. Harris. I know exactly what I'm doing."

Kevin and Stan had moved inside the yard.

"Need any help?" Kevin asked.

"I don't think so," Becky said. "You're leaving of your own accord, aren't you Mr. Harris?"

Henry grimaced as he brushed past the two men and limped out the gate. "I'm going."

Hawkman glanced up at Becky. "I'm not sure what to think about him. One minute I think he's innocent, the next I'm not sure."

Becky gazed toward the gate. "He always seemed so fond of my Mother. He's hard to decipher." She then glanced at her watch. "I've got to get back to work. Give me a call if you find anything."

He nodded and waved a gloved hand, then started digging again. After about another hour, Hawkman felt the shovel hit something, so he bent down and gently scraped away the soil with his gloved hand. When he discovered it was a bone, he dared not tug on it, or remove it from the soil as he might destroy some evidence. But he knew from what he could see this did not belong to an animal carcass.

Climbing out of the hole, he dusted off his clothes, removed the gloves and reached for the cell phone he'd placed on the small table. "Hello, Williams. You better send your forensic crew over to Becky Simpson's house. I think I've found some human remains."

CHAPTER THIRTY-EIGHT

Hawkman phoned Becky. "I think you better come home as soon as possible. It appears I've found some human remains. The detective will be sending his forensic people out, and I'm sure they'd like your permission to continue digging. Not that they need it, but I think it would make their job easier."

After hanging up, he walked toward the front with Scruffy at his heels. "You stay, boy. I'll be right back."

He closed the gate and strolled over to Stan's pickup. "I'm sure I've found something besides dog bones in the rose garden. Williams is bringing in his crew. As soon as the word gets out that we're digging in this yard, you're going to have to really keep your eyes open. I'm sure Henry will see to it the people involved will know. Pass the word to Kevin. Becky will be coming home shortly, so he'll probably be on her tail."

Stan picked up his cell. "I'll contact him right now."

Hawkman headed back to the side yard. Scruffy met him with pleading eyes and the ball in his mouth. Laughing, Hawkman gave the dog a head scrub. "You sure know how to tug at a guy's heart." He took the ball from Scruffy and tossed it away from the rose garden. After playing with the animal for several minutes, he heard the trucks and cars pulling up front. He pointed toward the back of the house. "Okay, boy, enough play. You go lie down for awhile."

Men and women with all types of equipment flowed into the area. Cameras flashed as they took pictures of the hole before anyone even attempted to climb into it. Becky dashed into the gate and hurried toward Hawkman.

"I got here as fast as I could, but had to park in Mavis' driveway. I couldn't even get near mine with all the vans in the way." She turned and watched the activity taking place. "Fill me in."

"Not much to tell yet. They just got here."

"What'd you find?"

"A bone in the dirt. I knew it didn't come from an animal, so I decided to let the Medical Examiner's Office take over."

They drifted toward the shade and watched the crew in action. Soon Detective Williams joined them.

"Before long, we'll know more about what you found."

They watched as one of the technicians climbed down into the hole. Within a few minutes, he hopped out and approached the detective.

"Sir, this is definitely a bone of human origin. We'd like to continue and unearth the rest of the body if there is one."

Williams glanced at Becky.

She grimaced. "Tell them to go ahead."

The detective instructed the men to proceed, and they immediately hoisted a tent-like contraption over the cavity. Williams had his officers tape off the area as a crime scene, then moved back into the shade. "So, it appears your hunch panned out," he said.

Removing his hat and wiping the sweat from his brow, Hawkman nodded. "It looks that way. Now, to prove it's Carole Simpson. It will sure help if the skull is still intact. If the dental records don't work, maybe we can find a forensic artist to reconstruct the face. Maybe I'm praying for too much."

Hawkman noticed Becky walk away. Her jaw appeared clenched and her mouth turned down in a grim expression. This was a heavy ordeal for her to bear, and she didn't need to hear their morbid discussion. He watched her meander to the other side, where she could view the excavation from a different angle.

Williams continued. "Not if we can unearth the whole skeleton. We'll just have to wait and see what they dig up. If our lab doesn't have the expertise to find the answer, we'll send the evidence elsewhere." Williams pulled a couple of lawn chairs under the tree, and the two men sat down. "By the way, I talked with the bank about LaVonne Adkins."

Hawkman's attention immediately went to the detective. "My word, in all the confusion I'd almost forgotten. What'd you find out?"

"Quite interesting. When the money came in, she'd left instructions for the bank to send it to a P.O. Box."

"Didn't she have to sign some papers?"

"I thought so, and asked the same question. But it appears Mr. Simpson made the arrangements. Since all this happened many years ago, the personnel has turned over and no one remembers handling the transaction."

"Have they heard from the woman since I instructed Becky to have the bank close the account."

"Yes. The bank manager said they received a call a couple of weeks ago and the woman identified herself as Ms. Adkins. She inquired about the account, and they told her the executrix of the estate had terminated it. They haven't heard from her again."

"Do you have the Post Office box number?"

"Yes, I even checked it out. Turns out Al Simpson paid for it on a yearly basis. It's still active, and won't expire for a couple of months."

"Has anyone ever seen this woman pick up the mail?"

"No. They're too busy behind the scenes. They don't pay any attention to people going to their boxes. And she probably went in the evening when they'd all gone home."

"Sounds like another dead end."

Both men glanced at the hole. The technicians, clothed in protective gear, had gathered around the cavity. They spread out a canvas nearby on which to place the fragments. One of them entered the aperture with his equipment and began slowly carving into the ground. The work tended to be slow, but they were carefully removing sections in whole clumps of dirt, placing descriptions on how the bones were positioned beside each segment. The photographer took many pictures of each one.

A couple of hours passed and Hawkman could see bits and pieces of bone protruding out of the hunks of soil. It appeared the skeleton had been nicely preserved after all these years. He even noticed scraps of cloth clinging to the soil. Then suddenly, something strange caught his eye. He walked over, bent down and without touching, observed some of the bones. "Williams, come here and take a look." He pointed to a row. "Doesn't it appear there are three feet."

Williams frowned and studied the parts, then turned to one of the technicians. "Aren't these toe bones?"

"Yes sir. It looks like there's more than one body."

Becky put a hand to her mouth. "Oh, my God!" She slumped down in a lawn chair, and dropped her head into her hands.

Hawkman rushed to her side. "Are you okay? You need a glass of water?"

Scruffy trotted up to her and whined, then gave her a wet kiss.

She finally raised her head. "I'm fine. But I think Scruffy and I'll go inside. This is too much for me to watch."

"I understand. I don't think we'll need you for anything. If so, I'll just come and get you."

"Thanks." She stood. "Come on Scruffy, let's go."

The two headed for the back door and disappeared into the house.

Hawkman walked out to the front and talked to his men. "One of you guys could go get some rest. At the slow pace this group has to work, it will be hours before they shut down. But I do think one of you should stay out here to keep an eye on things. With all this activity, someone could get to Mavis and we'd never know it."

Since Stan had been there the longest, they decided he should go and return in six hours to relieve Kevin.

Hawkman went back to the side yard.

Becky stared out the kitchen window at the crew working over the chasm. She knew the rose bushes wouldn't survive, and really didn't care. The thought of having any more such flowers in her yard, sent chills down her back. It felt like she'd been whirled into another world. She decided she'd better call Cory tonight after he got off work, and let him know what had happened.

She wondered how many bodies they'd find in her Mother's rose garden. It all seemed like a horrible nightmare. Her gaze riveted on the man in the pit. Suddenly, she felt her knees buckling and a scream caught in her throat. Feeling she might faint, she grabbed the cabinet as the technician placed a skull on the sheet of cloth in front of him. Becky forced herself to look away, but felt tears welling. Stumbling to one of the kitchen chairs, she sat down and covered her face with trembling hands. "Quit watching," she mumbled. "Stay away from the window."

CHAPTER THIRTY-NINE

The afternoon turned to evening, and bright lights were erected around the group as they continued their work. The opening had expanded and the mound of dirt had grown. Unfortunately, most of the rose bushes had suffered badly. The forensic crew had covered some of the bones with damp cloths and plastic, placed them in a tray, then carried the container to the van.

At one point Hawkman left and returned with numerous sandwiches and soft drinks. He handed one to Kevin, then made sure Becky got one, before giving the rest to the working men and women. The crew thanked him profusely, and stopped for about thirty minutes to devour the food.

"Very good of you to bring everyone grub," Williams said, as Hawkman sat down on the patio chair next to him.

"I figured they must be hungry. These people haven't even taken a break."

Williams smiled. "They love their work, and this type of job doesn't come often. So they throw themselves into it with gusto."

"How long do you think it will take to get a report on what they've dug up?"

"It could take a month or more. But I'm putting a priority on this and we should get some basic information within a week. The more detailed stuff will take longer."

"What do you mean by 'basic'?" Hawkman asked.

The detective shrugged. "Male or female bones. Maybe the approximate age and the length of time the bodies have been buried."

"How about the cause of death?"

"Depends on how obvious it might be. Like a bullet hole in the skull or a crack from a blow. We'll just have to keep our fingers crossed. Poisoning would take much longer, as they'd have to run a lot of tests." He scrunched up the empty paper which had held his sandwich and wiped his mouth with a napkin. "By the way, how are you doing on the investigation?"

Hawkman scratched his chin. "I'm getting there." Suddenly, someone tapped him on the shoulder. He glanced up to see Kevin.

"Could you come out to the front for a moment.

"Sure." He turned to Williams. "Excuse me."

Williams waved. "No problem. I'll be here when you return."

The two men walked out the gate.

"I didn't want to stay gone from the front too long, as I've noticed some unusual traffic in the area. I've written down the makes of vehicles, license plate numbers and the time they came by."

Hawkman moved toward the glow of light coming from the back yard and glanced through the list Kevin had handed him. His gaze focused on a particular make of car. He pointed to the entry. "Do you remember if a woman or man was driving this one?"

"A woman. The rest were men. However, no Hummer or white van came by."

"I know who owns this vehicle. Good work, Kevin. Keep that vigilant eye out for the next few days. Wouldn't hurt to keep a running list. It's going to take a while for this forensic group to get any results back. Meanwhile, we have to keep watch to make sure nothing happens to Becky or Mavis."

"Will do. Thanks for the sandwich; it gave me renewed energy."

Hawkman smiled. "You're welcome. Have to keep you on your toes." When he went back into the yard, it appeared the forensic crew were loading up their gear.

Detective Williams stood beside one of the members, discussing their departure.

He soon strolled over to Hawkman. "They've unearthed two full skeletons, and don't feel there's any more. The crew is going to wrap it up tonight, but will leave the canopy up and put barriers around the area. They'll send over a couple of techs tomorrow to make sure they haven't missed anything. Then they'll fill up the hole when they're done. Unfortunately, they don't think they can save the plants."

"Tell them not to worry about the rose bushes. Ms. Simpson will probably want to redo this whole area."

"You want me to go talk with her?" Williams asked.

"No, it won't be necessary; I'll inform her about what's going on."

After everyone left, Hawkman secured the gate, then went to the front door and knocked. Becky invited him in.

"Thanks, but I'm on my way home. I hope you're feeling better. I just wanted to tell you it appears they've completed the excavation of the skeletons and will be back tomorrow to check the hole. If they don't find anything else, they'll cover it up. However, they don't think the rose bushes are salvageable."

Becky listened, hugging her waist. "How many?"

"I don't really know how many of the plants were damaged."

"No, I don't give a damn about the bushes. I meant how many bodies did they remove?"

"Oh. Sorry, didn't understand. They think there were two."

"Who in the world would be buried there besides my mother?"

"I have no idea. But I'm going to try and find out."

"When will we know more?"

"If things go right, we should know something next week; otherwise it might be a month. The detective is going to hurry it along as best he can."

"Will you please let me know the minute you hear?"

"Yes. I'll check by tomorrow." Hawkman touched the front brim of his hat. "Goodnight, Becky. Try to get some rest. This has been a trying day for all of us. My men are on watch in front of your house twenty-four hours, so you should be able to rest comfortably."

"Thank you."

Becky closed the door and leaned against it for several minutes. Tears rolled down her cheeks as she thought about her Mother's burial ground. More than likely thrown in like a rag doll, then covered by dirt. Probably by her father.

She turned and hit the wood several times with her fist. "Dad, how could you have done such a horrible thing," she cried.

Her body wracked in sobs, she slid to the floor. Scruffy went to her side and whined. He placed a paw on her leg and let out a soft bark. She reached up and put her arms around his neck. "Oh, Scruffy, I hurt so bad."

The dog nuzzled her neck.

"How I wish you could talk. I'm sure you would have all kinds of stories to tell."

After several minutes, she got to her feet, went to the kitchen, took some napkins from the dispenser on the table and blew her nose. She couldn't help but stare out the window. When the team removed the lights, it pitched the whole yard into a black spooky sight. The moonlight glistened off the aluminum poles holding up the tent and cast strange shadows across the ground. She sucked in her breath when she spotted a spider's silvery web gleaming across the front of the canopy then down to the empty hole forming a grave web. She shuddered, pulled herself away, and ran a hand down Scruffy's back. "I've got to call Cory, but first, I've got to compose myself so I can carry on a decent conversation."

She fixed herself a stiff drink, took it to the den and sat down in the lounge chair with her pet at her feet. Pulling the phone base unit closer, she punched the memory button containing Cory's number, then pushed on the speaker phone. Cory finally answered after the third ring.

"Hello."

"Cory, this is Sis, you sound out of breath."

"Yeah, I was out in the back yard with Susan when I heard the phone ringing."

"How's she doing?"

"About ready to explode. Only a couple more weeks and we'll be parents. I hope she can make it without us going crazy. So what's going on?"

Becky related the events up until this evening. "This is really more than I bargained for."

"Oh, man, Sis. I think so. You said there were two bodies, uh, skeletons they dug up? I pretty well figure, from what you've told me, one is Mom. But, who in the hell is the other one?"

"We don't know. Hopefully, we'll have some information this coming week. Or it could be a month or more."

"You be careful. Obviously, Mr. Casey thinks the murderer is still alive. They could come after you."

"Yes, he's hired a couple of men to guard me and Mavis at all times. They stay out front in their vehicles night and day."

"Mavis? What does that old lady have to do with it?"

"Oh, I forgot to tell you. Mr. Casey questioned her and I guess she gave him a lot of information. Also, remember Carmella Jones, who used to take care of us, and has since passed away?"

"Yeah."

"Well, her stepbrother had saved a bunch of letters she'd written, and gave them to Mr. Casey. I guess they were pretty revealing. He hasn't told me their contents, but I have a sneaky suspicion he knows who murdered Mom."

"Why don't they arrest the son-of-a-bitch?"

"Not enough evidence yet. But I don't think it will be much longer."

"Man, you've really and truly opened a can of worms."

"Yes, I have. But don't you think it's about time we find out the truth?"

"You're right. You've got more guts than me."

She laughed. "I'm not sure. There were days when I was ready to trash the whole thing. I'm glad I didn't, even though it's scary and emotional."

"I'm sure it is. You take care of yourself. Keep me informed."

"I will. Give Susan my love and let me know the minute she goes into labor."

"Will do."

Becky had no more hung up, when the phone rang. She pushed the speaker button. "Hello."

A gruff male voice penetrated the air. "Hello, Becky, it seems you don't take heed. Don't be surprised in the morning if you find another body in that pit in your side yard."

CHAPTER FORTY

Hawkman had turned south on Interstate 5 and had no more reached the outskirts of Medford, when his thoughts were interrupted by the cell phone vibrating against his hip. He quickly yanked it from his belt and put it to his ear. "Hello, Tom Casey here."

When he heard Becky's frantic voice, he pulled to the side of the road. "Hang in there. I'll be back to your place within thirty minutes." After he hung up, he called Detective Williams. "Got a problem; this time it sounds pretty serious." He told him about the call she'd received. "I'm heading back to the Simpson house, but I think you better send a patrol out to Henry Harris' and check on him. Might even have a guy patrol their area. Also, if you can spare the man power, it sure wouldn't hurt to have one show his presence on Becky's street. I'm going to try and settle her down. I've got a guy there, but I don't want him to be the one they throw in the pit." He listened for a few seconds. "Thanks Williams. I owe you one."

After hanging up, he pulled onto the pavement, took the next off ramp and circled back onto the freeway. "Sure be glad to have my own vehicle again," he mumbled, as he pointed the red beast toward Medford. When he parked in front of the Simpson house, Kevin hopped out of his vehicle and approached the car.

"What's going on?"

Hawkman climbed out and stood next to him. "Ms. Simpson just got another threatening call. This one I don't like at all. Keep a keen eye open tonight. I talked to Detective Williams and he might be able to spare a man to help us out."

"That explains why all of a sudden the lights went on around her house. It's lit up like a shopping mall," Kevin said.

"She's scared and I don't blame her. A lot's been going on and her nerves are bound to be on edge." Hawkman turned and headed for the front entry. "I better go talk to her and assure her everything's going to be okay."

He pushed the bell and saw Becky peek out the window, then heard the lock click. She opened the door and peered at Hawkman with wide eyes. Her hands trembled as she pulled him inside and closed the door.

"Thank goodness you're here. I'm scared to death."

"Did you by any chance recognize the voice on the phone?"

"No." She shook her head. "He sounded like the other calls. I didn't even have time to record the message, as he just said a couple of sentences, and hung up." She brushed a hand across her mussed hair. "I don't know how much more of this I can take."

"I realize it's very trying. And you being alone in the house makes it worse because you have no one to talk to. Would you consider having Mavis here in the evenings until we get this thing settled."

She glanced at him, looking a bit startled at his suggestion. "You know, I hadn't even thought about that. It might be a good idea. Especially if she's as frightened as I am."

"I don't think much would scare her. And she hasn't mentioned receiving any calls, so she isn't feeling the brunt of it like you. She's lived alone for a long time, and from what she told me, been through a lot. Why don't I go over and talk to her. If she's up to it, I'll bring her over tonight."

"I'll get the guest room ready."

Hawkman left the house, and stopped to tell Kevin what he'd suggested to Becky.

"That would make our job a little easier concentrating on just one place, especially at night."

"Let's hope the little old lady goes for it," Hawkman said, as headed for the lighted entry at Mavis'. He'd just raised his hand to punch the bell when she opened the door.

"Hello, Mr. Casey. I saw you heading up my sidewalk and your forward gait told me you had something on your mind. Come in."

Hawkman stepped into the small entry and explained to Mavis what had happened. He couldn't see leaving anything out, as this woman showed a lot of wisdom and probably figured the incidents occurring next door would someday happen. "So how would you feel about spending the evenings and nights with Becky until we get this case solved?"

"Is she game for this plan?"

"Yes, in fact, she's hoping you'll come tonight. She's already getting her guest room ready."

"Bless her heart. She's got the right to be scared." Mavis turned on her heel. "Let me get an overnight bag ready, and my gun. Won't take me but a minute."

Hawkman raised a hand. "Hold it. Your gun? I don't think that's necessary."

She laughed and pointed a finger at him. "Mr. Casey, I've known how to shoot since I was a young girl. I've won many awards in my time. And not only that, I keep up with my practicing. I go once a week to the firing range, so I'm not a body one would want to mess with."

He shrugged. "You know, Mavis, it doesn't surprise me. Bring your gun."

"No need to tell Becky I have it." She chuckled. "It might frighten her, thinking this old lady might haul off and blast her."

Hawkman escorted Mavis, with her small duffle bag full of clothes and a pistol, to the Simpson house. Becky greeted them at the front door.

"Oh, Mrs. Watkins, thank you for coming."

"Please, call me Mavis. Since we're going to be roomies for a while, we might as well act it."

Becky laughed in relief. "I'm so glad you're here."

Assured Becky was in good hands, Hawkman left. While informing Kevin what had transpired between the two women, a patrol car pulled up alongside them. The men talked a few minutes and Hawkman told the officer about Kevin's presence.

The policeman assured them he'd patrol the street frequently, then drove away.

After scrutinizing the area, Hawkman finally felt comfortable about leaving and again headed home. The thoughts of the case rumbled through his brain. Tomorrow, he'd get on the road early; there were some items he needed to check out. The pieces of the puzzle were slowly fitting together, but the one thing throwing him the most was who shared the grave with Carole Simpson? He felt in his gut it somehow tied in with this case, but couldn't be sure. It depended on the placing of the bodies, and he sure hoped the forensic team could help him solve the mystery.

The next morning, Hawkman left home before the sun came up. He drove toward Medford, but this time he turned off before hitting the city limits and headed into the hills. If his hunch panned out, he'd find the Hummer. By the time he reached the territory he'd mapped out from the information he'd gotten at the courthouse, the sun had taken over, with only a few high clouds dotting the sky.

He slowed at the calculated section and searched the landscape for a home or cabin. A short distance ahead, he spotted a good sized cottage, resting on a hill surrounded by a cover of full grown trees. He drove forward until he approached a road that appeared to lead to the house. At the corner where the long drive connected with the road stood a mailbox. The name verified he'd found the right spot. A gate blocked passage to the narrow road, but he took a chance and checked to see if it had a lock. His luck with him, he swung it open and drove up the slight hill. Going slowly, he scanned the surroundings, not sure what he'd find.

When he pulled up to the front of the place, he noticed the drapes were closed on all the windows. Before getting out of the car, he flipped up the cover on his shoulder holster, then slowly approached the entry. He knocked loudly several times and when no one answered, he tried the door, only to find it securely locked. Strolling around to the side, he studied the garage, and didn't see a window, so crossed to the other side and found none there either. But his luck held out as he moved around to the rear and found a back door. He tried the knob and it opened. Taking his gun from his holster, he cautiously stepped inside. It took a minute for his sight to adjust to the darkness and what he viewed didn't surprise him. Holstering his pistol, he quickly examined the front of the Hummer and discovered a few small dents, plus bits of paint from his SUV. That's all he needed to see. He decided to get out before someone got curious about the bright red monster parked out front. Sure enough, as he walked around the corner, he spotted a dark colored vehicle kicking up a cloud of dust as it drove toward the house.

CHAPTER FORTY-ONE

Hawkman didn't want to look suspicious, so he hooked his thumbs in the back pockets of his jeans and casually walked around gazing at the front of the house. The black pickup came to a halt and a tall thin cowboy climbed out and moseyed toward him.

"Can I help you with something?" he asked.

"You the owner?"

"No, I'm the caretaker."

"This is really a nice spread. I've been driving these hills checking out real estate, hoping to find something to buy."

The man laughed. "I'm sorry sir, but this place isn't for sale."

Hawkman shook his head. "That's too bad. It's just what I've been looking for. You know of anyone wanting to sell a cottage comparable to this one."

"No. But I know of several lots for sale in the area."

"Nope, not interested in building. I want something I can move into and enjoy immediately."

"I see your point."

Hawkman sighed. "Well, thanks for your time. Guess I'll be on my way."

Driving toward the gate, he checked the rearview mirror and exhaled a breath of relief. The caretaker didn't seem concerned and had headed for the house. If he'd been caught in the garage, his lie wouldn't have worked.

He drove to his office and parked in the lot. Passing in front of the bakery, the aroma of fresh pastries swirled around his nose. "I'm so bad," he mumbled, as he charged into the store.

"Clyde, you're going to make me fat as a butter ball. You know I'm hooked on your good stuff."

Clyde guffawed, as he placed a tray of fresh doughnuts in front of Hawkman. "Sounds like a personal problem."

Hawkman grinned. "You got that right." He pointed to a couple of the delicacies and paid the baker. When he got upstairs, he turned on the computer and plugged in the coffee maker. As soon as the hot brew finished, he sat down at the desk with a steaming mug, took a big morsel of the still warm pastry and savored the taste. He then took the mouse and clicked on the icon of the Department of Motor Vehicles. Typing in his password directed him to a secured area where he had access. He wanted to verify the license plate number Kevin had given him last night belonged to the person he thought. Taking another bite, he sipped on the coffee as the computer did its job.

Before long, the information popped up on the screen. It didn't surprise him. The noose was tightening. It still baffled him they found two bodies in the grave. A suspicion about the other body kept rolling around in his mind, but he needed more data from the forensic people. Then he'd approach Henry Harris.

The next few days passed without incident. Hawkman kept in constant contact with Becky and his men working the area. No new bodies showed up in the pit. The forensic crew had returned, gone through the hole one more time with a fine tooth comb, then removed their gear and cleaned up as promised. Unfortunately, most of the rose bushes were thrown away, and only a bare spot of soil covered most of the side yard.

Becky told him she'd not received any more threatening calls. The arrangement with Mavis had worked very well. In fact, Becky said the woman would have her spoiled rotten before this all passed, because every evening Mavis had dinner on the table when she arrived home from work. Scruffy immediately took to their new friend and stayed by her side constantly. The dog only left her at bedtime when he went to Becky's room to sleep.

Hawkman decided to stop by Mavis' and talk with her about the things she'd told him previously. He first pulled up alongside Stan's vehicle. "I can't keep track of your schedule. So how's it going?"

Stan stepped out of his pickup, stretched his arms above his head, and twisted his body back and forth. "Not much action. Been pretty quiet the last couple of days. Any news from the Medical Examiner's Office?"

Hawkman climbed out of the rental car and leaned against the fender. "Not yet, but hopefully by the first of next week."

"Any ideas about those bodies?"

"I'd expect one is Carole Simpson. The other has me baffled. I'm hoping they can give me an estimate on how long the bones have been in the ground. That will help."

Stan glanced at him and grinned. "I've an inkling you've got a pretty good idea."

Hawkman nodded. "Let's just say I have a suspicion. To prove it is my next goal. But I need the information from the forensic people."

"Thought so. You've been very closed mouth, which is always an indication you're on to something."

"Am I that transparent?"

"Only to people who've worked with you." Stan patted the hood of the rental car. "By the way, when will the garage have your 4X4 ready?"

Hawkman made a face. "Soon, I hope. I'm not thrilled driving around a red bomb." He then pointed toward Mavis' house. "Has she left for Ms. Simpson's yet?"

Stan shook his head. "No, she normally goes over about four thirty."

"Good, I've got time to have a little chat with her. Talk to you later." He got into the car, backed up and parked in front of her house.

He rang the bell and when Mavis answered, her eyes lit up like sunshine. "Oh, Mr. Casey. You couldn't have suggested a better plan. I've enjoyed the evenings with Becky more than you'll ever know. It's so nice to dine with another person. Especially one as sweet as her." Then she flitted her hands in the air. "Oh my, where are my manners? Please come in."

Hawkman stepped into the entry. "I'll only keep you a minute. I just wanted to ask if you've spoken with Becky about any of the events that took place years ago?"

She looked at him with a shocked expression. "Goodness, no. That child isn't ready to hear all those sordid details about her father. Maybe later, but not now. She's a nervous wreck and has broken into tears a couple of times when she told about seeing the bones and skull come out of that horrible grave."

"I'm glad you've had the insight not to speak about them. Right now it's pretty crucial to keep the information to yourself."

She cocked her head and looked into his face. "You're finding out things, aren't you?"

"Yes, and the items you told me about are making a lot of sense."

She frowned. "The truth always hurts. And it will devastate Becky when it all comes to a head. I want to be with her when you break the news."

"I'll see to it." Hawkman turned and put his hand on the door knob. "Becky told me you were spoiling her rotten by having dinner on the table when she got off work."

Mavis' cheeks turned pink. "It gives me much pleasure to see her smile and maybe for a few minutes forget what's going on."

"You're a very kind woman, Ms. Watkins. I'm happy she has you available."

After he left, he recalled her words of the incidents happening at the Simpson home some fifteen years ago. He thought them more credible now. This woman, considering her age, still had her head on straight. He liked her.

As he passed Stan's vehicle, he gave a wave and drove out of the area. He'd only gotten a few blocks away when his cell phone vibrated against his hip. Pulling it off his belt, he put it to his ear. "Tom Casey."

"Hawkman, this is Detective Williams. Just got a short report on what the forensic crew has found so far."

"Wow, that's fast. I didn't expect to hear anything until the first of next week."

"Me either, but I told them to keep me informed on each step while this case moved ahead, as we needed the information as soon as possible."

"I'll drop by your office, I'm not far away."

"See ya in a few."

Hawkman arrived at the police station and hurried up the stairs. He hoped the reports would give him something he could use so he could start his interrogation of Henry Harris, which he figured just might lead him to the murderer of Carole Simpson. Even though he pretty much knew who'd done it, he needed Henry's story to corroborate his presumption.

CHAPTER FORTY-TWO

When Hawkman walked into the detective's office he found his buddy examining several reports strewn across his desk. Williams glanced up.

"These are interesting, and I hope they're going to fill in some of the gaps of your investigation. Maybe you'll be able to clue me in since the police are now a part of this mess."

Hawkman grinned as he scooted up a chair and sat down. "Let's see what we've got."

Williams pushed one of the chronicles toward him. "We don't have all the reports, but it's a start." He held up another handful of papers. "These state there were two complete skeletons in the dirt grave. It goes into detail describing the female and male bones. They discovered the male in much deeper soil, and the initial tests indicates it'd been there longer."

"Did they give a time frame on either?"

"Yes. But they're only approximates. The man's bones showed more aging and the forensic group estimate twenty to thirty years. The woman's, they're figuring ten to twenty. If you'll notice the note at the bottom, there will be more tests run later which will give a more accurate time base."

Hawkman nodded. "These dates suit me."

Williams leaned back and tapped his chin. "I see. So you have things pretty well resolved."

"I think so; I just needed some confirmation. Were there any signs of the causes of death?"

"Yes, there appears to be a bullet hole in the male skull." The detective handed him a picture.

Hawkman studied the photograph. "Someone was a crack shot. Right between the eyes."

Williams passed over another snapshot. "This surprised me. Looks like they even found the murder weapon. They discovered it buried beneath the male skeleton."

Leaning forward, Hawkman studied the image. "I'd say this is a Ruger P series pistol. Looks like the P85. I don't think it came on the market until about 1987."

"You're right. How'd you know?"

"Because of the way it's held up under the conditions. The P85 used an investment cast aluminum frame, and made extensive use of cast parts and proprietary Ruger alloys. Nearly all internal parts, including the barrel, were stainless steel, while the slide and ejector were carbon steel." Hawkman shook his head. "Looks like they decided to get rid of the gun as well as the body. Any ideas on the identity of the male skeleton?"

"Not yet. They're making inquiries as we speak to all sorts of services and looking for missing persons during that time frame. Also they have one of the computer artists working to put a face on each of the skulls. They feel they'll get a pretty good resemblance as both were in good shape."

"Excellent. Let me know as soon as you get those prints. I'll want to present the woman's sketch to Becky in hopes of proving, without a doubt, the woman is Carole Simpson."

"No problem. I'll give you a call."

"Any signs of what caused her death?"

Williams fingered through the rest of the photos and presented Hawkman with three takes of the head. "You can't tell much from the front lobe view, but you'll notice here on the side, and back," he pointed with a pencil. "It appears she took a hard blow to the head and it cracked her skull, more than likely causing a bleed, which probably killed her."

"Did they by any chance find another weapon in the grave?"

He shook his head. "No. But I think we can assume from the looks of the wound, it wasn't a stick."

"True. More like a hammer or pipe, which could be discarded more easily than a gun."

Hawkman glanced at the empty desk. "Is that it?"

"For now. They promise more to come."

"Is there a chance I can get copies?"

"Figured you'd want some, so I made extras. Those are yours."

"Thanks. These are going to help a lot." Hawkman stood and slipped the items into the folder Williams provided. "I can now proceed with my investigation."

"Mind telling me where you're heading?"

"Not just yet."

Williams frowned. "You sure don't appear to need our help."

"I don't want it to look like I'm accusing an innocent person. I'll definitely call If I need you."

The detective shrugged. "Okay, if you're sure you don't want me along."

"I don't think I'll need you yet, but the more dangerous stuff is just around the corner."

Hawkman left the detective's office, placed the folder on the passenger seat of the red bomb and drove away from the police station. His next stop, Henry Harris' place.

When he pulled up in front of the house, he noticed the gardener's truck parked in its usual spot. He doubted Henry felt like doing much work. The bell didn't work on their entry, so he knocked and heard the dog yipping. Lisa's heavy footsteps pounded across the wooden floor. When she opened the door, she scowled.

"What the hell do you want? Don't you think you've caused enough trouble for us already?"

Hawkman looked her straight in the eyes. "No, Mrs. Harris, whatever problems you and Henry are experiencing, were caused by your dealings in the past. Not me."

"Ha! That's what you say."

Before she could start her tirade, Hawkman interrupted. "I came to speak with Henry. Is he here?"

"He's resting."

"Please wake him. It's very important."

She stepped back and growled. "You've got your nerve. My husband got shot in front of your office, and now you want me to wake him? You're shameless."

"Yes, I am. If you don't let me talk to him, I'll call the police to handle the matter."

She put a hand to her throat, as fear flashed across her face. "The police?"

"That's right."

She disappeared around the corner of the room and returned within a few minutes, carrying the yippy dog and in a much more mellow mood.

"Come in, Mr. Casey. Henry will see you. Follow me. He's not feeling on top of the world, but said he would talk with you."

"Thank you," Hawkman said, as he trailed her down the hallway. He flipped on the recorder in his pocket, before they entered the bedroom.

Henry sat on the bed propped up by a stack of pillows, with his leg elevated. He stared at Hawkman through narrowed eyes. "Sorry I couldn't join you in the living room. My wounds are giving me fits."

"I understand," Hawkman said.

Lisa dragged in a straight back chair and put it near the bedside. "Here, have a seat. I'll get you something to drink."

Hawkman raised a hand. "No, thanks."

She let out a disgusted sigh and left the room.

Hawkman took the chair and rested his arms on his knees. "Henry, I'm sure you've heard by now, the Medical Examiners have dug up the rose garden."

He picked at his fingernails and nodded. "Yes."

"Do you know what they found?"

"Carole Simpson's body."

"We don't know for sure, but one of the skeletons is female."

Henry jerked up his head. "What do you mean, one was female? How many bodies did they find?"

"Two. One a female, the other a male. Who's the man, Henry?"

A flash of alarm passed across his face. "I have no idea."

Hawkman sat up straight. "Sure you do. Tell me how you saved Al Simpson's life."

Henry glared at Hawkman. "That has nothing to do with whoever was buried in the rose garden."

"Then what did Mr. Simpson do with the man you killed while saving his life?"

The color drained from the gardener's face. "I don't know what you're talking about."

"I'm through playing games, Mr. Harris. Do you want me to explain the incident?"

Henry glanced up. "Yeah, tell me, since you know so much."

"Years ago, you were known as quite a maverick and carried a gun. People had seen you out in the fields practicing your marksmanship. You were pretty proud of that Ruger P85, weren't you?"

Henry fiddled with the covers. "That was a long time ago," he mumbled.

"Where'd you get the pistol There weren't a lot of them around."

"I won it in a poker game."

"Do you still have it? I'd like to see it?"

He shook his head. "It disappeared. I think someone stole it out of my truck."

"I don't think so. They found the gun buried in the rose garden under the male skeleton. You and Mr. Simpson buried the man and the weapon."

Henry took a deep breath and exhaled. "No! That's not what happened."

"Then you better fill in the gaps."

CHAPTER FORTY-THREE

Henry wiped a hand across his face and grimaced as he shifted the wounded leg. "It began about twenty some odd years ago. I needed work real bad and wanted to find something that paid enough to keep my family together. I only knew gardening, and people in those days didn't have enough money to pay a lawn person. So, I approached some of the companies. The competition was fierce. No one wanted to hire just one man. I even tried to sign on with established landscaping firms, but they had all the help they needed."

Hawkman leaned forward. "You're beating around the bush, Henry. Get to the point."

"You need to know a little background."

"I've got the picture."

Harris nodded. "Okay, okay. I hung around with a bunch of derelicts near the Rogue Valley Freight Company, which wasn't far from the railroad tracks. Many of these guys were hobos who hopped on and off the freight cars as they pulled through. We played a lot of cards to pass the time. One night the stakes got pretty high and that's how I won the pistol. I carried it with me at all times and learned how to be a damn good shot."

"Get on with it, Henry. I don't have all night."

Harris raised his hand. "I'm getting there. One evening, right at dark, I walked past the freight company just as Al Simpson came out of the building. Out of the corner of my eye, I saw a shadowy figure come around the side of the structure acting strange."

"What do you mean?" Hawkman asked.

"Dodging around behind the bushes, trying to stay out of sight. Then I noticed he had some sort of pipe or club in his hand. This caught my attention immediately. I pulled my gun, and just as this person approached Simpson from the rear and raised his weapon, I aimed and fired. I got the the guy right between the eyes with one shot."

"So why didn't Simpson call the police?"

"He told me he didn't need the authorities. This guy was a hot headed immigrant he'd hired to do his home yard work and wouldn't be missed. He said they'd argued earlier and he'd fired him. The guy swore he'd get even." Henry put his hands up and let them drop to his lap. "Anyway, that's what he told me. I don't know if it's true or not, but I never questioned the story."

"How did you play into this scenario?"

"He told me to keep my mouth shut; he'd take care of everything and I'd have a job for life. When we stuffed the guy's body into the trunk of Mr. Simpson's car, I shoved the gun into the dead man's pant's pocket." Henry shook his head and stared at his hands. "I didn't want it anymore. I never figured on using it to kill someone."

Henry turned his head away from Hawkman. "I had no idea he'd buried him in the rose garden."

"When did you start working for the Simpsons?"

"About a week after this happened."

"Didn't you wonder why the rose garden had soft soil?"

"Not really. A body being buried there never entered my mind. The bushes were beautiful and I just figured they were well taken care of, and I vowed to keep them healthy."

"Yet, you told me Carole Simpson was buried there. What made you suspicious."

"I already told you, and it happened years later."

"Yes, you did. But I want to hear it again."

Henry repeated the story about the dumping of the fertilizer in the rose garden shortly after the news of Carole's disappearance. "Since no one ever heard from or saw her again, I figured Al killed her and buried her there."

"You have any proof he murdered her?"

He rocked his head to and fro. "None."

"When Carole stayed in the apartment at the back of this house, you told me the only person who came to see her was Al and Lisa's brother, the attorney. Are you sure there was no one else?"

"I can't be positive, because like I said, cars could go through the alley then. But as far as I or Lisa knew, those two people were the only ones."

"When Carole disappeared from the apartment, you said it looked like a struggle had taken place. Had Al been to see her?"

"Not to my knowledge."

"Who discovered her missing?"

"Lisa."

"Why would she go back there? From what you told me the two women didn't get along."

"My wife waters our yard, and takes care of the fish pond. She had Sugar, that's her dog, with her outside. The little mutt ran into the apartment because the door stood ajar. Lisa called her but she wouldn't come out, so she knocked on the frame. When no one answered, she went inside and discovered the mess."

"Did she touch or examine anything?"

"No, it scared her. She drove to the place I was working to tell me."

"So what'd you do?"

"I came home, and called Mr. Simpson. He told me Carole was okay and he'd pick up her stuff."

"Did you or Lisa see him come by and gather her things?"

"No."

"Didn't it bother you that you never saw Mrs. Simpson again? You were still taking care of their place, weren't you?"

"Yes, I've always taken care of their grounds, but I kept my mouth shut. As I told you, it weren't none of my business."

"If people thought Al Simpson murdered his wife, and you'd expressed the same conclusion, I don't understand why someone is trying to get rid of you. Doesn't make sense, Henry. What do you think?"

He took a deep breath and exhaled wearily. "I wish I knew

why they were gunning for me. I've wracked my brain trying to figure it out. I've never done anything to warrant getting shot at."

"Do you think it might be related to the migrant worker you killed years ago?"

"I doubt it. I didn't even know the man's name and how would they have known mine. Mr. Simpson and I were the only ones who knew what went on that night. I never heard a word about the incident and you're the first one I've ever told."

"Do you think Simpson told anyone?"

"No. He'd have been in more trouble than me. He'd have lost his job and it would have ruined his life."

Hawkman stood and walked toward the end of the bed. "Did he follow through with you always being employed?"

"Yes, I've never gone a day without work since I started. Even after his death, Becky told me I'd always have a job with her; as it was her daddy's wish."

"Were you and Al Simpson close friends?"

"Not really. I worked for the man and that's as far as it went."

"Did you two ever talk about the night you saved his life?"

"Never mentioned it again. You'd have thought it never happened. And after so much time passed, it seems like a fuzzy dream now."

"Did anyone ever come looking for the man you killed?"

"Not that I know of."

"Did your feelings change about Mr. Simpson after you suspected he'd killed his wife?"

"Didn't change one way or the other. I always figured life has its twists and turns. If he did it, he'll get his punishment in hell." Henry squirmed in the bed and let out a groan.

Hawkman glanced away. "Sorry, Henry, I know you're uncomfortable, but I need some answers. The more information you provide, the easier it's going to go for you.

I hope you realize you will be arrested for the murder of John Doe?"

"Yeah, I know."

"What if Al Simpson didn't kill his wife. Who would do it?"

"I tell you, it had to be Al. Who else would have buried her in their rose garden?"

"Someone very close to Al Simpson at the time."

Henry stared at Hawkman. "Who?"

"His lover."

"No one knows who she was."

"I think I have a pretty good idea." Hawkman stood and turned to leave. "Thanks for your time, Henry. I imagine the next people you'll see will be the police. I hope you've prepared Lisa."

As Hawkman stepped out the front door, he flipped off the recorder in his pocket, then the sound of a low rumbling engine piqued his attention, and he quickly scrutinized the area. To his left, he saw a car pull out from behind a clump of trees. The sun glinted off a rifle barrel sticking out the passenger window as it moved forward. He quickly fled back inside the house, and dashed down the hallway yelling, "Hit the floor."

He dove into the bedroom, and pulled Harris off the bed.

"What the hell!" Henry yelled as he watched Hawkman tackle Lisa as she stood gazing out the window.

"Stay down!" Hawkman demanded, yanking his cell phone from his belt and dialing 911. Suddenly, the window exploded, sending pieces of glass in all directions.

Lisa screamed and covered her head. Hawkman drew his gun, crawled to the gaping hole and cautiously peered out the corner, as he talked into the cell phone giving instructions to the police. Within minutes sirens were blaring from every direction and soon patrol cars surrounded the block. Officers, with guns drawn, cautiously approached the house.

CHAPTER FORTY-FOUR

Once the trauma subsided and Lisa, her dog, and Henry Harris were carted away by ambulance, Hawkman stood in the front yard with Detective Williams.

"I think you better keep a round-the-clock watch on those two until we find the murderer."

"Will do. Too bad you didn't get the license plate of the vehicle," Detective Williams said.

"It happened so fast. All I can tell you is, it was a late model dark green Chevy sedan with tinted windows. I have a suspicion the assassins were hired from out of town. They'll disappear and we'll never see the vehicle again."

"I'm sure you're right. They may not even get paid since they botched the job. One thing about it, you saved the Harris' lives, so they can be thankful. The only wounds they received were glass cuts, and I'm sure the woman will have to be sedated. She was shaking so bad I had to help the paramedics get her on the gurney."

Hawkman snickered. "Besides, I doubt one man could have lifted her."

Williams grinned. "I get the point." He turned and looked at his friend. "By the way, how'd you escape any glass cuts?"

"I managed to get a few scrapes, but they're nothing to be concerned about, " he said, raising his hands with trickles of dried blood staining the skin.

"Come on over to my car and I'll get some antiseptic out of my First Aid Kit so you can clean those scratches."

They strolled to the car and Williams handed him a small bottle with some cotton swabs. "So what were you doing here?"

Hawkman ran through the details of his interrogation of Henry. "I think Harris is prepared to be arrested for the murder of John Doe."

"What about Carole Simpson?"

After Hawkman cleansed his hands, he took off his hat and ran his fingers through his mussed hair. "No, he didn't kill her. He's sure Al Simpson did. But I don't think so."

Williams raised a brow. "Really. You got someone specific in mind?"

"Yep, but I'd like to approach the suspect first."

"At this point, considering it might be a bit dangerous, why don't I tag along?"

"Probably a good idea. I believe her husband is hiring the guns to protect her."

The detective jerked around and gave Hawkman his full attention. "You think a woman killed Carole Simpson?"

"Yes."

"Who?"

"Al Simpson's lover."

Williams raked his thumb across the two day stubble under his chin. "I didn't know you'd uncovered her identity."

"It took a little doing, but I've done a lot of research and the puzzle pieces are beginning to fall into place. I think I've got it pretty well thought out."

"Why don't we meet in my office." Williams checked his watch. "Say, in thirty minutes. It'll give me time to wrap this situation up, and then we can discuss the best strategy."

"Sounds like a plan. I'll run by and grab some sandwiches. I'm sure you haven't eaten all day."

"Does it show?"

Hawkman chuckled. "Yeah, you're drooling out the corners of your mouth at just the mention of food."

Williams chortled and turned toward the house. "I'll see ya in thirty," he said, waving as he entered the Harris' front door.

Leaving the scene, Hawkman kept a wary eye out for the green car, but saw no signs as he approached the main part of town. He figured the shooters had long gone once the police converged on the house from all directions.

When he went into Togos, a crowd of loud high school kids occupied the place and it took him a few extra minutes to purchase a couple of pastrami sandwiches along with two tall drinks. As he drove toward the police station, his ears rang from the kids' blaring voices talking above the gadgets they had plugged in their ears.

Balancing drinks on a cardboard tray, no one paid any attention to Hawkman as he went down the hallway toward the detective's office. He used his butt to push open the door and backed into the room.

"Where the hell have you been? I'm starving," Williams said in a gruff fake voice.

"I had to battle teenagers."

"Oh, that's right, it's Friday night. We better get busy, as all hell tends to break lose about ten o'clock, when these kids start feeling their oats." He unwrapped the sandwich and took a big whiff. "This smells delicious." The detective handed Hawkman a folder. "I forgot to mention these computer sketches came in on the skulls. It's amazing what they can do nowadays."

Hawkman took a big bite of the pastrami and opened the file.

"Does that show a likeness to Carole Simpson?" Williams asked

"I have no idea. I've never seen a picture of her. I don't know if Al Simpson destroyed all the photos or Becky just hasn't had time to display any in the house since her dad passed away. I'm sure she'll be able to identify her mother, as she seems to have vivid memories." Hawkman removed the image of the man from the file and handed it back to Williams. "I won't need this one. Becky wouldn't have any idea about this fellow."

"You think Henry can identify the John Doe?"

"I can tell you he doesn't know a name, and as far as getting a good look at him, I'm not sure. You'll just have to present it to him."

The two men finished their sandwiches and then plotted out the plan they thought best. They figured to implement it early the next morning.

Hawkman left the police station around nine thirty and headed home. He kept a close vigilance on vehicles around him, as he didn't cherish the thought of being shot at or run off the road. Arriving home without incident, he hung his shoulder holster over the chair next to the bed, undressed, put his eye-patch on the table, then flopped onto the mattress next to Jennifer and wrapped his arms around her.

She stirred and turned toward him, then giggled. "I can smell pastrami, it appears to be an aphrodisiac for you."

He arched his neck and gazed into her eyes. "Really, you think so?"

She ran a finger down his neck and onto his chest. "Yes, it never fails. When you've had one of those sandwiches late in the evening, you come home and attack me."

"You think I should change what type I eat?"

Snuggling against him, she reached up and kissed his lips. "Not at all, in fact, I think I'll buy some pastrami and make you sandwiches more often."

The next morning, Hawkman arose early, and peeked out the bathroom door at his beautiful sleeping wife. Grinning, he mumbled under his breath, "Oh, you wicked woman. How I love you."

Driving toward Medford, he kept an eye out for anyone tailing him. He felt a little uneasy about the proposed plan, but knew it had to be done quickly or else it would risk the lives of too many people. He didn't worry about Edward Barnett, because he figured no one knew Carmella Jones had ever written such intimidating letters to her stepbrother. But Henry, Lisa, Mavis and Becky were very much in danger. And what this villain had done so far, showed the person to be pretty ruthless and on the move.

Having called Becky the evening before, he'd told her he'd like to stop by early if this would be okay with her. She'd told him it would be fine, since she had to work this Saturday. Hawkman pulled up in front of the house, where Stan was on watch. He waved the folder in his hand and hurried up the walk. He met Mavis coming out the door carrying what he assumed to be her soiled clothes from the day before.

"Hi, Mr. Casey. Becky's waiting for you," she said, brushing past him and heading for her place.

"Come in." Becky called. "Hope you don't mind us talking in the kitchen, I have a few things I need to do before going to work."

"No problem. In fact, why don't you go ahead and do your chores first."

She glanced at him with a questioning expression. "Do you have bad news?"

"Let's say it might be a bit emotional."

Frowning, Becky poured them each a cup of coffee, turned toward the pantry and pulled out a big bag of dry dog food. She poured Scruffy's pan full, filled his water container, then carried them out to the back porch area, closing the door when she returned. "I've had a doggy door installed for Scruffy, and it's worked out great. He can come into the outer room without me having to run to the door to let him in or out."

She sat down at the table opposite Hawkman and gazed at the folder he'd placed on the surface.

"Open it," Hawkman said. "Tell me what you see."

Becky took the file with trembling fingers, and gasped when she saw the picture. Tears rolled down her cheeks as she held the photo to her chest. "It's my mother."

"I'm sorry I had to do this, but you had to identify her before I could pursue the case."

"Where did this come from," she sobbed.

"It's the computer printout of one of the skulls removed from the rose garden grave."

"Somehow I knew one of those skeletons was her. But this really shook me."

"I thought it might."

"Who was the other one?"

"A man you wouldn't know. He'd been there many years before your mother. Henry Harris killed him while saving your father's life."

Becky closed her eyes. "And Henry buried him there?"

"No, your father did. Henry had no idea what your dad did with the body until the skeletons were removed."

She stared at Hawkman. "You mean my father buried both the man and my mother?"

"I think so. But I'm pretty sure your dad didn't kill her. I think he was protecting the real murderer."

Furrowing her brow, she fumbled for words. "Wh-Who or why would my father have done such a thing?"

"I can't tell you yet. But maybe later today I'll have the information."

CHAPTER FORTY-FIVE

Hawkman wanted to make sure Becky had gained back her composure before he left. "Are you all right?"

"Yes." She finally looked at him with dry eyes. "May I keep this picture? Dad must have destroyed all Mother's photos, because I can't find a one in the house."

He nodded. "Of course. Would you like for me to have Mavis come back?"

Becky waved a hand. "No, no. I've got to go to work. It will help me get my mind off all this."

"I'll get in touch with you tonight, if things break like I hope."

She took a deep breath. "I hope I can handle the rest of the news."

Hawkman patted her on the shoulder. "You'll do fine."

When Hawkman pulled into the police station, Detective Williams stood in the parking lot talking to one of his officers. When he saw Hawkman drive up, he crossed the pavement toward him.

"Did you get the positive identification from Ms. Simpson?"

"Yes. The body is definitely her mother's."

"Guess we're on for this then."

"Yep."

"I've got a couple of men planted to watch the husband in my unmarked car."

Hawkman raised a brow. "Shall we go in my vehicle, the red target?"

The detective climbed into the passenger seat. "Might as well; we're not going to be staying in it. We can park a block away and approach the house on foot."

"It won't be necessary; she won't recognize us until we're at the door."

Williams grinned. "All depends if she's looking out the window. Few people would miss a six foot plus cowboy with a patch over one eye."

Hawkman gunned the car out of the lot. "You've got a point." He glanced in the rear view mirror and noticed a patrol car followed them out of the lot. "Are they supposed to be behind us?"

"Yeah. They're back-up. I thought it best to have them come along, just in case."

Hawkman and the detective cruised by the house and Williams let out a little whistle.

"Wow, that's some layout."

"I see the garage door opening," Hawkman said pointing. "We can't stop just yet. Looks like the husband's just leaving for work. I don't want him here while we talk with her. I'll pull around the corner where we can still see the front. Her husband will go the other direction."

Hawkman stopped the car and the two men sat back and watched the driveway. The patrol car passed, then turned at the next block.

"Why didn't you think it good idea to go see the in-laws first?" Williams asked.

"Because they really didn't know what happened, even though I'm sure they couldn't help but feel the tension. They were so concerned about their precious daughter getting pregnant, they pushed everything else out of their minds."

"This is definitely going to be quite a story if we can corner her into telling it."

"Okay, looks like the mister has pulled out of sight," Williams said.

"Let's wait until we hear from your men and make sure he's at work. I don't want him circling back and catching us talking to his wife."

Williams put his walkie-talkie to his lips and gave the men instructions to notify him as soon as Douglas Shepard arrived at the bank. He'd give the word if they were to arrest him."

Hawkman grimaced. "I don't like the idea of the kids being within ear shot, but there's not much we can do."

The detective waved his hand toward the house. "In that huge mansion, I think we'll be able to find a private place to talk."

Ten minutes passed and a scratchy signal came over the walkie-talkie. "He's here and going inside."

"Don't let him leave the premises."

"Got it. Over."

Williams slid the contraption under the seat and nodded toward the road. "Let's go."

Hawkman started the engine and pulled into the driveway, blocking the remaining car in the garage. The men got out, made their way to the front entry, and rang the bell They stood patiently on the porch, until a young woman in a white uniform finally opened the door.

"Yes?"

"We're here to speak with Mrs. Robin Shepard."

"You have an appointment?"

Detective Williams flashed his badge. "No, but she'll see us."

The young woman put her fingers to her lips and backed away. "Please wait, I'll go see." Leaving the door ajar, she dashed out of sight.

Soon, Robin Shepard, dressed in a wide brimmed white straw hat, fancy pink dress and matching high heels, arrived at the entry. Her long blond hair hung down one side of her neck. She gave them a forced smile. "Hello, Mr. Casey. Is there a problem? My maid acted scared to death."

"This is Detective Williams. We'd like to come in and talk."

She frowned. "I'm already late for a meeting. What is this about?"

Williams stepped forward. "You might have to cancel, Mrs. Shepard. We've got some serious business about the late Carole Simpson."

A flash of fear crossed Robin's face, and she folded her arms at her waist. "I've told Mr. Casey all about Carole Simpson."

"Do you want to talk here in the entryway or find a private room away from young ears and nosey servants?" The detective shot a thumb toward the young children standing in the hallway with a maid.

Robin whirled around. "Maria, take the children to the playroom while I talk to these gentlemen." Once they'd scurried up the staircase, she turned back to Williams and Hawkman. "Come with me." She led the men down a long hallway, her high heels clicking on the tile as she walked. After turning into a large study with shiny oak bookshelves on three walls, a huge television monitor with a line of overstuffed leather lounge chairs facing the screen, and a large oak lectern covering most of the wall on the opposite side, she closed the doors. She then pointed to a grouping of hard back chairs near a huge secretary. "We can talk in here without being disturbed," then she immediately headed toward the desk. "But first, I'd like to call Doug and have him present."

Williams stepped in front of her and put his hand over the phone before she could pick up the receiver. "No, Mrs. Shepard. What we have to talk about is none of your husband's concern, only yours for now. You're not under arrest; we'd just like you to answer some questions."

Clasping her hands in front of her, she glanced at Hawkman with alarm. "Mr. Casey, I don't understand what this is all about."

"You will as soon as you sit down."

A few moments of silence surrounded them, as they shuffled into their chairs facing one another.

Detective Williams took out a notepad and pen from his pocket. "Mrs. Shepard, I'm assuming you've heard by now, the

Medical Examiner's Office has exhumed two bodies buried in the Simpsons' rose garden."

"Yes, news travels quite rapidly in this town."

"Have you heard who the bodies belonged to?"

"No. Only that one was a man and the other a woman."

"The woman's body was Carole Simpson."

She covered her face with her hands. "How horrible for Becky."

"Mr. Casey would like to go over some things with you now."

Hawkman leaned forward and rested his arms on his knees. "Mrs. Shepard, when you were a teenager, you baby sat for the Simpsons quite regularly. Is that right?"

"Yes."

"As you got older, you found Mr. Simpson rather attractive, didn't you?"

Robin narrowed her eyes and glared at him. "Where are you going with such a question?"

"You didn't like Carole Simpson because you thought she was cold and calculating toward her husband."

"This is ridiculous." She threw up her hands in disgust. "I was just a kid. I snuck my boyfriends into their house while I baby sat, for Christ sake. I don't remember having any such feeling for or against Carole Simpson."

Hawkman leaned back in the chair. "Mrs. Shepard, when we talked several weeks ago, you told me Carole Simpson treated her husband horribly."

Robin glanced at her watch. "I'm already late for the meeting. How much longer are we going to be?"

"As long as it takes, Mrs. Shepard," Williams interjected.

"During the time of your baby sitting days for the Simpson's, you were seen climbing in and out of one of their windows in the wee hours of the morning. What were you doing there?"

She turned a surprised expression toward Hawkman. "I don't know what you're talking about."

"This happened many times and I have a witness who will swear to it."

Her mouth dropped open. "Mavis, their damn nosey neighbor," she hissed.

"You were Al Simpson's lover, weren't you?"

Her flaming gaze bore into Hawkman. "How could I've been. I wasn't even eighteen yet."

"You got pregnant, had an abortion, which Mr. Simpson paid for, then you blackmailed him because you were under age. You told him if he didn't send you a thousand dollars a month, you'd tell the whole world that he'd raped you. And you lied to me about the piece of paper you said you found in the house having LaVonne Adkins name on it. You were LaVonne Adkins. You've used the alias for years and Mr. Simpson sent you money to a Post Office Box in that name right up until a month before he died. You figured no one would ever suspect the truth."

Robin jumped out of her seat. "How dare you say such things." She turned toward the detective. "Don't you see what's he's doing? He's making all of this up because Becky hired him to find her mother and he's making me the villain so he can earn his money?"

Williams stared at her. "No, Mrs. Shepard, I don't see it that way at all."

She immediately went to the desk and picked up the phone. "I'm calling my husband."

CHAPTER FORTY-SIX

Robin Shepard's face turned pale as she gripped the side of the desk. The receiver dropped from her hand, bounced against the oak wood, then hung in limbo, swinging by its curled cord. "Oh, my God, he's been arrested. I've got to go to him."

Williams reached over and put the phone back on the cradle. "I don't think you should leave until you hear the rest of what Mr. Casey has to tell you."

Apprehension showed in her eyes, and her hands trembled as she grasped the back of the chair for support. She eased down on the seat. "I'm ready to hear the remainder of his lies."

Hawkman leaned forward again. "You thought you had it all planned, but somehow Carole Simpson found out about you. She called and insisted on a meeting at the apartment behind Henry Harris' house. Mrs. Simpson gave you instructions to come in through the alley. You hated her with a passion, because she was married to the man you loved, but you also feared what the woman might do to you."

Robin had her hands clenched so tightly into fists, her knuckles were deadly white. Her intense stare bore into Hawkman as he continued.

"When you arrived at the flat, you carried a pipe or a tire wrench. Carole felt like a spurned woman and probably lunged at you. The two of you scuffled until you were able to hit her hard enough to crack her skull, which killed her.

Robin jumped to her feet and came at Hawkman with both fists in the air. "No," she screamed. "She was hitting me."

Hawkman quickly stood, ducked Robin's blows, grabbed her wrist, and pushed her back into the chair. Williams quickly moved to assist, but sat back down when Hawkman had her under control.

She dropped her head into her hands. Tears ran between the fingers, and streamed down her arms.

"When you couldn't get Carole to respond, you panicked, left the rental, and called or went to Al Simpson. He assured you he'd take care of everything, which he did, by burying Carole's body in the rose garden in the middle of the night. You shoved the murder to the back of your mind as the years passed. The checks kept coming and life treated you good. Then Al Simpson died. Becky took over and hired me to find her mother. As I got closer to the truth, your world began to crumble."

Sobs wracked Robin's body.

"You told your husband what had happened in those youthful days, but he decided to let it slide and the two of you married. The money you'd saved looked good to him, and would get you two started on your climb up society's ladder. Something both of you wanted very much."

Robin sucked in a breath and glanced at the detective. "Are you just going to let him keep on telling these lies and accusing me of horrible deeds?"

"I think you should at least show him the courtesy of hearing him through," Williams said. "I'd certainly like to hear the rest of the story. Please continue, Casey."

"When the word got out that Becky had hired me, you and your husband devised a plan in hopes of frightening me off or get me fired. You started with sending menacing notes and making threatening phone calls. I searched through your trash cans, found the newspapers where you'd cut out the letters, and the latex gloves you'd used while doing this little number."

She jerked up her head and glared at him. "How dare you go through my garbage."

"That's part of my job, Mrs. Shepard. I investigated every part of your life. And it paid off. We found a thumb print on the inside of one of the glove that matches yours."

"I think I'm going to need a lawyer after all."

"Do you want to call one now?"

She squirmed in the seat. "As soon as you get through with this far-fetched tale."

Hawkman nodded. "You and your husband figured Henry Harris and Al Simpson had become close friends over the years, and since Mr. Simpson had died, you thought Henry might be spilling the beans. So your husband hired a gun to go after him twice. But both times failed. You also misjudged the relationship between Mr. Simpson and Harris. It was strictly business, and Henry knew nothing about your charade."

Robin exhaled, adjusted her hat, and pushed her hair behind her shoulder. "This is quite an incredible story. You have quite an imagination, Mr. Casey."

Hawkman leaned back. "I don't think so, Mrs. Shepard. In my work, I find out the facts. When your husband came after me in the Hummer, I later found the vehicle hidden at your country place in the hills. The police now have it in custody. The paint found on the front bumper matches the damage he did on my SUV."

She stood, her fists clenched at her side. "I've heard enough. I want you two out of my home immediately."

Detective Williams went to her side. "It's not that easy, Mrs. Shepard. I'm placing you under arrest for the murder of Carole Simpson." He read her the Miranda Rights. "Do you understand what I've just said?"

She nodded. "I'm calling my lawyer right now." Her hands shaking, she picked up the receiver and dialed. After speaking with the attorney, she turned to the two men. "He said he'd meet me at the jail."

Williams removed the handcuffs from his belt. She looked at him with horror.

"Do I have to put on those if I go peacefully?"

"Sorry," he said, as he snapped them on her wrist. He then led her out into the hallway. One of the servants dropped a stack of towels as she saw her boss being escorted away by the police.

"Jasmine, take care of things. I'll be back shortly. This has all been a horrible mistake."

Williams took her out the front door to the waiting police car. Hawkman stood to the side as the detective opened the back door, helped her into the vehicle, then spoke to the officer. "Take her to the station and book her for murder. I'll meet you in a few minutes."

"I need to contact my parents to come and take care of the children," Robin said in a quivering voice.

"Your lawyer will instruct you on what to do," the detective said. He shut the door, and the patrol car pulled away from the curb.

The two men climbed into Hawkman's rental sedan and headed for town.

"How the heck did you let your officers know to go ahead and arrest Douglas Shepard at the bank?" Hawkman asked.

"I figured the way things were going and observing Mrs. Shepard's body language, she would want to call her husband. So I text messaged my men to arrest him on assault with a deadly weapon. I figured that would throw her when she found out he'd been taken to jail."

"I didn't even notice you had out your cell phone."

The detective grinned. "You were a tad busy."

Hawkman chuckled. "You're right. I'm surprised she let me continue without wanting a lawyer present."

"I think curiosity got the best of her. She'd gone for many years with no one knowing what she'd done. I'm sure she wanted to hear how you could have found out so much in such a short time. That's why I didn't arrest her when we first went in. If I'd read her the Miranda Rights, no way would we have been able to get those reactions. Instead, we'd have had to take her in immediately. This will be one trial where you'll be a key witness."

"Yep, along with a lot of other people." Hawkman pulled in front of the station and parked. "How do you think Henry Harris will fare?"

"If a jury believes his story, he could get off scott free."

"You know, I believe him. I think he actually saw a problem and reacted. He's just a strange one, and hard to figure. But I don't think he'd kill anyone in cold blood."

"So what's your next move?" the detective asked.

"I'm going to go by and see Becky Simpson. She should be getting home from work soon. I think I owe it to her to let her in on the ground floor."

CHAPTER FORTY-SEVEN

Hawkman called Becky on the cell and discovered she'd be home in thirty minutes. This would give him time to have a leisurely talk with his men and relieve them of the surveillance duty. When he pulled in front of the Simpson house, he found Kevin on the job. They stood beside the car and chatted about the events.

"Looks like you've got this case solved, "Kevin said, shaking Hawkman's hand.

"Great job."

"Thanks. You want to contact Stan and tell him he's relieved of the task now?"

"Sure. I'll give him a call."

"You guys figure out your hours and I'll get your pay in the mail. Thanks for all your help. I couldn't have done it without you."

"Have to admit, this job wasn't too bad. The hours seem long when nothing happens during the night. But fortunately we didn't have any big problems."

"I need to speak to Ms. Watkins, is she still at her house?"

"Yes."

Hawkman just reached the door when it swung open.

Mavis put her hand to her heart. "Oh, my word, Mr. Casey, you made me jump. I had my mind on other things and didn't see you coming up the walk."

"I'm sorry. Certainly didn't mean to startle you."

"Come on in."

"I'll walk with you over to Ms. Simpsons'. The case has been solved and there are people under arrest. You probably won't need to spend the nights with Becky any longer. However, when we talked earlier, I promised you when I broke the news to her, you were more than welcome to be present."

Mavis put a hand to her mouth. "Did it all come true about what I told you?"

"Yes."

They moved down the path toward the Simpsons' house. "Oh, dear, this is going to be quite a shock for Becky. I just may stay with her tonight; she might need me."

"It's up to you ladies."

She remained silent, her mind definitely on something else, as they strolled up to the entry.

Hawkman glanced toward the driveway. "Doesn't look like Becky's home yet."

"Doesn't matter. I have a key. Let's go inside and wait." She fumbled in her pocket, then unlocked the door. Mavis immediately went to the kitchen and searched the cabinets. "Ah, here we go." Taking a bottle of gin from the top shelf, she went to the refrigerator and removed a large bottle of tonic. "This girl is going to need a drink. A gin and tonic will be soothing." She faced Hawkman. "What can I fix you?"

He raised his hands. "A tall glass of water. I have to drive home."

"Oh, that's right. Water it will be."

They both turned their heads when a door slammed.

"Mavis, are you here?" Becky called.

"Yes, in the kitchen with Mr. Casey."

When she entered the room, Mavis handed her a tall gin and tonic. Becky looked at it with a puzzled expression.

Mavis gestured toward the den. "Let's go sit down, dear." She pointed a finger at her. "And I want you to take a couple of good sized gulps. You'll need it before Mr. Casey tells you the news."

Becky dropped her purse on the table and followed Mavis. Once settled in seats facing one another, Mavis motioned to Hawkman. "Okay, Mr. Casey, I think you can start now."

He began with the letters he had from Carmella Jones to her stepbrother, Edward Barnett. "She wrote about her suspicions of Robin Kregor's behavior toward Mr. Simpson, feeling it a bit brazen for such a young girl."

"In what way?" Becky asked.

"She only mentioned one incident in her correspondences. It appeared Robin knew when your dad's birthday occurred and she brought over a box of gift wrapped chocolates with a card. Since your dad hadn't arrived home from work yet, she left it with Carmella. Not being able to stand the suspense, Carmella steamed open the envelope and read the note. Robin had written quite a love letter and signed it; "With all my love and I hope to be in your arms soon."

Becky looked at him with wide eyes. "Robin?"

"Yes. At the time, Mr. Barnett didn't take much stock in these missives from his sister because she was going through chemotherapy and he figured her mind had been affected. But I discovered after talking with Mavis, the letters made a lot of sense."

Becky picked up her glass and took another drink. "Go on."

"Carmella even thought somehow Henry Harris might be involved with the disappearance of your mother. She'd noticed one morning when she came to work, the rose garden had a pile of fertilizer dumped in the middle. Henry later came and smoothed it all out without a word to her about when the load had arrived. It was shortly after Carmella approached Mr. Simpson about the strange goings on, that he told her she was no longer needed. She had mixed emotions about her dismissal, and felt your father was jealous of the affection you children showed toward her. She even stated in the letters her suspicion your father had killed Carole. Mr. Barnett felt her writings were just an old woman's ramblings. However, I found them quite informative. Especially when she mentioned Mavis as Carole's best friend."

Becky glanced at her neighbor. "You never told me about being close to my mother."

Mavis reached over and patted Becky's arm. "Honey, we weren't. But I was probably the only person your mother ever chatted with across the fence. Yes, we had a few laughs." She looked up at the ceiling and tapped a finger against her chin. "I'd say we were in each other's houses maybe four times during all the years we lived next door to one another. We weren't bosom buddies." She shifted in her seat and leaned forward. "I was pretty much a night owl back then, and didn't require much sleep. I'd get up and walk around the house, then on warm nights I'd sit on the porch and watch the stars. Those are the times I noticed odd behavior around your place before your mother disappeared." She pointed to Hawkman. "Which I told Mr. Casey about and he's acted upon it."

Hawkman nodded. "Mavis noticed a young girl coming at odd hours of the night and climbing into the house through an open window. One evening, she decided to get a closer look and hid behind some bushes when the young female came out."

"You can imagine my surprise when I discovered her to be Robin Kregor,"

Mavis said.

Becky put her hand to her throat. "This is really hard to comprehend. To think our young baby sitter had an affair with my father. And to think he would participate in such behavior with an underage girl."

Hawkman glanced at Becky. "I never asked you this, but do you remember if your mother and father had separate bedrooms?"

"There weren't enough rooms in the house for Dad to have his own, but I know he slept on the couch in the living room for several months before Mom disappeared. I remember not understanding and asked Dad one night why he didn't sleep in his own bed. He told me his back had been bothering him and he found the couch more comfortable. I didn't question his story, being so young, but now I can see Mom had probably kicked him out."

"I wonder why he didn't just let Robin in the front door?" Hawkman asked.

Mavis sat up straight. "I can probably answer that one. She

never came at the same time. It varied. More than likely, she took precautions sneaking out of her own house too."

"How'd she get here?" Becky asked.

"She had a car, some older model her folks had probably bought. But she was bold enough to park in front of my house. Probably figured no one would ever see it, because she'd be gone by the time the sun came up."

Becky nodded. "Robin definitely had guts. She used to have her boyfriends over when she'd baby sit us." Then Becky turned and stared at Hawkman. "She was LaVonne Adkins, wasn't she?"

"Yes. Remember the little book you found with the strange codes?"

Becky nodded.

"While deciphering it, I discovered on one of the entries, your dad had carelessly written in Robin's name. This pretty well proved he'd been making payments to her since the day she got pregnant. Robin had blackmailed your father all those years until he passed away."

Becky gasped. "How evil. Do you know what happened to the baby?"

"She aborted. Your father paid for it. When she came home later, from wherever she went to have this procedure done, I think your father wanted to end the affair. Your mother somehow found out the identity of LaVonne Adkins."

Leaning forward, Becky's lower lip quivered. "Are you telling me, Robin killed my mother?"

Hawkman lowered his gaze. "Yes." He related the story of how the murder took place. Then he told her how Robin and her husband had tried to kill Henry, sent the threatening notes, along with the other incidents. "I knew I had to move fast, before something happened to you or Mavis. Even with my men outside, they might not have been able to protect you completely. When the detective and I talked with Robin and presented the proof, she didn't deny any of the accusations. Detective Williams arrested her today for the murder of Carole Ann Simpson. She and her husband will be in jail a long time."

Becky flopped back in the chair, her face ashen. "All of this hell happened because I wanted to find my mother." Tears trickled down her cheeks.

Mavis moved to her side and took her hand. "Honey, because of you, justice has finally been served after all these years."

Becky pulled a tissue from the box on the end table and blew her nose. About that time, the phone rang and she picked up the portable on the adjacent end table. "Hello." Her face broke into a smile. "Cory, what's happening? I can tell by your voice, you're very excited."

Hawkman and Mavis started to leave the room. Becky covered the mouth piece and called, "No, no. Stay. This is good news. I've just become an aunt."

When she hung up, her eyes twinkled. "My sister-in-law, Susan, just gave birth to a seven pound healthy little girl. Both are doing fine. My brother's ecstatic." She frowned. "I decided to wait a while before telling him what's happened. He deserves to enjoy this wonderful part of his life. The bad news can wait."

Hawkman smiled. "Congratulations. You'll be a wonderful aunt. I'm going to head home now. I think you'll be able to sleep well tonight."

Becky jumped up and held out her hand. "Mr. Casey, thank you for all you've done. I'm sure I owe you more than I originally paid."

"I haven't figured up the fee yet. When I do, I'll bill you by mail."

Mavis stood beside him, ready to exit out the door. Becky glanced at her. "Mavis, you aren't leaving are you?"

"I don't think you need me here anymore."

"Can't you stay tonight? It would really help to have you here."

"Of course. I'll go fix us some dinner. I know exactly what I'm going to prepare."

Tom Casey, private investigator, left out the front door with a grin on his face.

When Hawkman arrived home, Jennifer hopped up from the computer.

"I thought you'd never get here."

"What's the deal? "

"I just heard over the news about a fifteen year old cold case solved by private investigator, Tom Casey of Medford, Oregon. I didn't know it was all going to come down today."

"Me, either. But it sure did. With a vengeance, I might add."

Jennifer took him by the arm and led him into the living room to his favorite chair. She flopped down in her matching one opposite him. Miss Marple jumped into her lap and they settled in for the long story Hawkman began to tell.

When he finished, he reached over and gave the sleeping cat a head rub. "Miss Nosey, did I bore you?"

Jennifer laughed and put the pet on the floor. "How about some dinner?"

"I'm ravished. What are we having?"

"Sandwiches." Her eyes twinkled "I just felt in the mood for pastrami. Don't know why."

Hawkman raised his brows and grinned. "Sounds fantastic. And I have a wonderful idea for dessert."

ABOUT THE AUTHOR

Born and raised in Oklahoma, Betty Sullivan La Pierre attended the Oklahoma College for Women and the University of Oklahoma, graduating with her BS degree in Speech Therapy with a Specialty in the Deaf.

Once married, she moved to California with her husband. When he was killed in an automobile accident, she was left with two young boys to raise. She is now remarried and has had another son through that marriage.

Ms. La Pierre has lived in the Silicon Valley (California) for many years. At one time, she owned a Mail Order Used Book business dealing mainly in signed and rare books, but phased it out because it took up too much of her writing time. She's an avid reader, belongs to the Wednesday Writers' Society, and periodically attends functions of other writing organizations.

She writes Mystery/Suspense/Thriller novels, which are published in digital format and print. Her Hawkman Mystery Series is developing quite a fan base. She's also written two stand-alone mystery/thrillers and plans to continue writing. 'BLACKOUT,' Betty's story about a bingo hall (of the Hawkman Series), ranked in the top ten of the P&E Reader's Poll, and won the 2003 BLOODY DAGGER AWARD for best Mystery/Suspense. EuroReviews recently picked 'THE DEADLY THORN' (One of Betty's stand alone thrillers) for their 2005 May Book of the Month.

Betty Sullivan La Pierre's work is a testament to how much she enjoys the challenge of plotting an exciting story.

Visit her personal site at: http://bettysullivanlapierre.com